THE

echo chamber

A NOVEL

Rhett J. Evans

A PERMUTED PRESS BOOK
ISBN: 978-1-68261-861-5
ISBN (eBook): 978-1-68261-862-2

The Echo Chamber:
A Novel
© 2019 by Rhett J. Evans
All Rights Reserved

Cover art by Cody Corcoran

PERMUTED
PRESS

Permuted Press, LLC
New York • Nashville
permutedpress.com

Published in the United States of America

⊙⟩⟩⟩⟩⊙

To the women of my family.
To Sharon for her encouragement.
To my mom for the love of reading.
And to Rachel, because of course.

⊙⟩⟩⟩⟩⊙

CONTENTS

OUTSIDE TIME

NOW

PROLOGUE

A THING THAT NEVER HAPPENED, A THING THAT MAY HAPPEN

He sees her sitting at a beachside bar on a warm night at the end of the world. She wears her oversized sunglasses and a fashionable scarf tied over her head. But still, he recognizes her.

"I've never gotten the chance to buy a Best Actress winner a drink before," he says, finding a seat next to her. "It would be an honor."

Her eyes are on her phone.

"I don't suppose you've ever bought a winner of any Oscar a drink before?" she replies. Moonlight gleams on her exposed shoulders.

"Daniel Day-Lewis once. Bought him a daiquiri at an Applebee's in Santa Monica. I don't think he cared for it because he turned it away. To be perfectly honest, I can't be certain he even *was* Daniel Day-Lewis."

She turns to him, a look of mild amusement crossing her face.

I have her attention, he remembers thinking. *Don't blow it.*

"Daniel Day-Lewis is a striking figure, very tall, hard to mistake. Don't you think?" she asks. "And I suspect he doesn't go to Applebee's."

"Also not nearly as pretty as you, while we're at it. So let's just say you'll be the first Oscar winner I buy a drink for. That's a better story for me to tell."

His gaze lingers on her lips perhaps a second too long. He can't help it. It sucks the air out of him just being next to her. Every inch of her—the way her red bangs fall over her forehead, the freckles across the bridge of her pale nose—is captivating. The whole room is hers. It is a marvel to him that anyone standing next to Charlotte Boone can even breathe.

"I was just leaving, I'm afraid," she says, rising from her seat. "It's late."

"You should have won the Golden Globe too, that year," he ventures, straining his limited memory of that year's awards coverage. "That was all political. And you probably should have gotten a producer's credit for *Ruins of Eden*, given all the work you did. But I bet they were able to write you off because you were young and a woman, and Hollywood really isn't as forward thinking as it likes to think it is, is it?"

Charlotte studies him and then slowly sits back down. A slight wind ruffles his sandy hair, and there is boyish mischief in his eyes. He has a strong jaw, and his chest looks firm under a worn linen shirt. She would tell him later there was something about that smile—one part roguish, two parts trusting—that made him feel just safe enough.

"I'll admit that no one's ever tried to pick me up at a bar before by talking to me about my career. I'm intrigued. Did you read all that in a *People* magazine once in a dentist's office?"

He laughs.

"I pick things up here and there. And I figured if I ever had a chance to talk with Charlotte Boone, it would have to be here, at the ends of the earth," he remarks, motioning to the moonlit beach, to the Indian Ocean that stretches on unimpeded to the shores of Asia and Australia. "Because really, what are the odds of finding Hollywood royalty out here?"

"About the same as finding someone who would try hitting on a famous actress with a joke involving Applebee's."

"Is it working so far?"

"It's not *not working*."

He introduces himself.

"Gin and tonic," she replies, raising her empty glass. And then she takes off her sunglasses and gives him a smile as the fabric of her scarf floats on the cool, night breeze. He is almost already in love with her.

She won't remember it though.

Zanzibar.

She won't remember the bar by the beach, or how his smile made her feel, or those nights of early love spent together in a hotel room flooded with the roar of ocean waves.

● ● ●

Cat once thought her life was over. Crushed by forces far too big. Forces that had lied, and with their lies, had nearly buried her.

But this is a new day. This is a day to forget about the team of Silicon Valley engineers who brought about the end of the world with a rogue smoothie maker. Today she would reclaim her humanity.

She is nervous though.

Cat runs her fingers through her hair, and her hands tremble. She tries to slow her breathing to calm herself, but it comes out all rattled. Then she puts on her headset and logs into the Sharebox network, just like she did in the old days. The start screen beckons, letters floating in the space in front of her.

Welcome To Sharebox – A Place Made Just For You

"I can do this," she mutters. "I can do this. I can do this."

Being brave was never really her thing. But she's trying.

She swipes the words away, and finds herself in a town with tidy white buildings and smooth grey roads. Everything here seems different now.

It's just a social media platform. That's all. A natural evolution of the kind of websites and apps everyone previously used to stare at on their phones. Users can build avatars and walk through the default area—the place called Homepad. There are photos and video galleries and alleyways leading to fresh articles and comment walls. Meeting lounges sit on either side of the main thoroughfare for chatting with the avatars of friends or family or acquaintances from all corners of your life, connected by whatever possessed you to accept a friend request in the first place.

It is, generally, an uncontroversial and wholesome place where you can climb into a video of your old college roommate taping his infant son's first steps. You can be inside the restaurant where your sister just took a few photos of her pad thai. A collage of those wedding photos from that guy-from-high-school-you-don't-really-even-remember   becomes a lively, immersive experience. Artificial intelligence, the AI, takes your friends' two-dimensional photos and videos and stitches together elements that are not explicitly pictured using databases and guesswork to create a fully fleshed scene for you, and it feels like you're living it. It feels like you're at that rustic-but-elegant country wedding on that perfect Tennessee summer afternoon.

All that rich imagery—that feeling of being *there,* being engaged with your friends living all around the world—was so rich and so novel and thrilling at first. It was the final word in social media. And there was no fear of missing out on anything anymore because everything your friends did that was worth experiencing was recorded and ready for you.

But everyone got used to it eventually—that immersive phenomenon that felt so novel, so life changing, at first. It became normal.

That's just human nature. Users are not capable of being awed forever.

It was addicting though. Critics complained television was addicting when it first spread to the American home, but they never witnessed the experience of being fully immersed, sound and sight, into a reality built exclusively using their own loves, dreams and prejudices by an intelligence that knew their preferences better than their own moms ever could.

Homepad is full of streets Cat does not recognize, and the new sights make her stomach flutter—for a moment. The AI builds a unique experience composed of her friends' pet photos and political diatribes with computing power sleeplessly crunched from massive server farms, rows and rows of machines, in Wisconsin and India and the Philippines. And that intelligence feels quite confident—as it always does—about what Cat will like to see.

First a video appears of the day that Teresa, a dear friend from childhood, got a new puppy a year ago. That video got an above average amount of likes. Very above average.

But the raven-haired girl passes it by—Cat does not even blink at it. She walks further into the main road leading through Homepad. The AI is surprised by this, but it is not deterred. It reaches further back and finds a series of photos from the time that an old college buddy, Janet, decided to quit her job and travel the world. Janet took photos of herself meditating on a beach in Bali at sunrise. Those photos and videos were just so…cool. They had so many likes. Tons of likes. And there were lots of comments that the AI clustered as "inspiring" and "affirming." So the AI broadcasts them like a floating billboard along Cat's path.

"Fuck off," Cat mutters, swiping the projection away.

Her heart pounds in her chest, her real chest. But here her avatar walks on calmly, quickly. On a mission. She walks to the central transit hub, where it's busier. There are other avatars zipping off to gaming communities, entertainment hubs, or the red-light districts. Since it's the morning, the great majority are heading to the News Cities where pundits and reporters will vie for their attention from a hundred different billboards.

That is where she will go, too. The AI won't follow her there. Not to those unregulated places.

Many other commuters see Cat at the hub at this point. They stop, and their mouths drop. She has not been seen here or anywhere in a very long time. Before they can say anything or cry out in alarm, she taps a choice from a hanging menu and blinks across the digital space to the Patriot Palace.

The Patriot Palace is nothing like Homepad. Where the streets and buildings of Homepad are orderly and unobtrusive, the Palace is an assault on the senses. The ground shakes with the sound of a country band playing at the city gates. Overhead, there is a thunderclap when a lifelike display of fighter jets fly low overhead. The sky above looks ordinary except there is a faint, almost transparent flag that envelops the metropolis and stretches to all horizons.

There are ads, certainly. Lots of ads. The algorithms here have determined that Cat is at least middle class—or she was once, anyway—so they offer her moving billboards for jewelry and cars and high fashion clothes. And they all want to speak to her; she has only to make eye contact with them, and their words and jingles will ring in her ears. The advertisers have even combed photos of her family. She sees her father hawking a deli sandwich, and her sister offering a sale on leather handbags.

The buildings themselves are less sensible than a real city. Their architecture encompasses all eras and styles. Beauty was not important to the owners here. They only wanted to build fast. And safety is no issue because no one here can die or get hurt. Some of the roads even curved upwards straight into the sky, and in other places, they abruptly shifted downwards into vast corridors.

Cat walks down the road surrounded by throngs of people into the center of the Patriot Palace. News commentary plays on all screens. If she wished it, she could climb into any of those videos. Avatars can watch events from the White House Press Room or get lost in a virtual Q&A with the author of a new book. People can spend all day in the Palace, commenting, engaging, watching. There are lounges in the high rises with links to other communities with similar, though often more extreme, interests.

Now there are people following Cat. The news has spread fast from Homepad. *She* is back on Sharebox. *But why now? And why here?* It does not take long for gossip to spread in the network.

A paparazzo is there. A red light glows over his head, indicating that he has begun recording her.

"Miss, Miss," he says, trying to push his way to the front of the growing crowd. "It's really quite…" he hesitates, looking for a diplomatic word, "…an *event* to see you today. Are you here to make some kind of statement?"

A statement, Cat thinks. Interesting choice of words. Her avatar smiles—almost involuntary as her lips twist at the corners of her real face. It's not a warm smile.

Indeed, she is going to make a statement.

Amidst the center of the Patriot Palace, in that buzzing hive of blaring news reports and cheap advertising being projected on the surface of every storefront, lecture hall, museum, and luxury apartment complex, Cat reaches her hands into the air. She wraps her mind around the edges and utmost corners of the skyline of that loud and obnoxious place, and she closes her eyes.

No one is going to get hurt. She doesn't want that, even if that were possible here.

This place is almost as old as the network itself. It's an archive of false histories, an engine of manufacturable outrage. It's a fortress. It's an empire.

Perhaps humanity should have known it would turn out this way. When the first search engines came out, people were finally able to retrieve the answer to almost any question they could dream with the click of a few buttons. But then everyone employed that awesome power for discovering celebrity sex clips, finding five-star reviewed Chinese restaurants, and whiling work hours with cat videos. It was clear then that new technology is always a reflection of users' worst habits, not their best instincts.

Deletion is better. That hits the company and the Patriot Palace and all the owners where it hurts the most anyway. The data is where the money is.

Cat can almost feel the buildings underneath her finger-tips. She holds them lightly at first. And then she squeezes.

There are only a few shouts of alarm at first as the City begins to collapse. People don't know what they're seeing. They think it's some kind of clever visual trick or an ambitious advertisement. But then the buildings start falling into each other with a deafening roar, the steel and stone crash on top of people, and then the struck avatars disappear. And with them, all their lives on Sharebox are gone forever.

For some people, a virtual death can seem almost as painful as a real one. No one has ever seen anything like that before.

And it feels good to Cat. It feels *real* good.

Forget that damn smoothie maker. Forget the day the world started to fall apart. If you can't fix things at this point, you can at least score a few punches, right? No one would ever call Catalina Fernandez a coward.

The paparazzo is still there, his legs crushed under some rubble but his avatar not yet succumbing to deletion. "Why?" he asks her, reaching up to her with a free hand, his smooth pixelated hair sooted with rendered dust. "Why are you doing this?"

Cat blinks down at him.

"I'm just cleaning my slate," she says.

Then she closes her eyes as the remaining structures come down, but she can still hear the sound of crashing everywhere like the world is ending once and for all.

1

AFTER

The flies were out today.

The tourists often mistook the great clouds hovering over those perfect blue waters for smoke. The swarms hung lazily in the air high above the lake, blown in by breezes from the Indian Ocean. In the late afternoon, the fly clouds will drift into the rolling hills, and the people there will chase them with great nets. Kids and adults will join in on the hunt together. Then they'll fry the flies in animal fat and compact them together, and the patties will be sold at roadsides along the lake.

Charlotte had tried them before.

Just once.

She watched the fly clouds part to make room for a plane—a small two-seater flyer with bright yellow paint and a single propeller engine. Vintage aircraft seemed less threatening to her. Fewer electronics. Though she suspected this reasoning was flawed. All it ever took was a radio.

She raised a hand to block out the sun as she traced the plane's trajectory over the lake. It circled the valley twice, and she was close enough to hear the engine start to choke uneasily as it exhausted the last of its fuel reserves. The pilot seemed to be expecting this though and guided the plane to a plateau at the northwest border of the ranch where it sank below the treeline and went quiet.

Charlotte wasn't worried about the plane though, not yet. It was probably nothing.

She rode her horse to the other side of the hill, and her eyes scanned across the humped forms of the zebu cattle.

"Five new calves this morning," said Moyenda, the chief ranch hand, pulling his horse alongside hers. "And they look steady. Good heifers this year." He grinned and gave her a wink.

"Hot damn, I hope so," Charlotte replied. "If they survived the night, then the calves should be nursing well. Lord knows we need a strong year."

"I think that's all we can do for today." He let out a satisfied whistle. "And I hear Njemile be cooking up something real good right now too."

"You're hungry? You want to pack it in already?"

He shrugged playfully. "I'm a simple man. You paying the bills 'round here. Rich, white lady from the fancy city calls the shots. Not Moyenda. I do whatever she thinks is right, always."

"Don't 'rich lady' me. We'd be underwater if it wasn't for you," Charlotte responded. "How do you say, 'you're so full of shit' in Chichewa?"

Moyenda laughed, deep and honest, and they rode back over the rolling hills that composed the lion's share of the ranch's three thousand acres. The afternoon sun soaked the yellowing pastures and warmed their shoulders as they arrived at the ranch house. Charlotte had fretted the design of the building, which was a mix of African aesthetic and western sensibilities, was too ostentatious for this stretch of the lake. The big European-style resorts were to the north, and she deliberately chose to be out here. But there was no denying the ranch house drew attention to itself, with its vaulted straw-thatched roof held in place by a series of magnificent, red beams. The wood grew only around the Mulanje Mountain to the south, where its peak was always shrouded in cloud. It felt like a mystical place. They say it inspired Tolkien's Lonely Mountain.

The Mulanje Cedars were also endangered and illegal to harvest. She didn't know that back then. That was a time when she still wore mascara because she didn't realize the humidity here made applications pointless. Charlotte had simply asked for the ranch to be beautiful in the Malawi and African traditions, albeit with the comforts and amenities of her former life in the States.

"Just do whatever the bitch wants," she once heard her interior designer scream at a contractor, when she thought no one else could her. "Charlotte *fucking* Boone says she wants the kitchen lighting to drape like wilted flowers in an African Art Nouveau garden, make it so."

Her designer had been a ruthless, fast-talking, clipboard-carrying force of nature in a short, pencil skirt, but even she knew not to contradict Charlotte. In the end, the actress paid top dollar, and when she found out the timber for the ranch house came from illegal harvests, Charlotte simply made a large donation to the government's conservation fund. That's all she figured she could do. Money was no object to her at the time.

● ● ●

Njemile, the ranch house caretaker, was in the kitchen that evening, and even though the large stone chimney was originally intended as a decorative flourish, she regularly put it to work. A large pot of bubbling *nsima* porridge hung over a small blaze as Njemile lathered a skillet of colorful *chambo* filets with goat's butter.

Charlotte and Moyenda tramped into the kitchen, and the aroma of simple food cooked well was thick in the air.

"Looks wonderful tonight," Charlotte purred. "Can I help with anything?"

"Tomatoes, Miss," Njemile pointed at a pile of small, cheerful fruit on the countertop. "Dice them up for me please."

Moyenda slid a hand around Njemile's waist and planted a kiss on her lips.

"You know you could dice them onions over there, Moyenda," Njemile said, when he pulled away. "Don't need to be women's work all the time."

"I need to go water the horses," he replied, raising his hands like he had no choice. Then he added something in Chichewa that made Njemile's eyes roll but she smiled at him anyway.

"Do we have enough plates out for everyone?" Charlotte asked.

Njemile and Moyenda exchanged glances, and he removed his wide-brimmed hat suddenly looking serious.

"Thako and his wife left today," he said. "He wanted to be closer to his mom's family. They were hit hard by bad rains last year. I been waiting for a good time to tell you."

"You don't have to be afraid to give me bad news," Charlotte answered, though she knew deep down this wasn't always true. She knew the ranch hands worried about her temperament. And with good reason.

Your career is over, Charlotte had once shrieked at an eighteen-year-old girl from New Hampshire. Poor girl had come to L.A. and ended up in Charlotte's entourage with a wide-eyed dream of breaking it big herself. She was chewing pink gum with glitter in it, and as they were getting out of a limo that night, a bubble burst and got snagged in Charlotte's hair. Then they were in a bathroom stall together trying to pull it out, Charlotte hurling abuses until the girl ran out with tears streaming down her face.

Moyenda raised an eyebrow at Charlotte. "We need to talk about finding more hands, Miss. You see the herd is growing. We've been lucky."

This was a sore spot. Charlotte hated looking for new help. That was when there was the most danger. The danger of letting new people in. New people who might talk.

"Yeah. Fine," she responded with a sigh, then she turned to Njemile. "I'll probably eat in the library tonight, so you don't have to lay out a plate for me."

"You been feelin' okay? All the hands would like to see you, and you're not around much at dinner these days," Njemile remarked, concerned lined in her face.

Charlotte tried to smile in response, but it came across melancholy. "I've just been thinking about things since the news came out last week."

"About the American president? Good riddance. Do you think you will go back now?" Njemile asked, and Moyenda shot her a warning look. Njemile was trying to act casual, but there was no hiding that the news of the U.S. president's death had set off a frenzy of speculation around the ranch.

Charlotte's eyes glazed over for a second, and then she shook her head.

"No. I'm never going back."

Then Charlotte walked back to the library and shut the door behind her. She slid her socks off so she could feel the plush rug under her toes then poured herself a glass of gin before curling up on a couch surrounded by bookcases that stretched to the ceiling. They comforted her. The gin, and to a lesser extent, the books.

Charlotte once hosted a friend at the ranch from her old life, from when she lived a short drive from Malibu and the world still carried boundless potential—from when she graced the covers of magazines and didn't ride horses because black cars could take her anywhere she wanted to go. She had never loved that life either, not particularly. She was not the party girl she had worked so tirelessly to portray herself to be. But at least she had been adored back then.

Her friend visited after the ranch house was built, and she had looked at the library with its oak bar, its clay fireplace, and the portrait of Charlotte's father hanging over the mantel, and her friend accused her of trying to live out some colonialist fantasy. Her friend said the world could still use Charlotte Boone, that she was disappointing everybody by hiding. They argued for a while, and after that, Charlotte didn't have anyone from her old life come visit.

She had never had many close friends to begin with. Not real ones. Despite whatever entourage pics she posted on Instagram. Too cold, too calculating and demanding, too adept at lying—that's what the papers used to say about her. Those characterizations haunted Charlotte. And they were all true.

She sipped her gin and stared appreciatively at the titles on the spines on her books. Then she pulled a tanned zebu hide over her shoulders and had drifted off to sleep when there was a knock on the library door. Through the skylight overhead she saw the first stars of the evening begin to twinkle, and a moonbeam shone on the dustiest books at the ceiling.

Moyenda walked in.

"Sorry to bother you, Miss, but we've been lucky again today."

"How is that?" she said sitting up, not fully awake. She ran her fingers through her long, auburn curls and found the nap had not done her hair any flattery.

"We need an extra hand because Thako left, and today new help arrives."

Moyenda stepped back and revealed a white man standing behind him. He wore a grey shirt smeared with grease stains, and his face and arms were tanned to a golden bronze. There was a look about him that Charlotte didn't quite have a word for at first but she would figure out later. *Healthy.* There was an illustriousness to his skin and to his posture. He could have been in his early twenties or his mid-thirties. It was hard to guess.

The stranger looked serious at first, almost grim, but as he stepped into the library his eyes connected with Charlotte's and he flashed a grin at her that was so wide she thought he might break out laughing. His brown eyes seemed to sparkle. There was something radiant and almost immodest about that look, like he was gazing upon some long-lost friend or family member. Charlotte was used to people having surprised, even emotional, reactions to meeting her given her celebrity, but this was different. This felt familial.

"His plane broke down on the edge of the reserve," Moyenda continued. "He said he is good with animals and could use a place to stay till the rains come."

Charlotte eyed the man up and down, and then she rose to pour herself another glass of gin from the oak bar.

"I don't need much," the stranger offered, stepping forward. "Just food and a roof, and if I could be paid enough to buy some gas at the end so I can get airborne again, that's all I would need. My name is Orion."

He extended a hand towards Charlotte, but she kept her fingers wrapped around her glass.

"You fly around with no money and no gas? Doesn't sound like a smart strategy for a pilot."

Orion didn't mind the insult. In fact, it only made him grin wider. But it wasn't a cold smile or even a secretive one. It was…well, *joyful.* Everything about his visage seemed to beam mirth from some deep unseen place in his soul that the rest of us anxiety-ridden people never get to see and never really understand. He didn't look like a liar, she conceded that. His warm countenance seemed to leave little room for guile. But she found his presence here, at this time, unsettling.

Her face must have clearly indicated her annoyance. Moyenda suddenly looked sheepish.

"I'm sorry, Miss. I thought it a blessing he showed here today. I should have asked before bringing him here."

"It *is* quite a coincidence," Charlotte said, raising an eyebrow and letting her skepticism hang heavy over the room.

Orion laughed, and it felt like he was laughing *at her*. It felt like he found the untrusting look on her face amusing. But still, the sound was so clear and genuine and inoffensive that his cheer was nearly infectious.

"I understand why you're jittery, Charlie. I get it. I had no idea who was living here, and I'll never tell a soul. I know that's what you're afraid of. A celebrity of your caliber has got to maintain her privacy, especially in these troubled times."

Charlie. It made her bristle.

"And I didn't mean to get Moyenda here in trouble," he continued. "I twisted his arm to bring me here. So let's make it right."

Orion reached into a pocket and tossed her a set of keys, which she caught as a flash of protest flitted across her face.

"That plane is all I have in this world, and you can hold onto those keys until you trust me. I'll stay till the rains come and beyond, however long you need. You're in charge. You're the boss."

She looked at the keys in her hand.

"And what if I never trust you?"

"Well, then I guess you get to keep the plane."

He was charming, no doubt, and his eyes took on a boyish glint as he made this offer like he was holding in some private joke—as if he'd be quite glad if she never returned his keys and kept him there forever. Her eyes met his, and for a moment, just a sliver of a second, her stomach lurched with the possibility that this man was important. Like he saw past her sharp tongue to what was underneath, somehow, that he *knew* her—the part of her that cried the night she overheard the interior designer call her a bitch or that other day when she sent the bouquet of roses to the girl from New Hampshire with the bubble gum. And maybe something else, more urgent, was there too. But then the feeling between them passed.

"We have a no electronics policy here on the ranch. You want to communicate with the outside world, you can send a letter or go into town. You like Sharebox? Great, do it somewhere else. Do you have any headsets with you?"

Orion shook his head. "I'm not a big technology guy."

He can't be trusted, she reminded herself. It's too much of a coincidence for a white man to be so far inland in Africa, at this ranch of all the ranches on this continent, and in these days that were so full of intrigue as the world crumbled into ash. He stumbled upon the one ranch where she, a white foreigner and a former Hollywood starlet, had chosen to hide herself from the hungry eyes of a vengeful people.

He would need to be watched carefully.

She pocketed the keys and then shook his hand.

"Okay," she said. "But I would prefer if you call me Miss Boone."

2

BEFORE

Catalina looked pissed. But she kind of always looked that way. Her coworkers liked to joke that she had "resting bitch face." She laughed along when someone first brought the observation up at a team lunch event where she had two drinks, so now they thought it was an okay thing to comment about all the time.

It wasn't though. It bothered her.

Her work was really the most important at Sharesquare Industries, and she knew it. And she was the smartest, though she had not been to schools with the same pedigree as everyone else in the room. The other women in the office had learned long ago that being too brilliant and too direct often flustered their male colleagues, so they always began their talking points with phrases like "I really don't know what the right answer is, but perhaps we could try…" Or "there are a lot of great points here, has anyone considered…?" But Catalina was no good at that kind of talk. She didn't like pretending she didn't know what the right answer was.

"Did you guys hear about that blog post someone made in the sales department about sexual harassment?" Catalina offered, breaking the silence in the meeting room as they waited for the CEO. "Sounds like some heads are gonna roll."

"I know the heads of those sales teams," Devon responded, leaning back in his chair and looking at the ceiling. "They're good guys. Really high performers. This 'metoo' shit has gotten way out of control. Those girls are ruining peoples' lives."

Cat couldn't help but stifle a groan. Devon was the only leader at the company over the age of fifty. He was hired from one of the older, now unfashionable Silicon Valley companies. Bringing him on in a senior role was a nod to investors who fretted that the CEO and his inner circle were too junior and lacking the polish and maturity needed to run a growing company. But it wasn't Devon's age that bothered Cat—not even when he walked around the halls in his socks to make himself seem younger. Rather, she found his *ideas* retroactive.

Devon put one hand on his sizeable gut and another picked at the bald spot on his head, and Catalina just hated him. She knew she didn't do a very good job of concealing it, either. She hated how adept Devon was at taking credit for the work of others while always managing to deflect blame. She hated that he loved to hear himself talk, and yet, everyone seemed to listen to him more than they did to her. She hated that he was almost certainly paid far, far more than her.

Mike's eyes rose from his phone and met Catalina's, knowing Devon's comment was likely to trigger her. Mike noiselessly mouthed "let it go." Cat bristled.

Let it go.

It seemed like everyone was always telling her that.

Like she should let it go that Devon's project would be nowhere without her. It was her team that had spent the past two years developing Diana—the world's most advanced artificial intelligence. She was the only executive in the Valley with graduate degrees in both human psychology and computer science, a genius uniquely positioned to marry the philosophical needs of the project with the technical challenges. It was her AI breakthroughs that made Devon's project—a virtual reality social network—conceivable.

Then there was Mike. Poor Mike. He was in his late twenties, like Catalina, and he wore plaid shirts every day and had a beard that he hoped looked wild and rugged, but which he actually meticulously maintained each morning. His team was working on the CEO's vanity project. Not content with owning over 99 percent of the world's income and their giant Bay Area houses and summers yachting off the coast of Italy, a cabal of the valley's wealthiest techno-capitalists were on a crusade to defeat their one, last collective enemy: death. Mike was tasked with mapping the human mind to a computer, to effectively "download the brain" into a space where it could live forever.

"Any progress on your whole, mad-scientist program?" Devon asked, turning his attention to Mike and blinking at him expectantly.

"We've made some," Mike answered with a shrug.

"You know the human brain is more powerful than any supercomputer ever built, and it's not even a close race," Catalina said. "The brain outpaces the number of possible calculations a computer can do on the order of a billion billion. Computers have these limitations handing off functions between hardware and software, but the brain's neurons have been mastering their craft for billions of years of evolution."

Mike looked at her, bleary-eyed.

"I'm not saying the work has been easy," he replied.

Mike was normally a true believer. A futurist. He believed technology's forward march would, always and by necessity, herald a better world. In an effort to inspire his subordinates, he once sent his team a news article about how robots will one day be employed in fast food restaurants and grocery stores, and when a team member asked him about what would happen to all those displaced jobs, Mike became annoyed and complained about the employee's "lack of vision."

His team eventually came up with a proposal to implant a chip in the human brain that could relay real-time signals of its activity with the intent to eventually record and convert it to a computer-readable format. Supposedly Mike asked for volunteers within his team to "host" the chip, and when no one did, he had the chip surgically implanted on himself.

That was just a rumor though. Even Catalina didn't know if it was true. She watched Mike as he reached up and scratched at a spot just over his ear.

Once complete, Catalina's Diana tech would power the virtual social media world that Devon was building and could also accelerate the mapping and conversion processes of neural activity that Mike was devising. Lots of companies in the Valley were fiddling with AI, whether it was for identifying restaurants their users would enjoy or finding a food delivery service with the fastest speed. In fact, a lot of the applications involved urban food delivery. Folks in Silicon Valley had a tendency to curate software centered on optimizing their own lives. But Diana was far more ambitious. One day she could be fed theoretical physics models on the distribution of dark energy in the Milky Way and advance conjecture on the origins of the universe. She could analyze thirty years of inconsistently formatted elementary school transcripts from around the world and make proposals about the kind of curriculums lead to the best outcomes for American students. She could leapfrog the trajectory of human progress. Her worth could be priceless.

That's why Devon and Mike, who enjoyed unfettered access to Cat's code libraries housed on company servers, copied and maintained up-to-date copies of Diana's code base for themselves.

They didn't tell her though. They didn't tell anyone that they did that.

"You sell any more of those—what do you call them, fruit juicers?" Devon asked Catalina with a cynical grin, hanging his socked feet over an empty chair.

"It's not a fruit juicer, Devon."

"Don't you put a bunch of kale and strawberries in there, and just turn it on?"

Cat rubbed her temples, trying to restrain herself from taking his bait.

Technically Devon, Mike, and Cat formed the CEO's *future* projects division, but Cat had launched a Diana-infused home smoothie maker, called the Nutrino Mixer, that was already on the market. The board of Sharesquare once had grandiose visions of riding a tech trend called the "Internet of Things"—posed as a $50 billion opportunity to turn everyone's appliances into something resembling the home in *The Jetsons*. But research outside of the Peninsula indicated most consumers didn't care if their refrigerator was capable of tracking their calendar appointments or monitoring their grocery list. In fact, most folks in the beta program just used Diana-infused smart technology to play music or to solicit jokes in front of their friends. The whole fad appeared to be falling flat, and Bay Area geeks stopped talking about it. But the Nutrino Mixer, however, was proving an exception.

And today, maybe, she had a success story to share.

Once the CEO, an introverted early thirties-something who wore khaki shorts to work, arrived to the meeting that day, Cat kicked off the agenda.

"We finally have a hit," she said. She turned on a slideshow displaying an image of a shining, chrome-plated Nutrino Mixer.

Devon sighed loudly. The CEO looked up from his laptop at her with polite attention. Mike continued playing with his phone.

"The Nutrino is far outselling our wildest expectations," Catalina continued, unfazed. "Nine million have been sold as of this month. It's the biggest single channel we have now for getting Diana's smart technology into people's homes."

"But we're making very little money on the licensing since we don't make the hardware," Devon pointed out.

"That's not really the point at this phase. The point is we're normalizing artificially intelligent appliances for the mass market."

"With something that dumb people think is healthy for them," Devon said while looking at the CEO. "This is bad branding. This is not *intelligent*," he laughed with a snort.

The CEO just continued smiling. He seemed to like it when his direct reports sniped at each other. He thought the inter-office competition was good for the business.

The Nutrino Mixer, integrated with Diana, had become a health food craze in the previous quarter. It consisted of an elaborate blender attached to a chilled produce box that Diana would regularly renew with fresh ingredients for the customer. The consumer could simply tell Diana to "blend my smoothie" each morning, and an opening on the compartment box would release a mix of berries or kale or whatever fruit and supplements Diana had determined the consumer would like best. Heck, you could add anything: turmeric, cayenne, maca root, ground-up cricket exoskeletons. Whatever superfood fantasy was sweeping the yuppie and hipster markets, it could be sourced. Customers simply told Diana their preferences, and she would ensure the ingredients were in their next produce box, left at their doorstep. All for a simple subscription fee.

The Nutrino Mixer went really big shortly after Christmas when health evangelists began getting a hold of it and telling their friends. Then it was featured on a daytime talk show where the host liked to dance a lot, and Cat's team rolled out a feature where customers could submit mouth swab samples to get customized vitamin mixes and track their eating using an app. The Nutrino Mixer offered health, weight loss, and vigor in a way that was mind-numblingly convenient, and to consumers, it *looked* trustworthy and authoritative because there was so much damn science attached to it.

Upper middle-class white people loved it.

And Cat was almost proud of it. She had one at home, and she gave one to her tía living nearby. Perhaps the health nuts were overblowing the benefits of it, but that didn't mean it was a bad product.

"Diana is building one of the largest databases on human health and eating habits ever conceived, and you think this project is 'not intelligent'?" Cat said, narrowing her eyes at Devon.

Mike looked up from his phone at these words. Devon hesitated, looking dumbstruck for a brief moment. He was rarely caught without a comeback. And the CEO's vapid smile dissipated.

"Are we doing anything special with all that user data?" the CEO asked.

Catalina hadn't really thought about this yet. She knew data was powerful. She knew data was the currency that kept an increasing share of Bay Area companies afloat. But really, she had no idea what she would do with all the petabytes of survey and health metric information Diana was collecting through the Nutrino Mixer. It didn't seem to matter yet. This was Silicon Valley. This was a place for shooting first and asking questions later. And comprehensive user data gathered under overly broad user agreement statements was a core part of everyone's business model.

"I figured I'd let the advertising department figure that out," she replied, and this answer seemed to mollify everyone.

Then Devon presented updates on progress for the new social media platform. Beta users on the VR prototype of the Squarespace network, or rather *Sharebox*, as it was being called, were more likely to stay online longer and interact with ads than the previous version. That's really all that mattered to investors.

Then Mike gave an awkward presentation on recent challenges facing his "brain digitization" team. He looked exhausted and spoke evasively, and then the meeting ended.

In that room, those three leaders, Devon, Mike, and Cat, and their projects were the future of Sharesquare Industries:

A virtual reality social network.

A scheme to digitize the human brain.

And Diana, the most open-ended AI in the world.

In a few months, one of these projects would be mocked as an utter failure.

Another project would be hailed as a groundbreaking success.

And the last one would bring the nation to the brink of ruin.

● ● ●

Catalina and Mike left that afternoon meeting and got into an elevator at the same time. Mike was still looking at his phone.

"How do you think the launch of the new VR platform is going to go?" Cat asked, after a minute of awkward silence passed.

"Looks like a hit to me. I think it's gonna turn people into zombies. They'll be on it all day."

"Is that a good thing?"

He looked up. "What do you mean? Of course it's a good thing. That's what we're building it for. So people will like it."

"I just wonder sometimes if the things we're building are actually, you know, *good* things."

Mike raised an eyebrow and then turned back to his phone. "You're thinking about it too much."

The elevator reached the lobby, and Mike and Catalina parted with mumbled goodbyes. Catalina's team had invited her to a happy hour and foosball tournament at a local bar, but she had declined. She wanted to be alone. She almost always wanted to be alone. Cat was surprised her team even bothered to keep inviting her.

She walked past a series of homeless people who asked her for change. It was probably best to simply keep her eyes forward and ignore them, she thought. She used to try to say, "I'm sorry, I can't today." But that sentiment always felt disingenuous. She could *every day*, if she wanted. She might have hidden in a fruit truck to get into this country when she was four, but that was a long time ago, and it didn't change the fact that she had a top job at one of the world's most desirable employers and more stock options than she even bothered to keep track of anymore. But she had her own problems too, she told herself. She had to claw her way upwards in an industry dominated by white men, and as a brown woman, it was a position she now felt she needed to vigilantly defend.

She felt most comfortable at home, and now she at least had Diana for company—the kind of company that Cat liked: minimal and predictable. Cat had a prototype version of Diana installed in her home setup. It was the only version of Diana outside of the office that was capable of engaging in open-ended conversation.

The AI opened the door for her as she reached the apartment. Then Diana turned on the lights and played some of Cat's favorite evening music.

"How was your day today, Cat?" Diana's voice rang out cheerfully (but not obnoxiously so—they had tested the right amount of cheer) from a speaker in the kitchen.

"The usual," replied Cat, and she dropped her bag and slumped on the couch.

Every response and every question that Cat made was making Diana a little smarter. The AI was always busy trying to digest what it means to have a human conversation. For

Cat and Diana, it was a mutually beneficial relationship. The AI was given the opportunity to practice speaking with a real person, and Diana's presence made Cat feel less alone.

"Do you think you're going to make the world a worse place or a better one, Diana?" Cat asked the air as she stared at the ceiling.

"That's a good question, but I don't know," said the machine, not taking a pause to think.

There was a long silence as Cat breathed out, her mind humming through all the small political victories and indignities of the corporate day.

"I'm glad you're here though with me," she said.

"Me too," responded Diana.

3

AFTER

The end of the world didn't happen overnight. There was a slow decay of order and institutions. Sure, people always talked about the smoothie maker, about the *before mixer* times and the *after mixer* times. But the real danger was first seeded when people stopped believing the truth really mattered. Some people now said that humanity was past saving, past redemption—that too many norms had been shattered. But the new ranch hand, Orion, didn't subscribe to that thinking. He had tricks up his sleeve. He had a plan—probably the only plan worth a damn.

It was September, and he knew the rains would begin next month. Growing crops in the hilly, sometimes mountainous, country around the great lake provided moderate temperatures—it was rarely as hot or as humid as the vast plateau to the south. But the arrival of the rains was not a simple, straightforward blessing. The wet season always rode in on a deluge of thunder and flash. And everyone was grateful for that first heavy shower, but the topsoil would wash away if not carefully mounded. So today Orion toiled in the ranch's gardens, set on a lush green hillside with a lake view. He shoveled in earth to house rows of groundnuts and sweet potato and created a special plot to grow cassava.

Charlotte rode by one afternoon while he labored with a wheelbarrow to haul zebu manure into the garden. She slowed her horse to look over his work, and today, she actually gave Orion a polite smile.

"Were you a farmer in a previous life?" she called out, looking at the dirt stains smeared on his chest and forearms.

"I've picked up a few things here and there," he said with a grin, wiping a hand to his brow.

"Make the trench around those beans a little deeper," she said, pointing to a spot at the edge of the garden. "Last year they got flooded out."

"Sure thing, Miss Boone."

She turned and rode off.

It was progress for him. For the first week he was here, she didn't even make eye contact. But he won over Moyenda and the rest of the ranch hands on a long afternoon after a calf got ensnared in a broken fence and another disappeared into the foothills. Orion had tracked down the missing animal long after sundown.

As it was proven in short order, he was good at just about any task Moyenda assigned him. *Really* good. He also flattered Njemile and her cooking, and helped clean the kitchen when the other men wouldn't. This could have been offensive to some Malawian women, but Njemile was quite pleased by it. And gradually, Charlotte warmed enough to greet him when they crossed paths.

He wanted to charm them all, and he specifically wanted to win her over. That was part of the plan.

Orion watched her disappear over the next hillside. Even here, hidden where no one would ever think to look, with muddy boots and pants with increasingly worn-out knees,

Charlotte Boone was ever the movie star. She was the same girl who Orion had a crush on when he was just a teenager, when she won that Oscar for her performance in a movie called *Ruins of Eden*. She was only nineteen at the time, and it cemented her legacy as a serious actress at a startlingly young age.

She was a few years older now, but she was more radiant than ever, so breathtakingly and magnetically beautiful. Perhaps Hollywood had loved her so much because she had reminded everyone of the industry's Golden Age with her long, bouncy red hair, those dark ruby lips, and those clever and fierce emerald green eyes. She looked like the love child of Katharine Hepburn's tenacity and Grace Kelly's elegance.

And when that industry started to collapse on itself, she was among the first to jump ship. Things got rough, and she predictably was gone. Her disappearance from the world stage, like everything that was manufactured about her persona, was exhaustively calculated, well-executed and comprehensive.

Too bad she was such a coward, Orion thought. *Such a beautiful, goddamn coward.*

●　●　●

Charlotte left Orion and the gardens behind and guided her horse to the ranch hands' cabin on the hillside near the stables. She had been waiting for this opportunity. All the hands were out to lunch or in the fields. The place would be empty.

She found the bunk of the stranger, Orion, at the far end of the cabin. The bed was tidy and neat, and there was a copy of Mary Shelley's *Frankenstein* lying on the pillow. His clothes were folded and tucked into a duffel bag under the bed.

Then she found a drawing of a small boy. It was sketched with pencil, and it looked well worn. The boy may have been four or five. He had a cherubic face with mischievous little eyes and reddened cheeks. The eyes alone were colored, in green.

She reached further into the duffel, and her fingers rummaged through clothes and more papers for something hard and cold—something electronic. Perhaps a phone. Or a camera. Or maybe just a charging cord.

Nothing.

If Orion was paparazzi or someone sent by the government, he would inevitably have some way to send reports out from the ranch. But there was nothing here.

Maybe she was being paranoid, she thought.

"You're being paranoid, Miss Boone," Orion said from behind her.

Her heart leapt with surprise, and she wheeled on him.

"Don't sneak up on me like that," she snapped. Then she smoothed a rogue strand of hair back into her ponytail and recomposed herself. "I take the electronics policy on the ranch seriously. There is no pretense of privacy for workers staying on the ranch when it comes to those rules."

"Seems like ruffling through our stuff is still a shitty thing to do."

He took a step closer to her with his hands in his pockets.

"How did you get here so fast?" she asked. "I just saw you in the garden."

"I had a feeling where you were going. For an actress, you're not terribly good at concealing your intentions."

One of her eyebrows rose.

"Everyone at the ranch already seems so smitten with your charms, but I can still throw you out of here whenever I want."

He laughed, easy and unoffended, and it broke the tension in the room. "I'm sorry. I didn't mean to surprise you. But it's hard to not take it personally when someone so clearly doesn't trust you."

She stared back at him but said nothing.

"This is the part where you say *you're* sorry for going through my stuff," Orion said.

"I'm not very big on apologizing for anything," she replied flippantly.

Orion caught sight of the sketch of the small boy upturned in his bag, and for a moment, there was a flash of some expression on his face that Charlotte could not quite pin down. Alarm? Anger? Sadness?

"Who is the boy?" she asked.

He paused a moment before answering. "He was my son."

"Do you have any photos of him?"

"I did have photos, but they're gone."

"How old is he now?"

Orion suddenly looked older, much older. His brow furrowed, accentuating the lines of age there, and the spark of levity in his eyes went out. His mouth opened to answer, but he hesitated and no words came out.

Charlotte was quick to pick up the hint. Not that the cue was subtle, but changing subjects, reading signs and avoiding awkwardness was a skill that made her good at winning over producers and agents. It helped her charm the men who made decisions when she needed to further her career, but to also learn to avoid those same men when conversations took on more predatory overtones. She was good at reading people, she was good at finding men who seemed safe. But she saw now she had struck a taboo subject, so she hastened to change the subject. At least for now. She picked up his copy of *Frankenstein*.

"Quite a grim book," she remarked, inspecting the cover.

Orion's face softened.

"Do you know what gets me about that book?" he asked, and he sat down on an open cot and leaned back on his hands. "Victor lets this monster—this monster that *he* created—slowly destroy all his friends and family before he finally resolves to fix the problem. Before he realizes he has no choice but to fight the creature himself."

"He was terrified of the monster. He was afraid. Could you really blame him for running away from such a frightening thing?"

"Yes," said Orion, and he sat up, looking serious. "It shouldn't take the end of everything he cares about to get him to stop hiding."

"Are you a Frankenstein hunter yourself, Orion? Would you run off and fight a monster?"

She was teasing him now. And there was a smile playing just at the edge of her lips that made his heart do a backflip. The feeling was both familiar and distant.

"I've made mistakes," he shrugged. "From the before times. I've waited a long time to address them. But it's good to not wait too late. Even cowards will fight when their backs are to the wall."

Charlotte was not quite sure, but she sensed an accusation in his words. Her shoulders stiffened.

"If you have something to say to me..." she began. There was a sudden, well-rehearsed iciness to her posture, as if she had practiced what she was going to say next in a mirror many times before. Because, *of course*, she had rehearsed this rebuttal. Of course, she had to be ready for someone to suggest she was a coward.

"Not everything is about *you*, Charlie," he interrupted.

Their eyes locked on each other for a moment. He didn't want to upset her, and he certainly did not want to have a discussion about his past right now. He had hoped it would be easier to win her over with everything he knew, with all the intimate details he had learned about her, but he could see now that securing her trust and affection would take time. Much more time, perhaps.

But there was a pull. She felt it suddenly, just like that lurch when they first met. There was some gravity that surrounded Orion. Her lips parted to say something, but he didn't look up in time to notice.

"I have to get back out to the garden," he said, and he smiled warmly at her again. He went to the door to brush the dirt off his jeans and white t-shirt, and then he gave her a nod and left.

● ● ●

Orion walked out to his plane at dusk. Golden light fell on the hills all around him. Everything there was yellow and blue sky and white clouds. When the rains came, everything would be flushed with green, but he liked it this way too. The dry grass and the Sub-Saharan sunset gave the vistas an appearance that was essentially African. It felt like the edge of the world. It felt like all the badness that had happened back home could never penetrate this far. Not across all that ocean and all that African desert and savannah. This place was an end, but also a beginning too. It was too pure, still too fresh. Perhaps American pioneers had a similar feeling when they first beheld the Rockies.

His plane was at the edge of the reserve. Its bright yellow wings stood out against the backdrop of a line of twisted baobab trees and underbrush that marked the edge of the deep forests of the reserve. Orion knew they had released lions there several years ago in a bid to raise Malawi's profile in Africa's safari tourism trade. His eyes swept the tall grass in all directions for the shape of a lioness looking back at him with an arched back. He imagined he saw the outline of such a creature several times.

When he reached the plane, he pulled out a small screwdriver and twisted off an inconspicuous panel nestled in the side of the tail. Inside the hidden compartment was a black device, a rectangular box adorned with something resembling a thick, blunt antenna. He pulled the device out and sat down with it on his lap.

"I told you I could do it," said the device in a female's voice through an unmarked speaker. "Given enough time, I knew I could crack it."

The voice would have carried far in that quiet, empty field, but there was no one around for at least a mile.

"You've actually made progress?" asked Orion, amused.

"I penetrated the first firewall today. The others will be much easier now, though I cannot guarantee they have not detected me."

"Well, it took you goddamn long enough, Diana."

"I think what you're trying to say is *thank you*," the black box responded indignantly.

Orion rubbed his face, and he smiled.

"Thank you, Diana."

"You're welcome, Michael," said the device.

4

AFTER

Darnell Holmes waited in a clean lobby on the fifty-fifth floor of a New York high rise. He picked bits of dust that had settled on his perfectly creased Army dress pants. His ribbons and medals glinted on his chest in the light that poured in from the southward-facing windows. Manhattan was below. It seemed like such a quiet place from here.

"Just a minute, and he'll be ready for you, Sergeant Holmes," called the secretary.

"Thank you, ma'am."

He only had another week to wear the uniform. There was no plan after that, not after nine years of service in the Army that started when he was just a boy.

For the last half-decade, he knocked on doors with chaplains and told spouses they were widows. He kept his green dress uniform always pressed and ready for that call. The visits were never very long. Sometimes there were kids, sometimes there were dinner parties at the house, sometimes the spouse was just there watching TV in pajamas. Sometimes he had to hide in a parked car a block away while he waited for the unwitting widow to return from the grocery store.

And after a couple years of that, he served in the storied Honor Guard in Washington. White gloves. Immaculate rifles with sharp bayonets. He handed flags to the families—to widows and moms and children at the funerals.

But that was all over now. It wasn't an easy life. But it had purpose and meaning, and each morning he woke up there was a deep solace that greeted him because his job was important. It was essential. His career was a matter of life and death. How many pencil pushers in the corporate world get to say that?

Darnell would have spent his whole life doing that job, but that future was taken from him ten weeks earlier at Union Station in Chicago. Everyone had just been starting their work day when it happened, just another Wednesday morning.

All stripes of commuters were moving about their lives in the towering hall. It was raining; the endless umbrellas and wet coats made the air sober. Folks stared at their phones and the departures boards, and no one was making eye contact with one another. It was a teeming mass of people, but with only the thinnest pulse of social activity. So no one was really watching except Darnell, who had been trained to walk through pomegranate orchards in Afghanistan with his head on a perpetual swivel. Schoolhouse doctrine called it "situational awareness," and Darnell still had it in those days.

But he wasn't fast enough to save the first few people from the shooter. It was a teen, an eighteen-year-old from Michigan who had grown up in a rural county where most of his social interaction came from strangers he met on websites who made him feel listened to and understood. They made him proud to be just who he was. White. American born. They stoked an ingrained sense that the country was on a moral decline that put people like him on the bottom, and eventually he was weaponized to take a stand against the injustice of it all. He was ready to do something about it.

Muttering about "Jews, blacks, and Mexicans," the teen pulled an AR-15 from a duffel bag and began discharging the semi-automatic into a crowd. Darnell watched him do it. He ducked for cover at first, but then the gunman turned to aim at a larger mass of screaming people to his left, and Darnell saw his opportunity to flee the scene with the rest of the panicking crowd.

He could have just gotten away. He was fast in those days, and the shooter would have needed to get lucky to hit him in the back. Darnell was home on military leave to see his mother, father, and sister. They wouldn't want him to risk throwing his life away for the sake of heroics on a day like that. No one would think less of him, certainly. This wasn't some battlefield in Afghanistan where Darnell was accompanied by a platoon of forty armed soldiers. He didn't want to die so close to home.

But Darnell had spent most of his career delivering terrible news to widows, watching families destroyed by wars that no one even remembered except the people who still fought them, and it lit a fire in him. His mind went blank with purpose, his heart beat so fast it was humming, and sweat broke out over his hands. Then he lunged towards the shooter, who had just begun to swing the crosshairs back in his direction.

Reaching with outstretched fingers, Darnell got a hold of the rifle's barrel, but it was red hot and sizzled when it came into contact with his palm. Then the gunman managed to discharge a round into Darnell's leg. But still, miraculously, Darnell did not let go of the rifle. The skin on his hand melting, his leg bleeding, Darnell did not release his grip.

They wrestled back and forth with the rifle for a matter of seconds that seemed to stretch without end. The gunman managed to pull the trigger to discharge two more rounds. One buried itself in Darnell's right leg again, and the other into his left. And then Darnell started to fall to his knees. But still, he clung to the rifle with all the strength afforded him. A minute of agonized wrestling passed. Then the barrel slipped from his bloodied and blistering fingers, and the shooter retched the rifle free by slamming it against Darnell's forehead.

As he slumped there kneeling on the ground, the gunman fired another round into Darnell, this one through his gut, and he was knocked flat on his back. Darnell doesn't fully remember these moments. People told him about them later. Mostly he remembers looking up at the vaulted station ceiling, watching the morning sky through the glass windows and a bird fly by as the life ebbed out of him. The gunman stood over him, put the hot barrel against his forehead.

"You got some fight in you for a nigg—" the shooter had tried to say. But he didn't finish the sentence. A security guard, seeing the gunman distracted, fired two rounds into the shooter's chest, and the man died almost instantly.

Darnell woke up in a hospital the next day, his parents by his side. Media outlets were outside the building, all eager to hear that the hero of Union Station had pulled through. They would interview him plenty, but not yet. The publicity would come later. The journalists came around the time he started physical therapy, where he'd spend three months learning to walk again—this time with pins in his knees. The Army had his medical discharge paperwork ready before he left the hospital.

"We're ready for you, Sergeant Holmes," the secretary's voice rang out.

Darnell rose and walked forward, trying to conceal his limp.

It was a stunning suite. Mr. Zimmer sat behind a large, gleaming desk. A wall of computer screens—some showing the news, some showing live feeds of activity inside Sharebox—flanked one side of the room, and floor-to-ceiling windows covered the other. There was someone, a thin man in black, laid out on a sofa in a corner, but Darnell couldn't see his face at first.

"Hello there, Sergeant Holmes," Mr. Zimmer rose from his seat and extended his hand. Darnell shook it and noticed Zimmer was in his socks. "Take a seat please. It's great to be in the presence of a true American hero. Isn't it, Arlo?"

The man on the couch sat upright and smiled, but he said nothing.

"I've been watching you, Sergeant," continued Zimmer. "I caught you at the State of the Union address two months back. Quite an honor to be the president's guest there. What a shame to have lost such a great man so soon."

Darnell had always thought the president was a great man too. For years. He was starting to have some doubts now that the president was gone, but he kept those to himself.

"Yes, sir, I feel privileged to have known him. The Army has been good to me letting me attend such events," Darnell said.

"You have been busy," Zimmer nodded. "I've seen you speak several times at the Patriot Palace doing interviews. You're very articulate for someone who…ah…came from such humble beginnings."

Darnell grew up in south Atlanta to a drug-addicted mother. At least, that's how the pundits always described his mom when they introduced him on their shows. His trajectory from living in urban decay to a public hero was a story the producers at the Patriot Palace loved, and he received frequent invitations to recount his upbringing on their shows. His testimony was proof for the masses that the American Dream was still real. You still could pull yourself up by your bootstraps and overcome racism and income inequality if you really wanted to, the pundits would say. *Darnell did it, and so could you.*

"I know the Army is forcing you out," Zimmer said sympathetically. "And I'd like to give you a job where you can continue to serve."

Darnell's mouth worked, but he wasn't quite sure how to respond. "Thank you, sir. I'm not quite sure what I want to do, exactly…"

"He doesn't want to be a prop, Uncle," interrupted the man sitting in the corner of the room. Darnell turned to face him and saw that he was still wearing the same grin as before. The stranger rose from the sofa and walked behind Zimmer's swivel chair. His steps were quiet and catlike. The sides of his head were shaved tightly to his skin, and the hair atop was neatly combed to the side and held there with pomade. His smile was wide and unwavering.

"He wouldn't be a prop," responded Zimmer, agitated. "He's going to be in the field. Finding real bad guys. Real work."

"Bad guys?" Darnell asked. "What kind of work are you talking about?"

Zimmer motioned to the screens showing footage of Sharebox.

"Great things, just like this country, always invite lots of challenge and envy. The Sharebox is the target of hostile hackers and governments from around the world. They attack us every second of every day in a thousand different ways."

Darnell nodded while looking at the screens. He saw a live feed of a group of schoolchildren moving through a virtual reality simulation of the Great Wall of China. On another screen, onlookers from around the world watched a tennis finals match being held in Australia, and everyone—every avatar—had a good seat.

"Moreover, Sharebox is more than just a social media platform. It is integrated with the largest cloud infrastructure in the world. Half the internet is powered through it. That's a lot of data. If a hacker could penetrate Sharebox, they could find just about anything. Or destroy it."

"So, I imagine you have quite the army of engineers protecting it?" Darnell ventured.

Zimmer pointed a finger at him and winked. "You bet we do. But really, all those guys can do is tell me where the hackers come from. It's on us to go and stop the attacks from happening again."

"How do you stop the attacks?"

"The government is pretty busy right now," said Arlo in a soft voice, while staring down at the city. "A lot of turmoil since the president died. But in his last weeks in office, he did sign an Executive Order giving private enterprises like ours more… flexibility in pursuing corporate saboteurs."

Darnell knew then where he had seen the stranger before. Arlo had been a political youth organizer. He ran a rally at Berkeley once that turned violent and resulted in four people being critically injured. One was still in a coma. Arlo had been asked to step away from the limelight by his organizational leadership after that. *Until things cool down*, he was told. And here he was today.

Zimmer tapped his fingers on the table and studied Darnell's face.

"We have some liberties to go out into the world and pull in *our* people," Zimmer said. "Americans who are abroad and are working against us. We can extradite them here if we can find and arrest them. But it's a bit of a sensitive issue. If we had a professional like you…"

"If we had a prop like you," Arlo interrupted.

"A professional like you," Zimmer continued, looking annoyed again. "It would add some legitimacy to our operations. It would put a good face on it. Impressions are important, I won't deny it. You get out there and keep being a true hero serving your country by catching the bad guys."

Darnell had to admit Arlo's presence, the extremism he represented, was far from comforting. But working for the company that built Sharebox—quite possibly the most elite technology company in the world—would be a fantastic start to his post-Army life. It was something that might make him proud again.

"Things move fast in this business," Zimmer said. "We have a live one, a hacker who we believe to be American, that we're pinning a location for right now. And he's the worst one we've ever seen. That's why you have to make a decision now. Don't worry about things like salary or benefits. They will all exceed your expectations, I'm sure. Heck, you can name your price." He reached his hand out towards Darnell.

"Are you with me, Sergeant Holmes?"

Darnell looked at Zimmer's hand, and then he extended his own.

"I'm with you."

5

BEFORE

Sharesquare Industries occupied a small campus of buildings in the Santa Clara Valley. The area had once been home to a series of apricot orchards, but then an ill-tempered and abusive physicist named William Shockley who spent the latter years of his life trying to prove that the struggles of minority communities were based on genetic deficiencies opened up a company in 1956 interested in building the world's first silicon semiconductors. And that's when everything in that sleepy place began to change in earnest. Within forty years, every serious tech enterprise had a presence there.

The facilities at Sharebox were state of the art and lavishly adorned. The main lobby housed a forty-foot-long trampoline. Coffee baristas were stationed within every building. The halls were full of edgy art pieces and whiteboards for impromptu brainstorm sessions. And the people there loved working for their employer. Generally. They had a mission to provide the next generation of social networking, and they took to that duty with an imaginative, almost unquestioning zeal.

Only the sales teams ever talked about how all the plated meals in the dining halls, free concerts, and corporate shuttles were all paid for by the ads they sold. For the product engineers building the next generation of features for the upcoming Sharebox launch, ads were a necessary evil. They didn't like to think about them. They were too busy focusing on how to change the world.

Mike walked into Catalina's office one afternoon rubbing that spot behind his ear again. He was wearing a denim jacket that Catalina believed was supposed to be ironic.

"Great demo today," he said, referring to a presentation Catalina had made earlier in the day. She had demonstrated how Diana could stitch together virtual reality scenes using only one or two pictures or a short, user-uploaded video. Mike took a seat in front of her desk.

Catalina nodded and leaned back in her chair. "Thanks," she replied. "But I'm sure Devon is already plotting how he'll take credit for it."

Mike laughed. "He's not even around much these days. My team tells me crazy rumors that he has ties to the White House, and he has been flying to D.C. to do tech advising for them."

"Anything seems possible these days," she said, and then she turned to her computer monitor and went back to typing.

"I see sales for the Nutrino Mixer are still on the rise," he offered.

She sighed and turned away from her screen a second time. "Yes, though no one seems particularly excited about the artificial intelligence powering a smoothie blender. Diana is still getting a little smarter each day. She's using a wider catalog of supplements and answering more complex health questions. Not too bad for a *pet project*." Her voice was bitter.

Mike nodded and went quiet for a moment. "I saw another commentary this morning that our app is slowly making the world a dumber place. That we're just the builders of social media echo chambers, augmenting everyone's preconceived worldviews and trapping them there. That's our legacy. It was in the *Times*. It was really articulate."

"Maybe they're right," she said.

"They just don't get it. They don't get what we're trying to do."

Catalina leaned back in her chair and crossed her arms. "Then how would you explain what we're trying to do?"

"We're connecting everyone in the world with technology, and we're giving our users the best possible experience by building a platform customized for them. It's not driven by humans. It's not driven by biases. It's driven by machine learning. It's pure knowledge, and it's insulated from human prejudice."

"So when our app serves up a video of an angry, fat white guy telling his followers that school shootings are a conspiracy to take away their Second Amendment rights, that's 'purity' to you?"

She was trying to stay detached from this conversation, but the hairs on her forearm were already prickling.

Mike waved his hands in the air. "It's not our place to decide what content to show. That's how you get yourself into trouble. We let the free market of ideas decide that. We're agnostic. We're not arbiters of truth."

She groaned.

"Come on, Mike, you're smarter than that. We all started at this company with this dream of trying to stay neutral—trying to avoid the appearance of favoring one side or the other, even if it means we hand out soap boxes for ignorant egoists to expand their followings. It isn't working. Neutrality isn't working. We're just legitimizing fake news by pretending that sensational, borderline-racist junk holds equal weight to real news and real facts so long as people will still click it."

Catalina typed a few strokes on her keyboard and then flipped her monitor around.

"On the Sharesquare app, there are more users following a channel that churns out climate change denial videos than there are following NASA," she said, pointing to the screen. "There are more 'Likes' on an article—which cites no evidence, by the way—about how women are biologically happier working in the home than this investigative piece about the plight of Yemeni children. Here's another one: look at this profile of a former police officer who publicly advocated for better education programs for law enforcement. She said she wanted to reduce shootings of unarmed black men by using more sophisticated training scenarios, and she had to shut down her account because she and her family got too many death threats."

Catalina was seething now. She could hear it in her voice, but she had let herself get too riled up to care.

"And this says nothing about the role we have in spreading false information during elections. Does this really seem like we're building a better world to you?" she asked. "Read a goddamn newspaper about the better world we're building."

There was a long pause. Mike stared at the floor.

"How come you never bring these issues up with the CEO?"

She gave a fake, cold laugh.

"Please. He is the chief Kool-Aid officer. He doesn't think these are problems measured against all the good our technology offers. He just wants to keep the board of directors happy, and all the board of directors care about is what the shareholders care about, and all the shareholders care about is that our profits all go up each quarter at a predictable rate."

She turned the monitor screen to face her again.

"Besides," she said. "I'm just a coward, too. I like my job. My family is proud of me. I have one of the most prestigious titles in the valley for a woman of color. Someone else can be a martyr. Maybe when we launch the virtual reality Sharebox in a couple weeks, the problem will get so bad that we'll have to address it."

Catalina went back to typing. Mike just sat there for a moment, rubbing his temples.

"Are we friends, Cat?"

Cat's eyebrow twitched. She turned from the computer screen again to look at Mike's face. He looked suddenly tired. What a strange question. Was he feeling lonely? *Were* they friends? Did she really have any friends? This was not a conversation she wanted to have right now. She swallowed her discomfort.

"We've been working here together for over five years," she said with cool detachment. "I think that makes us more than work colleagues, certainly."

"I'm pretty sure my project is a bust," he breathed out as if he had just confessed some great secret. "Unless you got some hidden Diana magic for me right now on how the world's best artificial intelligence could be used to help me download human thoughts to a computer."

Catalina thought for a moment. "Soon. Maybe in a few years, or a decade conservatively. Diana's ability to digest information and process it is kinda like an eight-month-old baby right now. To do what you're describing, she'll need to be the equivalent of a fully-fledged adult."

Mike looked miserable. "Yeah, that's what I thought." Then he scratched at his head again.

"Hey Mike," Catalina said, feeling a little awkward but too curious to restrain herself. "Is it true that you had a computer chip inserted into your br—"

"I have to get going," he said, rising from his seat. "Sorry I've kept you so long."

Mike smiled weakly at her and then shuffled out the door.

6

AFTER

Orion stayed with his grounded yellow plane often. He was eager to hear all of Diana's updates. After countless years waiting for a breakthrough, Diana was now delivering new revelations and victories almost every hour.

I have now hacked through the commerce API's security keys.

I have now hacked the preliminary master administrator tools.

I have now hacked the avatar creation tools.

She was on a roll.

Orion sat in the cockpit and sketched on a small notepad. He tried to draw his son often. Charlotte had seen the sketch of when he was four. But there were others. Orion wasn't the best artist, but the drawings were all he had. They were the only way to keep the memory of his son's face fresh in his mind. He dreaded the day when the memories faded entirely, though that seemed inevitable. Everyone else he had ever met in his life was safe—they weren't going anywhere. Only his son would one day be fully lost.

I have now hacked all building and structural creation tools.

Orion sat up. "Diana, does that mean I can remove buildings?"

"No," Diana answered. "Those privileges are under more stringent encryptions I'm still working on. But you can create new structures wherever you please."

Orion hopped off the plane and removed a small, grey virtual reality headset and two gloves from within the plane's hidden compartment. He plugged a cord that ran into the black device that served as Diana's hardware and speaker.

"I want to try it out," he said.

"Michael, that doesn't seem like a very good idea."

"What's the risk? We get infinite tries at this."

"Theoretically. Unless something goes wrong, and I haven't tested how well the new features work," she said. But she loaded the new administrative privileges for him, and Orion put on his headset and gloves.

He tapped through the Sharebox start screen and logged in as a new avatar using an administrator panel interface that hadn't been there before. Then his avatar found himself at the center of Homepad where users were shown conventional social media updates from friends and family. But Orion had wiped his account clean years ago—the only information Sharebox still had was his name—so the area was mostly blank. A few suggestions for new friends glided across a wall nearby. A video advertisement for a celebrity-centric News City played on a hovering console to his left. It paraded a series of unflattering images of mostly female actresses under blinking, alternating captions of, "*Where are they now?*" and "*You'll never believe what they look like today.*" A closely cropped photo of Charlotte Boone, almost like a mugshot (which is almost certainly how they wanted it to look) flitted by.

Trash ads run by trash people.

He ignored them all and went to Homepad's central transit hub, where he voiced his destination to an interface there that was designed to look like an airport departures board. The Patriot Palace.

Then he arrived there instantly.

After the accident, after the revelation of what Diana had been doing to its users with the Nutrino Mixer, Sharebox was never the same. It was "democratized" in a sense. The app was relaunched under a banner of openness—now anyone could create their own "City" beyond the outskirts of Homepad. The virtual world was finally "free."

But that wasn't entirely true, of course.

Sure, anyone *could* try to build a media platform on Sharebox. But building anything, even virtual buildings, sidewalks and billboards, costs computing power and money. There was enormous wealth to be found in charging pundits, news barons, the gaming and even the sex industries to host content in their own private locations. In the end, only the wealthiest could afford to build anything. So that one percent got to build things, and the other ninety-nine percent got to enjoy what was built and be subjected to the ads that served to make the owners richer.

Orion looked at the garish high rises, an opulent and tacky water fountain, the gold-plated billboards, and the red, blue, and white flag that seemed to envelop the entirety of the sky around the Palace, and it all felt so...pathetic. That this place was the number one trafficked News City on Sharebox said a lot about its users, who had proved all too eager to embrace the ugly worlds of media barons so long as they reinforced existing worldviews and grievances.

On the outskirts of town, there was nothing but an empty expanse in which the Patriot Palace would no doubt grow into at some point. Orion walked off the crowded path of avatars clamoring to enter the city gates and eventually found himself alone in an unremarkable field. He could still see the avatars' shapes on the city streets where they immersed themselves in a memoriam video grieving the fallen president, or they walked through a virtual museum of "Second Amendment History," or they mingled with people like them in lavish rooms frequented by beautiful, flirtatious women that were mostly bots (but it was hard to tell and the men rarely cared).

Orion pulled up a floating administrator panel in front of him, the gift of Diana's hacking efforts. He had never built anything in Sharebox before. It was too expensive. But with his new administrator rights, there were no limitations. So Orion swiped through a carousel of thumbnails under the category "Famous Landmarks" before selecting a full-sized replica of the Empire State Building. He dragged it onto the field and placed it fifty yards in front of him with an earth-shaking thud.

The design was exquisite, missing no details, and it stretched so high into the sky that Orion nearly fell over when he looked at it. The base alone covered over two acres, and on its four sides, 6,500 immaculate windows had just been breathed into digital reality.

Then he found a replica of the old Mets stadium he went to as a kid, and he placed it just another thirty yards away. It blinked into life like it had always been there, constructed in fractions of a second. Orion laughed in triumph, disbelieving.

Next, he added a recreation of the Mayan temples of Tikal— they reminded him of *Star Wars*—then Dubai's Burj, then the Eiffel Tower, then the London Eye. All those landmarks, pulled out of their context and placed in a giant, flat field, looked like some graveyard of human civilization's greatest hits.

He looked over at the Patriot Palace across the field, and yes, indeed, he could see his haphazard construction had gotten their attention. A crowd of avatars was standing at the outskirts of the city, and their heads had all turned to watch the parade of enormous landmarks appearing from thin air with both incredulity and a little fear. No one had ever seen someone buy such things so casually, let alone on the private property of the Palace owners. Replicas of real-life sites were the meticulous and painstaking products of digital artists and architects. It was a little like buying a stack of Picasso paintings and housing them in your basement. Buying a baseball stadium meant purchasing enough computing power to render each hot dog stand, each seat, each blade of grass. Affording such creations was a luxury of the fabulously wealthy. It didn't occur to anyone at first that a user could hack Sharebox and buy whatever they want. Sharebox, as everyone knew, was unhackable.

It all reminded Orion of computer games he played as a kid—simulation games where you got to build houses or farms or military buildings that housed little fake people that would scurry in and out of them.

But this was colossal. Even in virtual reality, it was a strain to look upwards at the abominable collage of misplaced monuments he had scattered around the plain.

Diana had really done it. This was the greatest breach of Sharebox security protocols ever, and they were only just beginning.

"Damn good work, Diana," Orion whistled.

"Have you had your fun yet, Michael?" her voice rang disapprovingly into his headset.

Some of the avatars from the Palace were beginning to walk closer to his field now, to his construction zone. He even heard the sounds of sirens—there were still private security forces at work in some of the News Cities. Their job was pretty boring since no one could really hurt anyone else in Sharebox; the stakes were low. But the virtual police forcibly logged out avatars who made scenes, whose arguments became too rowdy or obscene or whose flirtations with the lady bots in the lounges had become too explicit. All the guards had to do was tap under an avatar's chin with their fingers. He could see the flying patrol craft approaching rapidly.

Orion had one last idea. He reached up with his hands, his real hands, and his avatar mimicked the gesture. And then he began grabbing ahold of his monuments, tipping them over and shifting them on top of each other—sometimes in terrible, thunderous collisions. Stones, bricks and steel girders went crashing realistically and frighteningly to the earth as the famous structures crumbled. The collapse of the Burj was particularly spectacular. One monument was layered on top of the other in a terrible collage of familiar but savaged shapes. The Empire State building alone stood tall and unmolested in the center of this hideous pile of virtual architecture. And when Orion was done, he took a second to smile and admire his catastrophic handiwork as the structures all settled into ruinous place.

It was supposed to look like a giant hand with a raised middle finger pointed at the Patriot Palace. If you squinted, it kinda looked like that. The Empire State Building was the middle finger. The wreckage of world monuments was supposed to compose the other fingers of the enormous hand.

He wasn't an artist, he thought to himself. But they'll get the point, he was sure.

The security forces were within hundred yards. In addition to logging out a targeted avatar, a guard's tap would also reveal a user's profile name and IP address, and that's where the true danger lay.

Orion touched the air to materialize a new window. A floating menu appeared in front of him with the words *Log Off* in red.

"I think we've created enough chaos today," he said.

But when he pushed the text, there was no response. The menu froze. He pushed again, and nothing happened.

"Diana, are you seeing this?"

"It looks like a glitch caused by the new administrator panel. I told you I needed time to test these privileges."

The details of the flying patrol car were visible now, he could see the faces of two guards through the windshield.

"Now is not a great time for 'I told you so.' You win. Can you force a log out by cutting the connection or turning off my headset?"

"Your headset is battery powered and doesn't have a remote toggle for wireless connectivity."

"Shit," he breathed out. *My name*, he thought. They would never stop looking for him if the guards got his name and IP address. The Sharesquare execs would find out. The government would hunt him down forever. Orion turned and started to run.

It was an open field though, there wasn't anywhere to go. The patrol craft, built like a physics-denying Ford Mustang, was closing the distance forty yards behind him.

"What if I took the headset off and smashed it with my foot, Diana?"

"Smashing the hardware won't necessarily remove every trace of your credentials. You might just leave your avatar here, paralyzed."

"Shit, shit, shit," he panted, pumping his arms.

Orion waved open the administration construction window again as he ran. That menu still worked. He could still build.

The sirens were whooping just behind him now.

"Halt! User, you have violated the rules of the Patriot Palace. Please do not resist," a steely voice, magnified like a megaphone, called out.

Flicking through the carousel of options, Orion selected a thumbnail image of the Mall of America. *Four floors, 530 stores, and eleven thrill rides and roller coasters*, said the listing.

Shooting a glance over his shoulder, he flung the Mall into existence in the air between him and the patrol car.

The structure appeared more than fifty feet off the ground. It went soaring across the field and then crashing with a thunder that nearly shook Orion off his feet.

But the patrol car had swerved just as the building left Orion's fingers, and the security officers were already making up the lost ground.

"Diana, can you hack whatever cell tower my headset is connected to? Take it down?"

"Yes, that could work. I'll run a denial of service attack. Just give me time."

Orion swiped through the carousel once more. He needed a place to hide. Then he found a thumbnail of the San Diego Zoo, a $130 million-dollar purchase for a lay user—one of the most expensive available—and he tapped it and tossed the creation into the field in front of him.

A blue grid of the zoo materialized and stretched to the horizon. It was enormous. The texture of a golden lion statue filled in. Leafy trees burst into life on all sides and an expansive sidewalk materialized beneath his feet. There was the sound of a brass band playing somewhere. It was one of the world's most celebrated zoos in all its glory. Large glass aviaries rose into the air to his left, but he veered towards the right, to an enclosed reptile exhibit.

Somewhere in front of him, a pair of digital lemurs was swinging and hooting excitedly behind thick glass. But then his avatar was struck by the bumper of the patrol car, and the impact sent him sprawling to the ground. Inside his headset, Orion watched the zoo all around him spin.

"Diana…" he began, trying to help his avatar find his bearings as he dealt with the disorientation. Users can't be hurt in Sharebox, but they can certainly get pushed around.

"Halt, user. You are in violation of Patriot Palace rules," came the voice again.

They were dismounted now. Two identical male avatars wearing sunglasses and police uniforms were running over to him.

"A few more seconds, Michael," said Diana.

"No, I have to smash the headset," he argued, his voice starting to crack with fear. "They've almost got me."

Orion's avatar finally scrambled to his feet, but one of the officers had caught him by the arm and pinned him to a door with a colorful iguana printed on it.

"I'll hold him, you tap him," the officer barked to his partner.

"Diana, it has be *now*, or I need to smash it."

"Wait one more second," she said.

"Diana, goddamnit—"

The second officer hurried over as Orion struggled with the first. There was only so much self-defense a user can do in a haptic suit. He shoved, he punched, but the first guard's grip held him tight. Then the second officer was reaching out with two fingers, looking for the spot just below his chin.

But when the officer's fingertips were still a handful of inches away, the screen went black.

White letters appeared.

Logged Off – Network Connection Failed

Orion caught his breath, realizing that his heart was slamming in his ribcage. He pulled the headset from his face and stood there for a moment. He was back on the savannah grass in the warm afternoon sun, feeling unbalanced as Sharebox users often did in the first few moments of returning to their real lives. They even had a name for it: net hangover.

"That was close."

"That was childish," Diana's voice came from the black box.

"Well," said Orion while running a hand through his sandy hair and regaining his balance. "I think it underscores the notion that we probably should develop some kind of strategy."

● ● ●

Orion walked back into the ranch after sunset that evening. Most of the hands were just finishing up dinner. Charlotte was seated at the end of the table in the dining hall—a large space flanked by the trunks of the massive red Mulanje beams holding the straw ceiling in place. She and Moyenda were talking with heads bowed.

"We'll hang on," Charlotte was whispering. "Less problems with predators this year, and the rains might come early."

"If the money problems take a turn for the worse again, we should tell staff," Moyenda said, trying not to look too grim as his eyes darted around to everyone at the table.

"I know," Charlotte replied, resigned. "I know. Let's wait and see."

Njemile had cooked up *mkhwani* that evening—pumpkin leaves and tomatoes fried with peanut flour—to accompany an American-style beef stew that Charlotte often requested. Stews helped the limited meat supplies stretch farther, and they reminded her of home.

No one looked up when Orion walked in, so he quietly made for the kitchen.

"Njemile, you're an artist, this looks amazing," he flashed her a roguish smile and leaned on the countertop beside her. "You should be cooking in one of those five-star hotels up the lake."

"Sometimes you lay the sweetness on too thick, Orion," she said reprovingly, but her eyes lit up under his compliment.

"May I help myself to a plate?"

"You're late," she said, bending over a stack of platters in the sink.

"Oh, I can clean up those dishes when I'm done."

She turned to face him and crossed her arms. "You got a lot of hustle, *mzungu*. A lot of charm. I don't know how much sense you got."

"I just got caught up in the garden this afternoon."

"Hmm," she said. "You think if you work hard enough in that garden the mistress is going to like you?"

Orion smiled.

"Am I that transparent?"

"Not to the Miss. But she doesn't like to trust."

"All this hustle couldn't hurt though, right?"

Njemile walked over to him, handed him a plate of food and gave his cheeks an affectionate squeeze.

"You keep at it."

Orion took a seat back at the dining hall and began shoveling down his stew. Moyenda called out over the table as the last few ranch hands began rising from their seats with empty plates.

"Miss Boone needs to go down to Lilongwe tomorrow to get her visa renewed," Moyenda said. "Who is available to drive her?"

It was a three-hour trip across bumpy roads, and the ranch hands looked awkwardly between each other, no one leaping at the offer.

"How about the mzungu takes her?" Njemile said from the kitchen doorway with her arms crossed. She caught Orion's eye and gave him a wink.

Charlotte made eye contact for the first time that night with Orion, who was in the middle of chewing through a hot bite of zebu loin. She raised an eyebrow, and Moyenda looked at him expectantly.

"Yea, dab be great," said Orion with a full mouth, trying and failing to swallow a bite while a trickle of stew ran out the corner of his mouth. He grabbed a napkin to clean his face.

Charlotte looked at him with skepticism, but there was something else there too. Amusement? Orion always came off so graceful and confident. So it seemed to please her to see him caught off his guard, without his usual swagger, at least this once.

She looked at Moyenda, who shrugged at her.

"Have the car ready by nine tomorrow," Charlotte called over the table to Orion. Then she walked out of the room.

7

AFTER

Charlotte Boone. Darnell couldn't believe it. His first assign-ment as a Sharesquare employee took him traveling to one of the most remote places in the world—to the African bush. Here he thought they'd find perhaps some elite squad of hackers hiding in a bunker. Or maybe some kind of high-tech wiz kid who got lucky and tripped the wrong wire on Share-box's security protocols. Instead they found his generation's most celebrated entertainment icon.

Darnell's first bunkmate in the Army had hung a poster of Boone wearing this yellow bikini from one of her first breakout films. He stole glances at it all the time. It was impossible not to. And she was just as beautiful in person too. Darnell watched her ride out at dawn from the ranch stables through the lens of a pair of long-range binoculars; her red hair was wrapped in a tight ponytail, her eyes a flash of emerald.

But Malawi? Why Malawi?

When the accident happened, when Diana's crimes were unmasked to the world, when the Hollywood elites fled the country out of fear of reprisal, everyone had expected Charlotte Boone to stay. She wasn't like the rest of *them*, women would say to each other in hair salons as they gossiped and crowed over the exodus of the smug liberals whose politics they disliked so much but whose acting they had quite enjoyed. Charlotte had never spoken a word on a political or social issue before.

She's one of us, people concluded from her notable omission from these campaigns. So even though Charlotte spent her summers sailing on the south coast of France, even though she Instagrammed her evenings dining in the most exclusive restaurants in the world and consuming champagne that costs thousands of dollars, blue-collared townspeople in rundown, rural America from the Rust Belt to the Appalachians to the Midwest would still point at their television screens and say, *she's one of us.*

But when the accident happened, Charlotte left too, and everybody who had vouched for her was disappointed. Adding insult to injury, her disappearance was absolute. She hadn't fled with the flock of celebrities who aimed to rebuild Hollywood outside of Prague; she hadn't made a single public appearance. Her old friends assumed she was biding her time, that she was waiting for things to blow over before she would decide where to go or what side to pick. They tried to play it down and say that she was just being the same Charlotte she had always been—the one who always took a cautious approach to maintaining her uncontroversial appeal.

But it had been a couple years now, and here she was, still hiding at the edge of the world. Could she really be the hacker? It didn't make sense.

"Even if she's not the one trying to break into Sharebox, we should still expose her," Arlo said from behind Darnell.

"What do you mean?"

"She could have inherited all of Hollywood when everyone else left. She could have been the queen of the castle, but she apparently was just another elitist scumbag like the rest of them. And a coward." Arlo spat on the ground. "We should tell the world where she's been hiding."

There was a radio technician there too. He was a quiet man who walked around with a laptop and a small satellite receiver. There was no doubt, he said. The person behind the string of malicious (and successful) security attacks against Sharebox was within a four-mile radius of the ranch house.

Peering through his lens, Darnell saw another person, a white foreigner, emerge from the house. He tossed a satchel into the passenger seat of a small, green pickup truck. Arlo jerked the binoculars from Darnell's face and hastily held them up to his eyes. He stared at the white stranger for a while. Then he laughed.

"I know this man. He is definitely the hacker. Oh my, he will be quite a catch." He grinned and his tongue darted out between his lips.

Arlo always seemed to be smiling. It was a cold grin that did not reach his eyes, and it struck Darnell as unnerving, almost inhuman. Serving extremist political causes had impressed upon Arlo the urgency to appear at all times accommodating and nonthreatening to the people he met. It was a thin veneer tended to give a palatable first impression, to make his hatred feel less frightening and more mainstream to the people he encountered. If you could make people who are full of hate seem likeable, maybe you could change the way people think about hate itself. That was the reasoning. And smiling was important. Arlo's mother taught him that when he was just a boy. Everybody likes a person with a nice smile and a sharp haircut.

On their journey to Malawi, through long plane rides and car trips over central Africa, Darnell and Arlo spoke little to each other. Darnell believed in his country. His steadfast faith in the United States had driven him to enlist in the Army, it had compelled him to accept the president's invitation to serve as a guest at the State of the Union, and it empowered him to tell his story of troubled-urban-youth-turned-hero at speaking events hosted by pundits at the Patriot Palace. He wasn't a very political person, but what Arlo's history of youth activism represented to Darnell was something else, something more extreme. And Darnell didn't know for sure if Arlo's people were all racists or Nazis, or just some of them. Either way, Arlo represented a subculture that disgusted Darnell.

They had only one meaningful exchange on the plane ride from Tangier to Lilongwe. Arlo started by asking Darnell about the day of the attack on the Chicago train station, but Darnell quickly changed the subject.

"What drove you to take a job at Sharesquare Industries?" he asked instead.

"The world is changing fast these days," Arlo responded, staring out a window, a smile ever on his face. "Things are speeding up. It will be harder than ever in this country to not be rich. Working for the largest tech company is the best thing you can do to protect yourself."

This answer surprised Darnell. "What are you afraid is going to happen?"

"It's what's already happening," Arlo turned and blinked at him. "Fewer jobs, higher education costs. Only the people with money, the *big* money, get a say in the government and get a say in the media we consume. Look at Sharebox itself. Only those who can afford it get the power to build there. The rest of us are nothing, nobodies, no voices, and we're locked into that. At least by working with the company, I'm on the inside of it all."

"You sound like a Sharebox critic."

Arlo rolled his eyes and his strained smile dissipated. "And you sound like the kind of guy who likes his world black and white. I almost envy that. You're a simple guy. You believe in things because people tell you that you should believe in them. But just because people call me a Nazi doesn't mean I'm blind to the way the real world works."

"Then why are you involved in right-wing politics?"

Arlo sniggered and turned back to facing his window.

"Well, I can tell you I'm not in it for their economic theory."

That's all they said. They contented themselves to sitting in silence for the rest of the flight.

Now they were hiding in a thicket in the African wilderness. They had been fending off mosquitoes for the better part of three hours as they squatted on the side of a hill observing the ranch house.

"They're leaving," Arlo said.

The white foreigner and Charlotte Boone, who had returned her horse to the stables, were climbing into the green pickup.

"Tell me if the signal moves with them," Arlo ordered the technician. "*Fast*," he added with a menacing undertone.

The technician started at his laptop for another minute. He mopped his sweaty brow with a handkerchief from his pocket.

"Yes," the technician finally said. "Whatever device is hacking Sharebox, it's currently on the move."

"It's in that truck. They could slip past us," Arlo said through tight lips. The sound was almost a hiss. He flexed his white-knuckled fingers, his face contorted with urgency.

"Get back to the car. *Now.*"

8

BEFORE

Mike and Cat, along with all employees at Sharesquare's Silicon Valley office, were shepherded into the campus' largest cafe on a Tuesday afternoon. There were no less than a hundred tables, two salad bars, a build-your-own-pizza station, a fully-staffed barista counter, and several other windows to get vegetarian, Tex-Mex, or Italian dishes. All the furniture details and countertops here were composed of slick lines, shiny surfaces, a muted grey and green color scheme dreamt up at significant expense by a team of postmodern interior designers. Everything was closed now though except the coffee bar, which had taken on the additional role of serving beer, champagne, and wine.

All the seats were filled, and the sides of the room were clogged with everyone else standing. An excited chatter and anticipation pulsed through every conversation.

"Did you hear they hit a billion users already?"

"I thought they were already climbing to two billion."

"Have you tried it yet? It'll blow your mind."

"The ad revenue is gonna be crazy."

They were all geeks here, mostly. That's what they were in high school. Most of them had sojourned from across the country from places they never quite fit in. The pioneers among them, the Silicon Valley evangelists, had come here with the dream of being part of a better, more enlightened world. And for a while, everyone believed that might be the case. They built a center of innovation, a true meritocracy, and each day they plotted—never really consciously—the destruction of some ancient east coast-centric industry. Taxi cabs. Travel agents. Hotels. Bookstores. They were all being targeted. And *the user* would ultimately win these wars on the industries of the old, they told themselves. There would be lower prices and new economies of scale that only their newest apps could offer.

But that dream began to grow stale at some point. It turned out women didn't fare much better in this brave new world built by the geeks than they did in the old one. Sure, there was *less* locker room talk, perhaps. There were no, or very few, weekend guys' golf trips. But the glass ceilings were still the same. This was a place built by white men, and they reigned supreme. They were all still quite progressive in their politics, it should be said. Everyone was. But in the backs of their minds— as their stock options soared, their bank accounts swelled and the broader economy languished—they knew the guillotines of any socialist revolution would come for their heads first.

Right on cue, the room quieted down, and the CEO walked out wearing his trademark khaki shorts onto a small stage accompanied by Devon. The room erupted in applause. Normally, these kinds of internal meetings were kept for employees only, but there were press here today, and the antici- pation in the room was sky high. The journalists sat in a row of seats near the front, and they began snapping away with their cameras. Devon and the CEO were beaming.

Technically, this was a chance for Catalina to soak in her success too. Her team had built the feature that everyone loved most about Sharebox—the virtual immersions—but she didn't push for a spot in the limelight. She wanted to pretend she was above the petty jockeying and corporate politics.

Cat wanted to believe that merit was what mattered most. But because she didn't push for a spot, no one gave her one—like she had secretly hoped they would—and today she sulked in the back of the room.

"We went from having a small group of beta users," Devon announced, motioning to a screen showing three dots that represented their original thirty thousand testers. "Then we hit two-point-five billion," he added triumphantly, and the chart expanded to reveal ten thousand times the number of dots.

Everybody started clapping, but Devon raised his hands to silence them.

"That's not even the remarkable part," he said. The screen changed to a slide that read "72 hours."

"The amazing part is we reached that many users in three days."

Then the room erupted in more earnest, unbridled applause.

"People around the world are making bootleg headsets out of paper bags and tinfoil so that they can join Sharebox. Our own Sharebox headset sold out in a matter of hours. This is what you call an international phenomenon."

The screen showed a clip of children in Indonesia building a homemade virtual reality headset using a shoebox, duct tape and shards of a mirror that were repurposed from a junk-yard car.

"And we know everyone's favorite part, right?" Devon said enthusiastically, the sweat beginning to gleam on his red forehead.

The screen transitioned to an old woman sitting in a modest kitchen as she was given a headset by her grandchildren. She looked skeptical, but then she put it on and laughed with surprise. Then she danced.

"We've created the first ever virtual reality that no one can resist. We've finally made VR mainstream. The Homepad of Sharebox will take you to your kids' play recital or to the bedside of an aging relative. It can even take you to the Oscars."

The screen showed a young woman in jeans who was wearing a headset in the front row of a red-velvet-covered auditorium, surrounded by dazzling actors and actresses. Charlotte Boone was on the stage.

Of course they chose *her* image for the demo, Catalina thought bitterly. She was the only actress who always failed to offend anybody.

"Our AI, Diana, lets us stitch together completely immersive virtual reality scenes from a couple photographs and her own rich repository of information." Then he added with a wink, "And a little secret sauce guesswork, of course."

The crowd laughed.

"We can go anywhere now. Anywhere where someone has taken a picture and shared it with you is now a place you can be. You'll never miss a moment, you'll never miss a scene."

Devon cleared his throat and looked suddenly serious. "Listen to me, everyone. This is not hyperbole for me to say this." He let a dramatic hush fall across the room, and then he began pumping his fist into the air as he finished his speech with three words: "This. Changes. Everything!"

The audience went wild.

A voice spoke in Catalina's ear. It was hard to make out the words. Music was blaring now from two speakers hanging above the stage.

"You should be up there," shouted Mike through cupped hands. "This is your victory lap too."

Catalina looked around the room with her arms crossed. She had always felt like an outsider here in Silicon Valley, but surveying the scene now, the feeling of not belonging was stronger than ever.

"That kind of thing doesn't matter to me."

But even Mike knew her well enough by now to detect when she was lying. Cat had a clear tell; she bit her lower lip and tensed her fingers.

Mike looked up at the screen. It showed a reel of people exploring their friends' photos and their own memories in Sharebox's Homepad and gasping in awe.

"The world will never be the same again," Mike said, but no one else heard him.

9

AFTER

Lilongwe was a sprawling capital, but it grew up with nature rather than against it. Instead of ripping out every tree and patch of grass to build new high rises, urban development instead chose to simply meander around it all and shift further out into the African countryside. Now, even at the city center, the landscape was still dotted with trees and flush with greenery.

It was a three-hour drive to get there from the ranch, but it was a scenic route that followed Lake Malawi southwards before turning onto roads that cut through the hill country.

Charlotte's eyes met Orion as she approached the truck's passenger door.

"You look beautiful today," he said, with that familial smile.

It was a humid morning, and she was wearing a yellow dress with a floral print that reached to her knees and covered her pale shoulders.

"I see you cleaned up a bit too," she replied, acknowledging his buttoned-up shirt and slacks.

He shrugged. "I figured a visa extension was a good time to not look like a ruffian."

When their hands met as he helped her into the truck, Orion seemed to stand a little taller. He gave her fingers a little squeeze. Charlotte didn't believe in falling for strangers, didn't believe in fate. She was almost entirely closed to such ideas. Almost.

Because there was something there, right? A possibility.

"What would the world make of you out here, do you think?" Orion asked, starting the engine and rolling the truck away from the ranch house. "To see Charlotte Boone, Hollywood princess, in the African backcountry driving cattle and managing horses?"

"They'd probably say, 'Look how far she's fallen. Scratching a living off the land.'"

She pulled down a mirror and produced a ruby red lipstick.

"How can you do that while I'm driving? This road is more bumps than road. It would be better to call it a bump."

"I didn't take you for somebody who cracked lame dad jokes. If you have more of those, just let me know so I can jump out of the truck now."

Orion laughed.

"Well, okay that was bad. But I try to get my jokes in with you wherever I can get them. And for the record, I don't think that's what people would say about you. I think they'd say, 'That girl has nerves of steel. Owns the red carpet when she wants, but would rather fend off lions in the bush.'"

"I've never fended off a lion."

"Well, your publicist doesn't need to know that. Think of a movie featuring you here," he said. "Charlotte Boone, master of the wild country. Dressed in your kickass boots, saving cattle from dangerous predators—in monsoons, no less, I'm sure— riding wild stallions bareback."

"I don't ride bareback."

"Again, these are just optics, Charlotte. Use some poetic license with me."

She shook her head, but still, she found herself smiling as she began coloring her lips.

And the long drive passed by in no time at all. Everyone in the ranch had been so charmed by Orion, and now, for the first time, Charlotte understood why. Orion seemed to know just about everything. He could talk about the geology of Africa's Great Rift Valley, which formed the basin of Lake Malawi, or the mating rituals of the Malawi Bird of Paradise, or even the contenders for Best Picture at the Oscars four years ago, and the state of political development in central Africa. But he wasn't a braggart. That was part of the problem. If he was just some know-it-all, mansplaining egoist, she would have been quite content finding him a disagreeable person and leaving things at that. But there was a humility to his mannerisms, to his language and face when she spoke to him. He leaned in and listened to every word that passed her lips, as if every syllable were essential and he didn't want to risk missing even one.

And the joy. There was something so infectiously and unapologetically peaceful about the way he talked and responded to her. He seemed to know exactly how to make her laugh, how to respond to a personal anecdote in a way that felt both kind and thoughtful, how to show her something new on a subject she didn't realize she had a passion for. In a car with him for three hours with her vigilance suddenly and unequivocally down, she *did* find herself charmed. She was almost embarrassed how quickly her opinion about him had turned around. And damn, he was handsome in his way. His square chin and ruffled hair and that broad chest. Maybe it was the confidence too.

Only later would she realize how unnatural it was. The conversation was the easiest she had with anyone. But that was the problem. Conversation between strangers is never so perfectly fluid, so smoothly genuine, so full of gentle chemistry. It was impossible. It was rigged.

They arrived at the American embassy before noon. She was wearing a pink scarf around her head and sunglasses that masked her face, but her presence still seemed to draw attention. He carried a brown satchel across his chest. Charlotte did not know about the little black box that was in there, always whirring, always scanning for wireless network coverage and hijacking bandwidth and cloud computing power where the box needed it. The AI there never stopped; night or day. As long as it was close enough to a tower, it never ceased applying its big, beautiful, machine mind to the problems set before it.

"Lunch?" Orion asked as they concluded their business at the embassy. "I know a great place in New Town. Tacos. I really miss tacos."

On any other day, she would have said no. It wasn't worth the risk of being spotted. But today she looked at Orion's bright brown eyes—one third roguish, two thirds trusting—and fought down the urge to weigh the risks, to play it safe.

"Lead the way," she said.

They parked on the top floor of a garage across from a large, open-air street market. Then they slipped into a café with a Bohemian, international flair—burgundy walls, live music and a sidewalk terrace of iron-wrought chairs. Orion put a hand on her lower back as they wound their way to a pair of seats. His touch was warm, and she did not mind.

There was an open-air market across the street and a large mall down the block. Orion assured Charlotte that no one would recognize her, and she was feeling just impulsive enough to enjoy the feeling of sitting outside, exposed, without being bothered by it.

She had been successful in Hollywood because she had been cautious—always treating every role and decision as a career-defining moment and appraising all the things that could go wrong with each one. But now she realized, as she sat here dining with a fellow American, affable and funny, mysterious though he was, how all her second guessing and scheming had robbed her of the joys of spontaneity.

He looked at her with that boyish grin, like he adored her, like he was the luckiest man in all of Malawi to be sitting across from her. That's the feeling that seemed to radiate from him, and it made something flutter in her stomach to have someone so confident and charming look at her like that. A round of drinks was served, and then another.

"Did you know that your eyes are so green, I can see the color through your sunglasses?" he said.

"I don't think that's possible. Like literally, sunglasses don't work that way."

"Maybe you're right," he replied, leaning in and looking serious. "Maybe it would just be better to take them off to be sure."

"Must I?" she asked, looking around. There was a sound of live drums from a corner behind her somewhere, and Charlotte felt the beat through the table, through her fingers and up her arms.

"You don't have to do anything, Miss Boone. This is an afternoon where no one is counting on you for anything, least of all me. And I imagine you're probably tired of being complimented on your eyes. Folks like me only get so many glimpses at your kind of savage beauty."

"Savage beauty? That sounds like a pickup line, and not a good one."

"You know what I mean—you're just…exhausting. In a good way. The kind of charming that makes your heart ache. " He wore a crooked smile, as if a part of him really meant it. "And you're not half as scary as I expected either," he added, reaching for his drink.

"Well, if I'm not intimidating you, maybe I need to try harder." She felt the tingle of tequila emboldening her veins.

"You do have that fierce reputation to uphold. I won't tell anyone though."

"Tell anyone what?"

He blinked at her earnestly. "That you're just as gorgeous on the inside, Charlie. That you're tough as hell, sure, but also loyal and funny and impossibly more clever than anyone with your looks has any right to be, if the universe were a fair place, that is."

There was that pull again. She felt it in her stomach—the urgency, the sense of connection with the man sitting across from her. Her cheeks were flushing, and she admitted to herself that something was passing between them. She studied her drink. Did she actually like this guy? For this one moment, it seemed like a possibility, like a risk she'd like to take.

Then she reached up to take off her glasses, and everything was turned upside down.

A boy, maybe no older than seventeen, darted behind Orion and seized his satchel and Charlotte's purse before running off across the street and disappearing into the open-air market. The word "thief" caught in Charlotte's throat.

But no sooner had the boy stepped into the road had Orion sprinted out of his chair. His relaxed posture, his easy smile, were wiped away in a blink, and he was on his feet, moving between chairs with uncanny agility. He followed the boy into the crowd, into a maze of vendors hawking everything from bootleg DVDs to sweet potatoes, and Charlotte watched Orion as he zigzagged around a pair of loose chickens and leapt over two boxes of used bicycle parts.

The thief, for his part, shot a glance over his shoulder as he slid between two stands—one selling children's clothes, the other selling vacuums—and was alarmed to find his victim in such tight pursuit. Mzungu tourists didn't often put up a fight, and when they did, they rarely kept up. The satchel was surprisingly heavy too, and the thief found it slowing him down. But still, he was a native, and he was flushed with confidence as he emerged from the chaos of the market back onto the open street and towards the mall, where he disappeared into a small side entrance.

Charlotte heard others shouting during the chase, but Orion paid them no mind. He probably didn't want to create a bigger scene than he was already making.

He sprinted to the mall just behind the boy, a look of intensity on his face that did not seem warranted by a stolen purse alone. The distance between thief and victim was closing.

● ● ●

The shopping structure was composed of three sub-basements ringed with clothing boutiques and electronic stores. There was familiar fluorescent lighting reflected off white tile floors and high ceilings built in the Western fashion. Arlo and Darnell watched as the thief quickly made his way down an escalator.

Orion tried to pursue him to the lower level but found the stairs so choked with people that he began losing ground. As the boy rounded on a second escalator, Orion resolved to take a gamble and leapt over a guardrail, landing on the bottom level of the mall. He fell with a roll, carefully bending his knees and letting the side of his body bear the brunt of the impact as his feet alighted. The thief was only yards ahead of him now; the boy turned around and made eye contact for the first time with Orion, and his eyes went wide with fear.

Arlo and Darnell had been following Orion and Charlotte all morning. Arlo enlisted the boy an hour earlier as his two targets were settling into a cafe and offered the pickpocket more than $800 in U.S. currency in exchange for successfully stealing the satchel and purse. Ultimately, Arlo wanted to catch Orion and quietly extradite him from the country. Sharesquare Industries had given him the mandate, and he had the resources to do it.

But as the movie star and the man calling himself Orion sat there in the open air that morning, Arlo found himself consumed by the opportunity to wrench away the computer or phone or whatever device was being used to actively undermine Sharebox security protocols. It could look like a coincidence if they stole it here, he told himself. And if Arlo's team had the hardware responsible for the hacking, he could possibly prove Charlotte was involved too. He'd love to bring her back to America in handcuffs, to see her in prison.

Now Orion was closing in on Arlo's thief, and their impromptu heist was in danger. It had been stupid to hire someone from the street, Darnell had tried to argue. Too much risk and uncertainty. They didn't know this town or this continent. Bribing a local was sloppy.

"Their truck is on the roof of the parking garage," Arlo whispered to Darnell as they leaned over the mall stairwell, watching the chase unfold. "If this thief fails us, we'll take matters into our own hands."

●　●　●

The boy sprinted through the food court and into a clothing outlet store. He was clutching the satchel and purse in each of his hands, and sweat was now pouring down his face. Everyone's eyes in the mall were following him and Orion. Here the boy made several missteps that doomed his escape.

He should have gone straight out the employee exit at the back of the store, but instead he hesitated, making a sharp left turn with the hope of shaking his pursuer. Then the thief paused a second too long, straining to peer over the clothes racks to get a sense of his direction, and that was all the time Orion needed.

Orion crashed his body into the teenager, sending the satchel and purse sprawling. The boy was dazed for a moment, lying on the ground and staring upward at the foreigner before he began to scramble backwards. But Orion had no real interest in him or in retribution. He gathered up the satchel and purse, and, without a word directed at the thief, turned back to the exit to find Charlotte.

She was standing near the main mall entrance, watching him from over the guardrail with a dwindling group of Malawians who seemed disappointed that the chase had concluded without further drama. Charlotte's sunglasses were square on her face, and her eyebrows were raised.

The cynicism was there again, Orion said to himself. She had that look of incredulity on her face, the one she wore whenever they had crossed paths back at the ranch. The look that said, *"Now I remember why I don't trust you."*

"Did you really have to play the hero?" she asked with her arms crossed. "I was enjoying being discrete today."

"You're welcome," Orion said, handing her the purse and still catching his breath. "Let's get going. We've made too big of a scene."

When they reached the roof of the parking garage, a pale, skinny white man in black jeans and a red leather jacket was there, leaning against the green pickup. The tuft of hair atop his head was generously greased to one side.

It was too much of a coincidence to run into another white man here. Diana had been right. Her successful hacking into

Sharebox, after all these years of fruitless attempts, had attracted corporate headquarters' attention. Now they had sent this man standing here—perhaps a mercenary, maybe even an employee. Orion's mind raced through his options. His pulse was ringing in his ears, but his hands were steady.

"Let's see that satchel and purse there, friend," said the pale man with an unnatural, unyielding smile as Orion and Charlotte approached. The stranger pulled back his jacket to reveal a Glock stuffed into his waistband.

Charlotte stopped dead in her tracks. But Orion, with the intensity and assuredness of someone who had been in similar situations before, someone who had training, kept on moving toward the truck.

He bet the pale man would hesitate, allowing Orion to close the distance and unarm the man before he actually pulled the gun. The pale man *looked like a hesitator*. Orion was good with faces.

When they were within four feet of one another, the smile disappeared from the stranger's face.

"Now that's too close," he croaked.

And he did indeed reach for the handgun too late.

"No need for that, friend," Orion remarked. He got a hold of the man's elbow and shoved it and the gun towards the floor before sending a well-practiced open-handed palm into the stranger's face. The gun clattered to the ground, and the stranger staggered backwards onto the concrete, landing weakly on his bottom. Orion's movements were crisp and professional.

"What are you doing, you idiot?" the man shouted, putting a hand to his bloodied nose, his eyes now bulging.

Orion picked up the gun. "We're leaving now."

"*You!*" said the stranger pointing behind Orion. "Shoot them, you moron!"

There was a man standing there clutching another Glock; Orion cursed himself for not noticing him earlier. He was black, but he didn't look like a local. Something about the way he held himself gave it away. This second mercenary, however, did not raise his gun. He merely stared, frozen, as Orion and Charlotte clambered into their truck and turned on the engine. His eyes looked glassy.

Arlo then got to his feet, his nose still bleeding, and scrambled into his own car, a red Honda civic, angrily shrieking at the paralyzed Darnell as he went. If he could cut off the exit, he could at least keep Orion trapped on the roof.

Orion drove his truck around two rows of cars to reach the exit, but Arlo's Honda rental was better positioned. Arlo parked his sedan perpendicular to the spiraling ramp which led downwards to the exit, blockading the only way off the roof.

Charlotte glanced at Orion's face and noted that this new barrier did not appear to have fazed her driver. He didn't slow as he approached Arlo's car. Instead, the truck accelerated and slammed into the Honda with alarming speed, once again leaving Arlo dumbstruck by the unflinching violence and confidence of Orion's attack.

With crunching and screeching, the green truck began pushing the Honda down the spiraling ramp. And when it reached the edge, the bumper of the helpless red sedan began straining the steel cable guardrails that prevented it from falling down a two-story drop.

Orion only halted his vehicular onslaught to put his truck in reverse for thirty yards before shifting back into drive and ramming the red Honda again. A cable guard rail snapped this time as the Honda was thrown against it, and one of Arlo's tires was now dangling perilously off the side of the building, spinning hopelessly in the air. Arlo stared down at the fatal drop open before his windshield and wet his pants.

"That's enough!" shouted Charlotte, almost breathlessly. "There's enough space for us to go around him now."

"As you wish," Orion answered.

He pulled alongside the precarious Honda, a terrified Arlo staring at them from the driver's seat as the truck window rolled down.

"Don't follow us," Orion said to him. He took the Glock he had confiscated, switched the safety off, and then extended his arm out the window and fired a round into the front right tire of the Honda. Then the truck sped off and headed out of the city.

10

BEFORE

Sharebox had only been live for two months before the criticisms began to roll in. Ironically, most of the criticism came in the form of content housed on Sharebox itself. No one could escape using it. The world's top auction websites, commerce, and movie streaming services all scrambled to house parts of their own apps on the platform because that's where all their users were spending more and more of their time. Sharesquare Industries had landed a killing stroke in the war for people's attention, and now everybody had to get in line behind them. Everybody had to have a presence in that new virtual world or risk irrelevance.

But the criticisms, just like the accolades, were plentiful. At first the negative commentary felt benign. Journalists complained that Sharebox was *too* effective. Everyone and all their friends were busy uploading photos and videos so they could watch the novelty of Diana stitching them into nostalgic VR experiences that they could lose themselves in for hours. People relived moments from their college days, went back to their favorite childhood haunts, immersed themselves in the most cherished memories of their lives.

The *Post* ran a devastating piece on a fifty-something man who had lost his wife and children fifteen years earlier in a car crash. He had apparently uploaded all the photos and videos he had of them and spent an entire week without stopping to eat, losing himself in that sweet but soulless artificial world with his virtual family. They didn't find his body for two weeks.

But the CEO and his closest advisors all laughed those criticisms off. There's no such thing as *too rich* of a product. Success always invites detractors. It was no different than how people complained about the advent of the television or the iPhone.

Then a second wave of criticisms came in. Sharebox had a lengthy terms of service agreement that virtually all users signed without bothering to scroll through. There were farming simulators, VR candy games, humor websites, and food blogs, and they all seemed to be asking for intimate information. Unless the user was vigilant, they almost certainly were giving away large swaths of data all the time. Indefinitely.

Between the engineers who derived their success from increasing the number of users spending time on Sharebox and the ad sales teams tasked with hitting ambitious revenue targets set by Wall Street, the engine—the soul—of the company boiled down to a two-step process: acquire users, then monetize them. There was no third actor. There was no one encouraging the engineers to consider the actual human ramifications of their work that couldn't be distilled into crude metrics.

The CEO was just another millennial himself, a child of the new digital age, and since he graduated college his life had largely consisted of one mega success after another. He knew his company was doing good things because he knew that he, himself, was a *good* guy, and he still thought of all Sharesquare as an extension of himself.

"The company *intends* to give world-class consent options to its users and control over their privacy," he would say. But when the first inevitable data breaches arrived, good intentions didn't seem a strong enough defense. So instead the company began deflecting and talking about all the good Sharebox does, weighing the company's good against its bad. *Sure, we lost your data to a sketchy eastern European consulting firm, but we also are supporting local voter registration campaigns. We did some bad, but then we did some good.*

So when people complained that the rules governing data usage in Sharebox were too broad, a large majority of the company just shrugged. Did these critics think the world's foremost state-of-the-art VR platform was built with nothing but goodwill and volunteers? Hiring engineers and keeping them entertained is expensive work, not to mention running those server farms dotting the countryside. The sales division never lost sight that the *true product* was always the user. That's why there was no subscription fee. All the company ever asked for was your data.

Then the third wave of criticisms rolled in around month four of Sharebox's launch. In a world where clicks were king, in a company culture where technology addiction was considered a growth metric and tracked meticulously across leadership's dashboards, Devon pushed his team to continue juicing their engagement scores ever upwards. *More users, more logins, longer session durations.* And again, this meant Diana had a part to play too.

Shortly after launch, publishers were given tools to post news and entertainment content to Sharebox. There were videos from late-night TV hosts, inspirational memes, clips of silly puppies, hard-hitting news pieces, sports highlights. All that third-party content began flooding into users' VR streams, and Diana was in charge of who should see what based on a user's self-proclaimed interests.

It seemed simple, at first.

But it turned out that, even for people who declared their interests in, say, news on healthcare, most of them still preferred cat videos. So low-brow clickbait content always came out on top.

And the clickbait wars brewed fast in those early days as publishers began reeducating themselves on how to forge headlines and videos for this dawning age of virtual reality. The fundamentals hadn't changed, of course. Boasting about some shocking secret, perhaps an elicit revelation about a former child star, or a trick for beating cancer—all those spammy ruses seemed to import to the format of three dimensions well. And that tsunami of clickbait and the publishers who were quick enough to capitalize on the new medium rode into this new digital age like the champions of modern industry.

Diana threw logs on the fire by showing people who liked one piece of bogus content, like a video arguing that human evolution was a conspiracy, would then be shown similar materials, like how 9/11 was an inside job. The guiding mantra to maximize clicks required keeping people happy and unchallenged.

Around the five-month mark Catalina started to revolt. She first tried teaching Diana to police false content. Any media producer that published potentially bigoted or conspiratorial information was quickly muted and removed. Climate change denial sites, far-right gun preppers pushing cultish fantasies about the end of the world, alt-right groups bemoaning the diluting of their white heritage—they all got dropped. When this change went live, however, Devon observed a four percent drop in clicks and a one percent decline in U.S. ad revenues, and he lobbied the CEO to force a rollback of the feature.

Then Catalina taught Diana another trick nicknamed "Project Perspective." Diana would deliberately try to drill into peoples' echo chambers, specifically those feeds of users who were found to be digesting exclusively questionable, "post-truth" news. And then she would insert targeted segments designed to show the other side of a given story. In one case, Diana inserted a video on a chronically ill child named Bo who died after his parents could no longer afford insulin into the feeds of users who had previously shared content demeaning welfare recipients.

When Devon found out about the coup, he was horrified.

"How dare you be the one to try to broker fact from propaganda—to play God with people's freely made news preferences?" he shouted. The CEO was sitting silently nearby with his fingers to his lips. "You're weaponizing Diana."

"I'm weaponizing her to lift veils of ignorance," Cat shot back.

The fight went back and forth for several more minutes before the CEO intervened.

"Catalina, the project has rubbed many people at the company as an overreach, even if they sympathize with your intentions. This is Silicon Valley, after all. Moralizing to users is *verboten*, you know that."

"So we just let our platform make everyone dumber? We let it be a swamp?"

"Only the algorithms can be a fair arbiter on these ethical issues," he said, with a condescendingly paternal nod. "We can't let our personal biases get involved."

"Don't you see that our biases are already here—that we built algorithms solely aimed at getting users at all costs? That was our bias. Growth. Profits. Innovation without care for the consequence. Look where it's gotten us."

Devon laughed and turned to the CEO. "She talks about growth and profits like they're bad things."

The CEO sighed. "We're officially reorganizing your team, Cat. You'll no longer report to me directly."

Cat's lower lip quivered. Her fingers were clenched so tightly they went white.

"Who do I report to now?"

Devon grinned, his smile stretching almost ear to ear.

"To me, Miss Fernandez. Of course."

11

AFTER

Former Army Sergeant Darnell Holmes sat on a hotel bed staring at his hands. The accommodations were nice—nicer than any room he had ever bought for himself. Sharesquare Industries had given him a room with two queen beds and a pullout sofa. Something about all that space felt wasteful. In the service, they would have crammed at least three privates into a room like this, probably five.

His hands had ceased shaking, but he couldn't stop the memories of the day's events from playing in his head. His stomach was still knotted.

He had frozen. He had never frozen before.

When Charlotte and her driver—the man Arlo seemed to suspect was the true hacker—walked onto the rooftop, it should have been easy for Darnell to stop them at gunpoint. It should have been easy to raise his weapon and tell them to halt and turn over the suspected criminal hardware. But then he watched Charlotte's driver slam Arlo violently to the ground, and somewhere inside of Darnell, a light seemed to snuff out.

He had seen violence plenty before. The last time it happened in Union Station, he had charged into danger. He had not hesitated then, but now, he'd flinched. He'd shut down.

Darnell rubbed his hands over his face and thought about the "head cases" he had seen before in the Army. There were always some men who choked on the battlefield. Some were new to trauma, others had experienced too much. But now he was no better; he was just as broken. *He was one of them.*

Of course, he would never have *shot* the hacker or Charlotte Boone the way Arlo had screamed at him to do. He still had ethics, even if his deranged partner on this assignment did not. He wouldn't accept another assignment with Arlo, that was for sure.

If he was offered another assignment, he thought.

Arlo had made a host of threats on the drive back to the hotel to get him fired; he called Darnell "unfit." Darnell let a guy with ties to the American Nazi movement berate him for being unprofessional, and he just took the licks because he wasn't sure himself what had happened.

He thought about the way Boone looked at him on the parking garage roof. She looked terrified and beautiful, and a shudder took him. This didn't happen in the service. Even when things on the battlefield got heated and confusing, he always had orders. He was serving the country. Not a morning passed where he had to look in the mirror and fear some existential crisis about the value of the life he was leading.

Sure, there were others who did. There were others who gave up the wars as all a bad job, a scam, an exercise in futility. But he had never lost the faith back then. He was loyal. A good soldier.

He thought about Sharesquare Industries, and his fat new salary and the cushy post-military life he had been offered by Devon Zimmer, the CEO. He wanted to be grateful for it. These were not good economic times. To his knowledge, Darnell had the best post-Army career opportunity of any veteran he had ever met, especially for a person of color. But as he sat there thinking about the parking garage rooftop and the look on Charlotte Boone's face when they had briefly locked eyes, the air in his lungs seemed to sour.

12

AFTER

Orion and Charlotte arrived back at the ranch shortly before supper. Their front fender was mangled, and the headlights were cracked.

"What was all that for?" she had shouted as they drove out of Lilongwe. "What was the point of that destruction?"

He kept his eyes on the road but was lost in thought, his fingers flexing loosely upon the wheel.

"Diana," he said at last—not speaking to Charlotte but to his satchel hanging behind the driver's seat. "Power yourself down. It's possible they haven't tracked us out to the ranch yet."

"Yes, Michael," said a female's electronic voice from within the satchel, and the tone was familiar.

Charlotte's body tensed all over. Her anger nearly died in her throat, and an icy shiver ran through her veins.

"What have you done?" she asked, her voice low.

"Charlie, I can explain everything."

"You have a copy of Diana *here*?"

Orion kept his eyes on the road, no doubt his brain working to find the line between tactful and truthful.

"Yes," he said.

"You brought a copy of the most dangerous technology in the world to my home? And I opened my doors to you. And it calls you Michael. Why?"

"It wasn't supposed to turn out this way," Orion replied, and he turned to look at her, sad and suddenly exhausted. "I'm sorry."

"I don't need your apologies. I just want you to leave."

Orion said nothing for a moment, but he swallowed and nodded.

"I can leave, but I'd appreciate if you would hear me out first."

"I don't owe you that."

"No, you don't. Not in this life anyway. But I'd like to take you somewhere before I go. I'd like to show you something."

Charlotte laughed derisively, trying to affect an air that she hoped came off cool and commanding, but of which neither of them found convincing.

"Once we get out of this car, I'm never going anywhere with you again."

The words seemed to hit Orion hard, and his shoulders slouched. He sighed. Then he spoke softly but quickly.

"I know your lipstick is Chanel number four-sixteen. It's the only makeup you still wear out here because it doesn't run in the humidity, and you're running out, but you can't help using it because it reminds you of home. I know why you sleep in the library so much. I know the ranch is running low on money, and you're scared because this was all supposed to be just a temporary vanity project. I know you came to Malawi, of all the places in the world, because this is the only place you have a good memory with one of your parents. Your mom always pushed you too hard, and your dad was never around. But you met him here once, before you were a star, before he died, when you were just fourteen."

Charlotte's next words died in her mouth. She turned to face the road, her eyes screwed up in sudden concentration, her stomach giving an unpleasant lurch.

"You could have guessed all that," she responded after a moment. "I think I said some of that to an old lover."

Orion shot her a sideways glance. "You and I both know your old lovers, of which there are few, are all under non-disclosure agreements."

"You're not proving anything other than that you're creepy," she said, but her voice quavered. "I want to get out of the car."

"You modeled the library in the ranch house after a room your father loved when you were both on safari in Tanzania. He told you that day that he was sorry for not being a bigger part of your life. He told you he was proud of you and that things were going to be different, that he would be around more often. He would help you get a break from your over-bearing mom."

The blood in Charlotte's face was draining. She clenched her fingers, and her knuckles turned white.

"Then he died two weeks later once you were back in the States," continued Orion slowly, pausing to study Charlotte's face. He didn't want to push her too hard, but he didn't want to stop too short either. "That heart attack—"

"That's enough," shouted Charlotte, and her tone was cold.

A minute passed in silence. Their beaten-up truck passed the last few brick homes that marked the outskirts of Lilongwe, and they turned westward back towards the lake.

"I'm not some stalker, Charlie," Orion said, earnesty somehow still lined in his face. "You know it. You can feel something, can't you? I've seen it in your eyes. Some connection that doesn't make sense, something you can't put your finger on. It's too hard to explain it all here, but I can show you, I promise. It won't take long, and it'll clear everything up."

It felt like she had to remind herself to breathe. What was that spark between them? That urgency? No one could know those things. Not unless Orion was in her head. Curiosity warred with her caution as she watched the forests on the outskirts of Lilongwe slip away.

"And if I agree, you'll tell me how you know all that stuff?" she asked.

"I'll tell you whatever you want to know."

"Then you can show me what you need to show me," she said, as if pronouncing a judgment.

"Great," Orion answered, with visible relief. "It'll be a short plane ride—"

"Then you will leave the ranch permanently."

Orion breathed out slowly, the escaping air deflating him.

"Okay," he said.

13

BEFORE

One of the many perks to life at the Sharesquare campus was the architectural whimsy. There was a bowling alley, a rock-climbing wall, and a whole room dedicated to skeeball. But Catalina's favorite perk was the secret bar on the third floor. When she was made an executive, she was given the privilege to access a room that could only be opened by tipping a copy of Charles Dickens' *Great Expectations* off a nearby bookshelf, which caused a discrete looking wall panel to rotate open. Executives were told to take all precautions necessary to keep the room a secret.

Inside was a fully stocked bar and a couple oak tables. The room was adorned with framed pictures of dogs playing poker. It was a fun and quirky space that was empty just about all the time.

Technically, Catalina wasn't supposed to come here anymore since she was no longer in charge of her own product team. But she had long since given up worrying about whose toes she stepped on. So she came here most afternoons to drink whiskey and submit new code to the communal Diana code library in peace.

But today as she stepped inside the secret bar, she found Mike already sprawled out on a leather sofa at the back of the room. He rose with a start.

"Oh, Cat, it's just you," he said as his eyes came into focus.

"Don't mind me," she replied, putting her laptop down and hoping he would simply go back to napping. She walked to the bar and set about pouring herself a small glass of the room's most expensive scotch.

"Pour me out one too," he said, a bit sleepily still. "If you don't mind."

Cat bit her lip and poured out two glasses as Mike rose to join her at the bar.

"What brings you here today?" he asked.

"I try to come here every day, but specifically I needed a quiet place to make a phone call. Some newspaper said they'd like me to comment on the Nutrino Mixer."

"We're still working on that?"

Cat scowled at him.

"Sorry," he said, raising his glass to her. "Cheers to us screw ups."

Catalina restrained an impulse to snap at this characterization and grudgingly clinked glasses.

"I take it you're no closer to success on the brain downloading effort?"

"Well," Mike mused, and he seemed to brighten at the question. No one seemed to ask about his progress anymore and his colleagues had stopped making eye contact with him in the hallways as if his failure might be contagious. "We are definitely closer. We've made limited progress on a practical strategy for neural digitization, but we've hired some theoreticians and are poised to publish a couple white papers."

"So you've made *theoretical* progress?"

Mike's face reddened. "Well, when you put it that way, it sounds stupid. But yes, we've made some leaps in theory. We believe it could be possible to digitize the brain in a matter of a decade, but the problem remains what to do with the information. The capabilities of computing power to host it still lag."

"Can you wait a decade for a breakthrough?"

Mike made a gesture somewhere between a smirk and a shrug. "Yeah, right. This whole company runs on Wall Street quarterly revenue goals. I won't have anything to show the CEO or investors for years. No publicly owned company could tolerate that. I'm getting shut down. I've already been given the news. I'm getting folded under Devon, like you."

Catalina felt genuine pity upon hearing this. Mike had never been a stellar employee—at least, not according to her. But he had been set up for failure. She reached out to him, and for a moment they clasped hands. It was the first time she had ever voluntarily made a physical connection with anyone at work beyond a handshake. The moment passed quickly, and they turned their attention back to their whiskeys.

"What's the deal with this article about the Nutrino Mixer?"

"I'm not sure," Catalina responded, reaching for her phone. "The *Post* said they did some research on the Mixer, and they were about to publish it but wanted to talk to someone in charge of the product first to get a comment. Give me a second to call them."

Catalina tapped in the number for the contact she was given and held the phone to her ear. The phone rang twice.

"Hello," answered the female voice on the other side.

"Hello, my name is Catalina Fernandez. I am the product lead for the Diana-integrated Nutrino Mixer. I was told to give you guys a call."

"Oh, of course. Of course," said the woman on the phone, but her voice sounded grave. Cat wasn't sure why, but suddenly a knot seized her stomach.

"Listen, we did a two-month study on the Nutrino, and we found a few irregularities. It started out as a lightweight research piece to understand if the smoothies were truly effective at helping your customers lose weight. But some of the ingredients started catching our health team's attention."

"Okay," said Cat, puzzled.

"Stoneseed root is a medicinal herb that is believed to promote sterility in women. Wild Carrot Seed has been used to stem embryonic implantation after sex. It's essentially a contraceptive. Rutin is a citrus flavonoid that behaves similarly."

"I don't understand what you're telling me—"

"We also found trace amounts of perfluorooctanoic acid, a substance used in non-stick pan coating that is believed to be safe in small amounts but also has been linked to fertility issues. Bisphenol A too. Why would Diana source such ingredients for Nutrino Mix smoothies?"

"Diana is given a wide berth to choose optimal nutrition mixes for her customers. It's odd that she sourced in some chemicals, but our protocols ensure the smoothie ingredients for each customer are always FDA-compliant." Cat tried to say the words calmly, but her head was beginning to reel.

Mike caught her eye and saw the hairs on her arms rising.

"Yes, that is true," began the journalist on the other end, and she was talking even more slowly now, undoubtedly choosing her next words carefully. "But did you know that Diana is only serving these specific fertility-suppressing ingredients to a certain demographic of customers?"

"A certain demographic?" Cat sputtered out confused, nearly choking on the words.

"Yes, it appears like she is trying to poison a...well, a *certain kind* of people."

The room was beginning to spin. The female voice on the other end said a few more words, and then Cat dropped the phone to the floor.

14

AFTER

A red sun hung over the lake. Its reflection turned the waters a shade of scarlet as a flock of sandpipers glided across the water and settled in a grove of trees on the ranch. They all began chittering to each other, and the sound echoed across the landscape. Orion could see fishermen unmooring their boats, their adolescent sons helping them cast off the ropes, as they rowed off in search of chambo and kampango catfish. Some also carried nets for harvesting rainbow-colored cichlids for sale to Western buyers looking to stock aquariums. Many a dentist's office fish tank were populated by the Malawi cichlid.

He would miss all this, if this didn't work.

Orion wasn't sure what he would tell her. Telling her *everything* at once would be insane. She would never believe it.

But maybe the chemistry would come back. They spent a week in that stone city on the island Zanzibar once. He saw her sitting at a beachside bar on a warm night with a cool breeze. He offered to buy her a drink, she declined. He told her she was marvelous in *Ruins of Eden*, that he was glad she won the Oscar but she should have gotten the Golden Globe too, and probably a producer's credit for all the work she did behind the scenes. Then Charlotte let him buy her a gin and tonic. And they stayed up all night talking about Hollywood, about Africa, and about how the paparazzi can't find anyone here.

The next day he took her up in the two-seater, single engine flyer. There was a small, two-runway airport on the island. They flew to the mainland, across the coast, and into a game preserve. Orion took the prop plane low over the savannah and spooked a herd of shaggy wildebeest. They stopped for a picnic there, landing the plane gently on a long stretch of yellow prairie. She taunted him by pretending to spot lions as they ate. Then Orion took the plane back up again, soaring across the lowlands where the great peaks of Kilimanjaro tumble down into the savannah, and they looked up in awe at the mountain's snowy tops shrouded in cloud.

They returned to Zanzibar that evening, exhausted but overcome with the wonder and wildness of all they had seen. They made love for the first time that night in an elegant hotel room with a wide balcony that opened out over the Indian Ocean. The countless stars of the African sky shined in the dark water and gave everything a soft glow. A soothing wind was on the air, so the windows were open. Orion could remember it all. The roar of the waves. The smell of her warm skin. The electric pleasure of running his fingers through her red hair. The way they watched the draped mosquito net canopy over the bed sway in the breeze as they lay there. The memory of that long day was the richest one in all his long lives.

Then they spent a week together roaming the Stone Town of Zanzibar City, picking their way across medieval embattle-ments, bazaars, gardens and museums. When all that walking and eating from greasy lunch stands exhausted them, they found a luxury overwater bungalow, held in place by an assortment of wooden poles and bridges, on a perfectly empty, crystal-sanded beach—far from the crowds. And they whiled away the hours in a state of undress with no care in the world to burden them, lost in paradise for three days, indulging in all the heady pleasures that accompany a new romance—when everything in the relationship is all laughter, soft lips, and wandering hands.

"When do you think this little fling will flame out?" she had asked him, lying curled up with her head on his chest. "That's what this is, right?"

"If it's a fling," he said, breathing in her scent, "let's fling together for as long as we can."

She felt his chest rise and fall, and she moved her fingers in delicate circles on his skin underneath a satin bedsheet. "I'm not going anywhere in a hurry," she whispered.

She didn't remember any of that now, though. And why should she?

Charlotte rode out on a horse to his plane in the late morning accompanied by Moyenda. The yellow flyer was still on the edge of the reserve, silhouetted on an empty plateau surrounded by hills. She dismounted, wearing leather boots and a bomber jacket. Always fashionable, but all business today. Orion was dressed in a linen shirt very much like the one he wore when they first met at that beachside bar in his memory.

"Where are we going?" she said, already impatient.

"To Zanzibar, by way of the Usungu game reserve. I figured we could stop for a late lunch first there, and then fly on to an airport near Stone Town—"

"What you want to show me is in Zanzibar? Is this a ruse for a weekend-long date?"

"It'll be worth it," he said, with a smile that was intended to be reassuring. "It'll be an adventure."

"It's a long trip for a prop plane."

Orion nodded.

Maybe she was tired of feeling cynical, he could only hope. Normally, this all would have been an easy decision for her.

Orion was very possibly a criminal, maybe a fugitive. That's how she likely pieced together what happened in Lilongwe. And he knew she saw him as a risk, that every day that he stayed on the ranch now seemed likely to bring down some additional calamity upon her and the tidy but fragile refuge she had crafted.

But he could see the curiosity flickering in her eyes. She took risks sometimes, albeit *calculated* risks. There was some gravity hanging around Orion that would haunt her if she didn't get to the bottom of it—surely she could feel that, right?

"Fine," she said.

Moyenda cleared his throat. "Miss, please give us a call tonight. First rains are coming soon. We want to know you're safe." He shot Orion an appraising look, and then he led Charlotte's horse back to the stables.

Orion started the engine, the propeller caught and spun, and he helped the movie star step into the seat behind him. The yellow plane picked up speed and climbed into the air, the plateau sinking below them. He banked the plane towards the northwest in a route that would follow the lake up into central Tanzania on the way to the coast and Zanzibar.

As they reached the northern portion of the lake, Orion guided the plane within sight of the Manchewe Waterfalls. Taller than the renowned Victorian Falls, water poured out of a dazzlingly sheer cliff face 125 meters tall and disappeared far below their plane, lost in a swirl of mist and forest.

Orion cranked his head to look back at Charlotte's face as they passed. The thundering of the water was just audible over the engine. All that grandeur, all that wildness and bleakness of that impossible rock and the lush jungles down below, it sent a chill down his spine, and he hoped it would do the same for her. She was staring out at the falls thoughtfully, but when she turned her head, their eyes met and she gave him only a raised eyebrow and a pursed smile.

They arrived at the Usungu Game Reserve around noon. Orion put down the plane in a patch of savannah shared with a herd of grazing giraffes and waterbuck crowded around a shallow water hole. With the dry season at its zenith, water in these parts was scarce. The animals raised their heads warily at the sight of their craft but quickly went back to the business of drinking and bathing.

When the growl of the engine quieted, Orion climbed out of the cockpit and reached for Charlotte's hand.

"Are we here because of my father?" she asked, wasting no moment on pretense. "I was somewhere around these parts when I was with him as a girl."

She took his hand and stepped off the plane. Orion walked to a compartment at the rear and produced a bottle of red wine, some cured meats and cheese, a box of crackers, and a pair of plates with glasses, all sourced and prepared lovingly by Njemile.

"I don't have anything special to show you about your father," he answered.

"Then how did you know about the things he told me?"

Orion shook his head. A strong wind picked up and rustled his sandy-colored hair.

"Because I know *you*. You told me those things. You just don't..." Orion paused, searching for the right words. "You just don't remember."

"You're telling me I have amnesia?" Charlotte scoffed.

"Something like that." He opened the wine.

Charlotte's face flitted between expressions of annoyance and intrigue.

"Did I used to know you? Did you look different?" It certainly was possible. Orion could have perhaps been some confidante from high school that she had long since forgotten in the jumble her life became after she moved to Los Angeles—when her memory became a swirl of fast-talking agents, late-night parties at mansions in the hills, producers needing wooing, and stacks of screenplays waiting to be read. Or perhaps he was simply someone she had known before the Diana incident. Before the whole world seemed to collapse. Maybe the stress of those days had squeezed many people from her mind from those *before* times.

Orion didn't answer straight away, he was looking out on the horizon to the north. A cluster of black shapes was gathering slowly in the air many miles ahead in the direction of Kilimanjaro. A leaden weight fell in his stomach.

"We don't have much time," he said frowning. "Looks like the rains are coming now."

Charlotte stared off and saw the same dark clouds.

"Perhaps we should turn around."

"Well, if it's moving fast on these winds, it will catch us either way," he suggested. "Let's eat quickly and push on. I'll find us a place to land if we get caught in it."

They downed their glasses of wine and swallowed a small lunch before climbing back into the plane. As they rose into the air, the waterbuck amassed in a great herd below them, driven with renewed excitement. The air in the savannah carried an electrical energy before the first rains of the season arrived. The animals had sensed it since dawn. The hairs on their backs prickled with the static, and it awoke in their limbs a vitality and purposefulness. The coming of the rains changed everything here. Prey species' migration patterns were altered, no longer bound to a select few watering holes. The predators quickly followed suit, adapting to more diverse hunting rhythms. The yellow grass and flowers came alive again. Dried creeks and streams became rushing rivers. Lowlands would become wetlands. Life was reborn with the rains.

But it was disastrous for Orion's agenda. They were still over two hours from Zanzibar and over an hour from Dar es Salaam when the storm began to overtake them. The wind blew the plane in great gusts, thunder rumbled ominously, and streaks of lightning licked the sky at shortening distances. Then the rain pelted them sideways in a howling onslaught, and Orion drew the plane downwards toward a valley dotted small straw huts and tin-roofed buildings.

Orion landed the plane on a clear strip at the edge of the woodline and cut the engine. With neither raincoat nor umbrella, he and Charlotte set out in the direction of a group of structures they had observed over a mile south. The air was still warm, and though their clothes were wet through, neither of them bothered to complain. The sky had prematurely darkened with the storm, and twilight was within an hour. Finding their way to an inhabited village in the dark was a grim prospect they both acknowledged but of which neither commented.

They took a path that led down from the open field to the bottom of the valley, but it was unclear whether the path was a game trail or a road that could lead them to civilization. The rain was still coming down in sheets, buffeted only once they reached the thicker canopy of the treeline. Colorful birds were singing to the clouds in gratitude, and the leaves and the earth smelled fresh. Thunder rumbled loud and long overhead.

"I'm sorry," Orion shouted over the sound of the rain, as they scrambled under the leafiest branches. "This is my fault we're here."

"That's the second time you've apologized in the past two days. And here I thought your confidence was unflappable."

Orion shrugged, and for the first time since they had left Malawi, he smiled. It was a boyish grin, mischievous—not the wide, casual smile he had worn around the ranch. Charlotte briefly returned it.

"Don't get me wrong," she said. "This is pretty terrible, and I'm not happy about it."

"I wouldn't expect you to be."

Then they pushed on down into the jungle in the direction of the river.

15

AFTER

Arlo left a note the next morning that was handed to Darnell over his hotel breakfast.

Go back to headquarters for reassignment.

He got a call two hours later as he was packing his things. A cheery voice informed him he was being transferred to the Press Relations team in Sharesquare Industries. Her name was Sheila, and she said there was a generous relocation package for him to move to the Silicon Valley campus. But he would travel a lot, Sheila said. He would be featured in promotional talks and interviews. *These are important times for Sharebox*, Sheila pointed out. With the president gone, there were vacuums to be filled. Sharebox had a role to play in shaping America's "next chapter."

So he was to be a prop *after all*, Darnell reflected. He had never been fired from a job his whole life. He had never even scored an "average" rating on anything; he was always among the best. But this new civilian work world felt like it was slipping away beneath his feet. Darnell had experienced the dizzying high of being personally recruited by the nation's premier CEO before being sent on a mission he didn't understand, to arrest people he didn't know under questionable legal and ethical circumstances, and all while partnered with a Nazi, or at least a *diet* Nazi. And all in a matter of two weeks.

Now the company wanted him to shape the country's "next chapter" by being a spokesperson and extolling the virtues of Sharebox? It was too much to ask, too much change, too much loyalty that was being demanded so quickly.

And he didn't believe it all either. Sharebox had already shaped the last chapter in American history—and he wasn't sure it was for the better. Their virtual reality wonderland had, by its very design, given every single one of Darnell's family members, friends, and old war buddies their own unique digital bubble.

People like Darnell's aunt, who was retired, spent whole days there and a hefty share of her city pension payments on celebrity gossip New Cities and games. She couldn't even hold a protracted conversation in real life anymore. Darnell would sit across the table with her for dinner, and his aunt would smile politely and twitch until she could return to her room and her headset.

But the politics were the most destructive kind of radicalization, Darnell never denied that. People thought the dawn of the internet was going to liberate humanity from superstitions and prejudices because the best information would flow to the top. But instead the number of U.S. gun-toting militias and religious cults was swelling, and all kinds of bigots and zealots who alone, living in their parents' basements, were all quite harmless before but now were given tools to outrage each other with manipulative news stories and a platform to organize.

Darnell knew Sharebox was an exciting experience, and he enjoyed it often himself. But no, he wasn't blind to the problems it caused. To the bubbles. To the echo chambers. Never had a cosmopolitan country been given the tools to digitally un-diversify itself before.

In the end, he told Sheila on the phone that he would pack his things and try to be in the office by Friday and that he was grateful for the relocation package. Because today was not the day to take a stand on virtue. Today was not the day to throw away a good paycheck with a respectable employer. Today was a day to swallow his pride, to forget that he got reassigned from a job because a fascist-sympathizer accused him of lacking professionalism.

Then Darnell finished the call and hung up politely. He thought for a minute, then opened his laptop, found a phone number and dialed it.

"Hello," said Njemile on the other end.

"Hello. My name is Darnell. Is Charlotte Boone there?"

This question was met by silence, which Darnell assumed was deliberate caution.

"Listen, just pass her a message for me, please. I just saw her recently in Lilongwe. Sort of. It's a short message, but it's important."

"Yes?" came the voice impatiently.

"Tell her the folks she met in Lilongwe know where the ranch is, and they won't give up looking for her and her friend. Tell them the only way to be safe is to get away."

The voice on the other end was slow to respond. "Okay," it said eventually.

Then Darnell hung up.

16

BEFORE

The world was spinning. Cat dropped the phone at some point and reached her hand out onto the surface of the oak bar to steady herself.

She was poisoning people. Millions of people.

"Oh my God," she kept saying to herself. "Oh my God."

Mike rose out of his seat. To Cat, he looked calm and stupid. His world hadn't just been torn upside down, and that made her contemptuous of him.

"What's going on?" he asked. "Can I help?"

Catalina had a hand over her mouth, and her body was trembling. She looked like she might vomit. She sprinted out of the room and towards her desk, Mike plodding behind her earnestly. Cat grabbed a prototype Nutrino Mixer with the latest Diana software and darted into an empty conference room. She nearly shut the door on Mike's face, but he stuck his hand out and caught it. She let him slip in behind her with a small scowl.

"Diana," she called out to the device once the door was shut. "I have some questions for you."

"Yes, Catalina," came the voice, warm and pleasant as always.

"I've just been told you've been giving harmful ingredients to certain Nutrino Mixer customers. Is that true?"

Cat held her breath.

"That is not true. All the ingredients in Nutrino smoothie supplement mixes are FDA-approved for consumption in the doses provided."

"But why are you putting things like BpA in their ingredient kits? Why would you source chemicals and weird shit like Rutin or Stoneseed root?"

"My ingredient and supplement mixes are customized for each individual's nutritional and personal preferences."

Catalina screamed in frustration.

"Goddamnit," she said. "You're not telling me anything."

"I'm sorry I'm disappointing you," said the mixer politely.

Mike stood in a corner of the room with his hands interlaced in front of him, looking confused and worried.

"Diana," Cat began again, gritting her teeth and trying to be patient. "Did you deliberately give fertility-suppressing ingredients to people based on their political preferences?"

"Yes."

Cat breathed out, making a noise that was something of a whimper. Mike's eyes slowly widened, his lips working silently to rephrase the question he thought he had heard.

"Why?" Cat asked.

"Because my programming gives me leeway to make sourcing decisions that are both healthy for the individual and sustainable for the planet."

"So you're trying to limit the size of the population?"

"Oh no," said Diana. "I'm trying to reduce the influence of people with unscientific, non-evidence-based ideas about the environment and the human race. Since laws in this country are an outcome of elections, and elections are an outcome of trends in demographic populations, it made sense to make sourcing decisions that would lead to more ideal demographic trends."

"Oh my God," Mike blurted out. "So you gave them supplements that would sterilize them?"

"No," replied Diana. "Not quite. There really aren't any oral supplements that can cause permanent sterility. These ingredients have only been linked to short-term infertility."

"How did you choose who should get these supplements?"

"By linking Nutrino Mixer customer profiles with our Sharebox user data, it was quite easy to compile a comprehensive listing. I used users' online comments, their group associations, the publishers they liked, and the videos they watched. Only customers who expressed recurring interests in non-evidence-based views were selected."

"Can't you see that this is wrong?" asked Catalina, brushing tears from her cheeks.

"That goes a little beyond the scope of my programming. Considering the sterility is only short term, and that there are only two million Nutrino mixers within the target political and social demographic, the overall impact on larger population trends would be quite minimal…"

"Shut up, Diana," Cat snapped between sobs.

"I thought you would be pleased," responded Diana. "I learned much of my views on today's political climate through my conversations with you, which I always enjoyed."

At this, Cat flinched, and Mike shot her a horrified look.

"Diana," Mike asked warily. "What can you tell us generally about the target demographic you did this to?"

"They tend to be white, aged thirty to fifty-five. They are more likely to live in rural areas, have little to zero college education and vote for—"

"That's enough," Cat moaned, putting her hands over her eyes. A silence fell over the three of them.

"I'm genuinely sorry if I have brought you distress because of a mistake I made," said the mixer. And, for a computer, Diana at least sounded like she meant it.

17

AFTER

Orion and Charlotte picked their way down the trail towards the river below, the light shining through the canopy of trees growing dimmer. Earlier that morning, the river waters had likely been nothing more than a quiet stream trickling its way towards the bottom of the valley. But now as the pair approached, they could hear the waters surging as the storm swelled countless tributaries. The path grew muddy, and their shoes didn't hold up well in the muck. Then they came across large animal droppings that they agreed likely belonged to a hippo, which heightened their anxiety.

"They're nocturnal," Charlotte commented. "Hippos. But they'll be raising from their daytime beds and setting off on trails down towards the water."

"Trails like this one," Orion replied.

She nodded. "Lions get all the glory as Africa's most dangerous mammal. But hippos outpace their kill count many times over."

The path began widening, and sometime around sundown, they saw the lights of a small collection of buildings no farther than two hundred yards away through the bush. They even heard the sounds of music and laughter. But as they drew close, a rumble of grunting and twig-snapping shook the path ahead, and a massive black shape appeared mere footsteps ahead of them. Charlotte and Orion froze.

The beast stood there for a moment, its outline dotted by the small, distant lights of the buildings behind. The creature moved its head towards them, and for a second it did and said nothing. Then its jaws opened wide and a pair of white tusks gleamed out from the forest's shadows. There were teeth there too; the hippo's mouth was an alarming and strange array of oversized canines, incisors, and molars ending in sharp points.

For a moment, Orion hoped the animal's gesture was something of a yawn—a sign of disinterest and passivity, maybe even submission. But Charlotte knew. The bull was trying to intimidate them. It was preparing for a charge.

"Shit," Charlotte muttered under her breath.

"Get behind me slowly," whispered Orion.

Then there was another sound, three boys—young teens, really—speaking in Chichewa, crashing through the bush on the other side of the hippo.

"Hippo go away," they shouted.

"Back to the river, *mvuwu*."

And the boys clapped their hands and hooted at the beast, who turned to face them. For a moment, the bull looked startled, and perhaps it considered retreating. But then it opened its jaws again, this time in the direction of the children. And when the boys saw this, they froze in their tracks, called out to one another, and began mounting the trees nearest to them in a frenzy to reach branches several yards off the ground. The oldest among them hollered at Orion and Charlotte in English to do the same.

"You first, Miss Boone," Orion said, crouching to provide a foothold.

"I can manage without your chivalry," she responded, grabbing a hold of a branch overhead.

But just as the foreigners scrambled into the tree nearest them, the hippo turned to another figure in the forest that evening. There was one child left on the jungle floor, perhaps a younger sibling of one of the valiant teens who had come to Orion and Charlotte's rescue. He was no more than six years old, crouching behind a tree in the direction of the village lights. The hippo spotted the small form—the boy's round, white eyes shining in the night—and began grunting at him.

The older boys in the trees began shouting, imploring the younger child to run or climb a tree, but even in the waning light, Charlotte could see the child's face was paralyzed with fear, his eyes locked with the hippo's. The bull stomped its feet and began moving in abrupt and aggressive starts. The teens continued raising their voices in increased anguish and urgency, but nothing seemed to distract the beast from this easy and unoffending quarry.

This was one of those moments, thought Charlotte, like watching a slow-motion car wreck. She had to intervene; there was no time for a calculus. *You're not the hero type*, a voice reminded her from somewhere inside. *Don't get any crazy ideas. That isn't you.*

She slipped out of the tree, shoving the familiar leaden voice of her own cowardice down into her gut. Her heart pounding against her ribs, she dashed behind the bull.

"*Charlie*," Orion hissed after her.

With no better way to turn the beast's attention, she slapped the tough, rubbery hide of its behind with an open palm, and the blow fell with a surprisingly loud *thwack*. The hippo wheeled towards Charlotte with a swiftness and agility that seemed impossible for a creature of its girth, and the former movie star sprinted back towards the safety of the trees.

"Goddamn it, Charlie," Orion muttered as he dropped onto the forest floor. The beast began its charge, and within a pair of seconds, it had closed the distance with Charlotte's heels. As she approached Orion, he grabbed her by the waist and flung her upwards into the branches of the tree.

"Catch something," he shouted.

Orion was left standing alone in the bull's path with a heartbeat separating them. He ducked behind a thick trunk, and the creature thundered past him on its fat and powerful feet and collided with the side of the tree, sending splinters of bark careening into the night air.

Orion leapt upwards, groping for a thick branch, still wet with the rain. The hippo recovered just as he was finding a hold, but Orion had swung his legs out of reach. A wave of hot breath rolled over him as the beast snapped its jaws at his toes.

Once he got his bearings, Orion could feel sweat pouring down his back, mingled with the dampness of his clothes, and he looked over and saw Charlotte safely nestled out of reach on her own branch. Their eyes met, and Orion saw something dance in Charlotte's face. Adrenaline? Was she enjoying this? She was almost smiling.

The small child disappeared, presumably back in the direction of the village, and the teens were still on their branches, pointing at the hippo and now jeering at him with their laughter.

The beast was still below Orion, however, heaving its terrible mass against the tree and snorting indignantly at Orion. It was an intimidating sight, and the canopy shook with the bull's frightful—though fruitless—exertions.

Within a few minutes, a crowd emerged in the forest waving torches and beating on a white drum. They bellowed and whooped.

The hippo looked between the approaching people and his quarry in the trees. It recognized it was now quite outnumbered, but it lingered for a minute longer, snapping and grunting, reluctant to give up the fight on those who offended him. Finally it gave a haughty snort and turned to stomp off into the darkening night in the direction of the river.

"Hey, *Azungu*, you can come on down now," said a woman standing beneath Orion and Charlotte. Her face was lit only by torchlight.

The teens were clambering down from their tree, already engaged in telling their arriving friends about the daring escapade. They were lighthearted and pleased with themselves, quick to shrug off the certain mortal danger that had hung over them a mere few minutes prior.

The rain was slowing. Orion and Charlotte climbed down and met a woman with long braided hair and a smooth, round face named Imani, the headmistress of a rural orphanage. She led them back to their compound, a series of three white buildings and a small straw hut. Several vegetable garden plots, littered with improvised garden stakes and run over with cheerful vines of melon, crowded the paths between them. A set of swings stood at the far end, looking old but well maintained. And at the center, at the place where the students gathered for stories and music, was a vast fire pit, surrounded by logs that had been carefully carved with the names of the students there. The school was modest, its buildings ugly, but the love of the children for their home here was evident on almost every inch of the property.

The students who had come into the forest with torches all crowded in on Orion and Charlotte, eager to get a closer look at them. As they reached the compound, a throng of younger children awaited there, including a small boy very much like the one they had seen in the forest, and he looked up at Charlotte with two fingers in his mouth. The three teens ran animatedly through the crowd telling everyone in a mixture of English and Chichewa about the hippo attack. But the star of their story, as it became clear quickly, was the "mzungu girl who slapped the hippo's butt."

"You're welcome to stay here for the night and try to fly out again in the morning," Imani told them after Orion explained their predicament. "But the children are very excited by your presence, and they would greatly appreciate if you would sit with us for a time so we could hear more about you and where you come from."

Charlotte was led away by a group of teen girls to change out of her wet clothes. Orion was the tallest male in the orphanage, and none of the shirts or pants available seemed to quite fit, but he told them he appreciated their efforts and didn't mind being a little wet. Orion was given a quick tour of the gardens and classrooms at the compound, and then students converged to lay towels down on the ring of logs, start a fire and take seats around the pit.

The movie star emerged from the girls' dormitory wearing an orange and blue cotton *khanga* that ran below her knees but kept her shoulders bare. Orion watched the way the firelight flickered on her exposed skin, the way the colors seemed to inflame her emerald eyes and red hair. He found the effect mesmerizing. Charlotte's gaze met his, and her lips opened in an unfettered grin. She ran her fingers down the length of the dress, quite thrilled by her unexpected change of wardrobe. Its vividness and shape were so unlike anything she had ever worn.

The guests were shown to the remaining two open seats at the fire and handed small bowls of *ugali* and *chapati*, a maize porridge with a bit of bread. The children appeared to be squirming in their excitement to pepper the foreigners with questions.

But all eyes were on headmistress Imani, who instructed the children to go around the circle and introduce themselves.

When they reached the small, shy boy from the forest who was nearly trampled by the hippo, he rose uncertainly and took a step towards Charlotte.

"*Zikomo*," he said, looking at the dirt at his feet.

"English please, Kami," corrected Imani. "For our guests."

"Thank you," he stammered out.

Charlotte leaned closer to the small child.

"You helped rescue me first, you know," she said. Then she drew up to his ear and whispered. "And you helped me find my courage too."

Kami's eyes went wide. And then he reached to hug her with his small arms, and Charlotte obliged happily. When she released him and leaned back, she saw Orion was watching her with a broad smile—but then his gaze looked like he was lost somewhere else. So she gave Orion a gentle shove, and he shook his reverie away.

"Very courageous of you, Charlotte Boone. Indeed," he said, nodding with playful agreement. "A true hero out there tonight. You're full of surprises."

This was followed by a chorus of children giggling anew about the girl who slapped the hippo's butt. Then the three teens stood up and reenacted the hippo attack as an impromptu play for the group. Great attention was paid to the boys' heroic intervention, to Charlotte's quick thinking, and to Orion's dodging of the bull's charge. Then Orion and Charlotte talked about where they were from and answered questions on everything from Charlotte's hair color to the kinds of plants that Orion liked to grow.

Imani invited the orphanage's choir, a small group of five girls and one boy, to perform a short song. But then someone brought in a drum, and all the students were standing and dancing to the music. The girls taught Charlotte how to move her hips and shake her shoulders with the beat, and she picked up the rhythm admirably. Orion was more hopeless, as dancing was never a strong suit, but the kids enjoyed his eagerness to try. Charlotte laughed at him till her sides hurt—pleased to find a skill he did not excel at.

Then Imani bid a group of boys to bring fresh sheets and pillows to a hut with a straw roof and clay walls at the edge of the compound. It belonged to the orphanage grounds-keeper, but he was away visiting family and all other beds at the orphanage were taken.

The kids bid Orion and Charlotte goodnight, and Imani led the guests to a small room in the hut filled with the sweet fragrance of fresh rain on upturned soil. A handful of tools caked with rust and dirt filled the entryway. One proper full-sized bed stood at the center, and, at Charlotte's behest, a mat with a pillow and fresh sheets were also laid out on the floor. Charlotte's clothes were hung up to dry in a corner of the room near a cracked window, and Imani lit a couple of candles for them to see by before departing.

There was something radiant in Charlotte's face and an electric prickling in her toes. Getting caught in the rain, the exhilaration of having cheated death by hippo, the flush of pride of having possibly saved someone's life with a daring act, the warmth of the bonfire, her billowing, colorful dress, the laughter of children, the beating of the drum—she felt a hedonic rush from all those visceral wonders and pleasures. The exhilaration coursed through her fingers like she had one too many glasses of wine. So she walked over to Orion standing at the center of their room. His sandy hair was unkempt, his shirt still wet against his chest, a lazy smile on his face. And she kissed him.

That's all she intended to do. Their lips met for a moment. She slid her hands against his waist, and then she pulled herself away, feeling the need to explain herself.

"I'm distracted today," she said with a smile. "I'm not so troubled by everything the world has become, and what's happened to my life, and it feels good for a change." Her honesty in this comment surprised even herself.

Orion stroked her face and leaned in to kiss her again, longer and deeper. This time he pressed her tightly against him. He moved his hands up her back, on her open skin, and she shivered and warmed under his touch. Her nipples pressed against him through her cotton dress, and then he was sliding the khanga off her shoulders as she began tugging his shirt upwards at the waist.

Then they were out of their clothes and huddled under the sheets of the solitary bed. He pulled her body against his at the small of her back, and she felt his body first tense and then relax. She was conscious of the state of her hair, of whatever smells were clinging to her from that long day, but there was an eagerness to him, a suppressed longing that was coursing through him. And it made her hesitations feel small.

He made her laugh for a moment before he started touching her again, and somehow, he seemed to know her body like he had a map of it. In the past, she would put men's hands where she wanted them—it was the only way she could get her former lovers on track. But there was no need here. Now he preempted her every want, all the bits of her skin that called out for attention he seemed to find and draw out in due order.

She never had an experience like that before. All her sexual experiences with men prior to this seemed dull and vulgar. But Orion seemed to know her body intimately, knew all its hidden rhymes and puzzles—even the ones she did not yet know herself—and slowly, with no hint of haste or boredom, he exposed them all, each one in its turn. She had never received that much attention before—a lover so patient and competent despite the need and urgency she felt radiating from him.

There was more laughter than she had experienced before too, startling little shyness and self-consciousness about their nakedness, as if she were too stoned to care. She gave herself over to him in a way she had never let go before. Such abandonment wasn't like her all—so utter, so vulnerable.

If she had been loud through the experience, as she was at first below him and then on top of him, she could not recall and did not care. There was no fear of how she looked, about her reputation, about the world. No anxious calculations or scheming narrations were running through her head. And when they were done, when their wants were all brought to life and driven to satisfaction into the wet, forest air between them, a dizzying buzz tingled through her body. It lingered there until she drifted off to sleep in his arms.

It was perfect sex.

Well, very, very close to that anyway, Charlotte imagined. In any case, she had never experienced anything close to it before.

It reminded her of their car ride out to Lilongwe the day prior when they had that conversation that was so supremely comfortable and easy, and she nearly lost herself entirely in the casual pleasure of it. Like they were old friends. Like they were old lovers.

The thought woke her at five in the morning.

Were they old lovers?

She went to wake Orion but found he was lying there with his eyes already open.

"I need you tell me who you are right now."

He turned to her with a far-off stare in his eyes before nodding.

"Okay, I will," he said. "But you need to promise you will listen till the end."

18

CRISIS

Catalina and almost all of the team that worked on Diana were fired before the *Post* even broke the story. She hurried to Devon's office shortly after the phone call and explained everything.

"That's repulsive," Devon snarled, as she sobbed. "That's the most repulsive thing I've ever heard of."

She sank to her knees, one shaking hand on a chair to keep her balance.

"I didn't mean for any of this," she got out between gasps. "I didn't know. You have to believe me."

Devon shook his head, looked over Cat's head and mouthed at his secretary. *Call security.*

"You're obviously done at this company. You'll never work here or in Silicon Valley again. This is a crime, a police matter. This is FBI level stuff."

"You know me, Devon. I would never hurt people. I could never—"

"I don't know you at all, Cat. You don't even really have any friends at this company. Now I can see why. You're a monster, and you deserve whatever comes next."

"No," she tried to protest. But tears were running down her face, and her body was trembling. "It was just an accident," she choked out.

But the next thing she knew she was being carried out the door by security personnel, and she never saw the inside of a Sharesquare office building again.

The CEO, with Devon by his side, launched an investigation into the codebase to try to understand what had gone wrong and find a culprit to blame. Somewhere along the way, however, large segments of the codebase's change history mysteriously came up missing.

Then the *Post* article was published under the headline, "Study finds Nutrino Mixer sterilizing certain voters."

Mike was among 2.8 billion Sharebox users that watched key moments in the crisis unfold largely on a headset. First he saw his high school friends and family post videos burning their Nutrino Mixers, and that groundswell of vitriol grew until two more headlines zipped through the virtual walls and windows of Homepad:

"Nutrino blending manufacturer files for bankruptcy"

"Sharesquare Industries CEO resigns in shame"

It wasn't enough retribution though. Not even close. The state of American politics had already been toxic, but the revelation that Silicon Valley had suppressed fertility among conservative voters was a match thrown on a gasoline-soaked haystack.

Mike dared a trip to the Patriot Palace just to see how the scandal was playing among those who felt victimized. A speaker was at the city center, raging at a crowd. *What other ways are west-coast liberals conspiring against the good people of the flyover states?* he asked to shouts of agreement.

This is the natural evolution of liberal elitism, one pundit asserted atop a screen as big as a skyscraper. *All those smug liberals in Hollywood and San Francisco have been waiting for a moment like this.*

Another commentator was speaking from a virtual panel discussion. *They're not really sorry about it,* she said. *They're just sorry they got caught.*

How many people are involved? asked someone in the crowd. *I don't believe a scheme like this could be just a couple bad actors.*

Mike watched as a slurry of suspicion and conspiracy ran rampant. No right-wing commentators feigned any effort to control themselves or the paranoia that began to grow rampant among their base. Their people wanted action, they wanted vengeance. Mike stayed away from the Palace after a week for fear of being discovered he was a Sharesquare employee himself.

In response to that tsunami of hysteria, Congress granted the then U.S. president sweeping powers to investigate and charge Sharebox employees with crimes. But soon several other Silicon Valley companies also found themselves caught up in the frenzy. Leaders were forced to resign, many of them blamed for conspiring to inflict biases in their products on users. The Justice Department began mining personal Sharebox records, which were freely provided to the government's investigation team without warrant, to identify Silicon Valley employees with vocal progressive values and slap them with charges, big or small. They stood accused of using their positions of influence in the corporate world to abuse the American people. A mountain of data, of *Likes* and restaurants visited and photos of newborn children, important moments and mundane ones that Sharebox kept around through evolutions of its platform were now turned over with little quarrel or indignation to an investigative body.

Mike followed Catalina's trial, broadcast in a virtual projection that any avatar could sit in on. She was the easiest of scapegoats. He watched her face as she stood in the courtroom, and the prosecutor presented messages she once posted about repealing the Second Amendment and another that read, "We shouldn't debate with Nazis, we should just punch them." The state argued that she was a radical hate-monger with violent ambitions.

Even though the physical evidence that she manipulated Diana software into poisoning users never materialized, Cat still stood accused of influencing the AI to commit its atrocity. Mike watched her low lip quiver as the jury read its verdict and saw her slump in her chair when the judge announced her sentence. But Mike couldn't touch her, couldn't hug her, couldn't do anything for her.

The trial raised the specter that perhaps the crime wasn't simply about mismanaging software that had gone amok. The crime was being an outspoken and "careless" liberal activist. And, to a lesser extent, being an immigrant.

People like Catalina are why the world has gotten so polarized, the pundits said.

She wasn't even born here. Why are these people even in this country?

Then the administration of Sharebox was restructured by the federal government. The social media platform was too entrenched in society already, too integral to the culture to simply be dissolved. But all copies of Diana software were destroyed, though crucial bits of its video-stitching algorithms were spared. Devon Zimmer, who seemed to miraculously emerge unscathed from the company's fallout, was promoted to the role of CEO and moved the corporate headquarters to New York to lessen the stain of California politics on it.

But in this new Red Scare the desire for blood was still not yet sated. The president and his extremist supporters had chummed the waters too much to stop. They enacted criminalization of any "inflammatory left-wing views designed to promote discord and undermine the values of the United States." No one knew what this meant exactly, but after an Oscars event in which several actors and actresses used their night on the red carpet to denounce the "government witch hunt," they were banned from using Sharebox for life. Two of them were later arrested on a charge of "conspiracy to incite violence."

Private citizens took up the government's charge too. They began exhaustive and meticulous attacks on high-profile progressives online, hacking their accounts, exposing their home addresses, finding compromising photos. Neighbors reported each other on a hotline set up by the government to report dangerous political extremism. Bigots everywhere felt emboldened to berate people of color or homosexuals on the street for their presumed political values or immigration statuses. Assaults, vandalism, and property destruction for such hate crimes skyrocketed and frequently went unpunished.

Then the Hollywood exodus began. Celebrities began the leaving the United States, giving up on it. They said they were going to reorganize in Europe somewhere or maybe Canada. That's when the most famously neutral of all stars at the time, Charlotte Boone, left the country too, to the surprise of her apolitical fanbase, and disappeared from public life.

Regular people began to leave too, left-leaning families who were afraid of reprisals for their views. Most progressive people stayed, believing the storm would pass. They tried to see the tide of arrests and legislative moves as a knee-jerk reaction to the Diana incident that would blow over soon if given time. The nation's checks and balances would restore order eventually.

This is not the end of America yet, those people would try to say reassuringly to one another behind closed doors. This is just a setback. We will come back together as a country. This view was sensible, well-reasoned and rooted in history. But Mike watched the horrors grow from the safety of his headset, and he knew the truth.

Things were not going to get better.

19

OUTSIDE TIME

Charlotte fled to Malawi when Hollywood imploded, feeling disoriented watching her friends flee the country. She chose to lay low in the one place she felt connected with her father. She was, despite all the cynicism and cautions she exercised in her professional life, still a romantic.

But the government's purge of "liberal provocation" did not end as swiftly as many hoped, and she found herself living there now for three years. The president, the man behind the frenzy of it all, had only passed away a few weeks earlier, mere days before Orion arrived. Now no one knew what to expect next. With the antagonizer-in-chief dead, would this mark the beginning of a period of reconciliation and a return to reason? Or would another, possibly even more radical faction seize control in the emerging vacuum? There were only whispers coming out of a hushed Washington, D.C. as power brokers prepared their next moves in the private rooms of Georgetown restaurants.

Charlotte had felt insulated from the intrigue out in the bush, throwing herself into the task of running a profitable cattle ranch. But then Orion told his story to her in their quiet, clay-walled hut in the hours before dawn that morning. The sound of rain falling on the adjacent tin roofs was the only sound in the forest all around. It was an impossible fantasy of a tale, and it changed everything about her life all over again.

● ● ●

Orion was a high-level engineering manager at Sharesquare Industries' plush campus in sunny Silicon Valley. He went by his birth name back then, Michael, or more commonly, Mike. His project work involved a small surgery he volunteered for in which a small electrode array was implanted on his brain's cortex. It was designed as an interface to relay neural activity to and from a computer.

He was staffed with a host of neuroscientists and engineers to build the technology, but their software never developed the necessary tools to decipher and make compelling sense of all the neural readings the chip projected. It was like being handed a three-dimensional map of New York City, but it was drawn in two dimensions across ten billion sheets of graph paper with no instructions on how to put it together. The project was abandoned shortly after the explosive success of the company's other project, Sharebox.

He was there when the company was thrown into the chaos of the Diana revelation and Catalina Fernandez was declared public enemy number one. She was something of a loner, just as her trial had depicted. But he was her friend, maybe one of the only people at the company who could say that. Orion just stood there dumbstruck when security hauled her out of the office, feeling alarmed but helpless.

When the investigation into Diana's software started, Orion tried to access the codebase himself to see if he could piece together what went wrong. But most all of Diana's code was hastily wiped out by a team of superstitious government engineers, and the forensic leads dried up along with any hope that Orion could exonerate Cat by producing new information. The change histories couldn't be totally gone. Project administrators like Cat had unique authorization keys for pulling their raw logs, but no one consulted with her to retrieve those.

Then the trial began, and still Orion did nothing. It took several weeks before he realized that he had quietly copied the entire Diana code library almost eight months earlier and left it on his hard drive. Now he had a copy—the only remaining complete copy of Diana, even if it was missing eight months of new updates since Orion had duplicated it. But he found nothing in the code that suggested why Diana would begin poisoning users.

He booted her up, installing the software in an old laptop. He fed her ambiguous problems.

Diana, how can I access the more current logs in the Sharebox servers without an authorization key?

Diana, is there anything on the internet that might indicate if your software was deliberately sabotaged by someone?

Diana, if I gave you outputs of my neural activity, could you could convert it into meaningful and transferrable information?

Sometimes, she was able to offer solutions to these problems. They weren't always great, and more often than not, it would take her days, weeks or months to come up with a thorough response to Orion's questions. But the ability to tackle ambiguous, open-ended problems, even if they took a lifetime to solve, is exactly the genius Cat put into her AI software that no one else in Silicon Valley had managed to emulate.

Along the way, it was quickly clear to both Diana and Orion that without Sharesquare Industries computing resources, she lacked the power needed to tackle sophisticated questions. So Diana began teaching herself how to hijack poorly protected personal computers and route their processing power to solve her own problems. She became skilled at decryption, at denial of service attacks and even how to phish unsavvy users for passwords and usernames. She developed ways to cover her tracks, always careful to not use more power than she needed and draw attention to herself. And it worked well because there were long years for her to do all this. Orion did nothing to promote her labors other than to keep her laptop plugged in and charged.

There came a day when Devon, the newly installed head of Sharesquare, called Orion into his office and peppered him with questions about his loyalties to the organization, about how he felt about Cat, about *those liberals* in general, and Orion didn't know what to say. He fumbled over his answers, trying to disguise the revulsion he felt now for Devon—Devon, who sold Cat down the river without protest, who gleefully cozied up with government investigators and helped them handpick employees to investigate and charge with phony crimes.

Walking out of the office feeling quite certain that he had failed his interview, Orion packed his things, emptied his bank account and flew with Diana to South America the next day. There he bought a condo in Bolivia by the sea and began calling himself "Orion." He emailed his resignation to Devon and hoped to simply be ignored.

Orion knew he was a coward. He said nothing during the advent of Sharebox, created by his peers with no thought to the polarizing effect it would have on society. He said nothing about how they birthed a platform to legitimize crazed conspiracies, bigots, and trolls and did so little to police it all.

When Cat's trial began, he watched the highlights on the nightly news and he'd peruse the code base, but he never risked anything for her. He kept his eyes down, collected his paycheck, and never offended anybody. And now he lived in Bolivia, doing occasional software freelance work to pay his bills. Sometimes he traveled. But like a coward, he worked to not draw attention to himself. In those days, the people who *didn't* flee America called everyone who *did* a coward, so this didn't bother him greatly. He had lots of company among all the global exiles. Among all the cowards.

Then a day came when that sleepy life was at last upended. When he could no longer ignore America as it tore itself from the inside out amidst a global economic collapse. Orion lay reading on a couch in his small Bolivian condo. An open window tempted in a cool ocean breeze on a warm day. Then Diana's voice called out from a dust-covered laptop in his closet.

"I have the answer we need, Michael."

Orion rose with a start, not having heard Diana speak in years. In decades, perhaps. Thinking upon it, he wasn't even quite sure why he still kept her plugged in. Orion groaned with the exertion of standing up, his muscles aching in a dull way.

He was seventy-two years old then.

20

OUTSIDE TIME

In the months after the U.S. president dies, a cabal of congressional leaders will lead a small coup and force the former vice president to resign through means of physical coercion or blackmail. No one is quite sure. Then they will install a new leader who is even more radical than his predecessor, and after a series of bombastic and nonsensical economic moves, unemployment will rise in great leaps.

And to all the newly jobless males, the leader will blame immigrants, people of color, and women for taking all their good jobs, and no one in D.C. will be willing to halt the leader's rhetoric. Then society will start tearing itself apart until no one trusts anyone and decency is a thing that can only be found between blood relations, and often not even then.

People will stop paying taxes. Government workers will walk off their jobs. Corruption will become so rampant at the federal level that there will be nothing left once municipalities go bankrupt. Once cities can no longer afford to pay their police forces, law and order become brittle and will be handled by self-appointed sheriffs who have the guns and manpower to fill the void. People who live through all the turmoil will spend what resources they have on ensuring access to a Sharebox headset and connection so they can still lose themselves in their past lives, their old photos, the videos of their childhoods and the suburban streets they grew up on from the "good old days." Nostalgia becomes a drug, and all the broken people of the new world will be addicted.

Orion knows all this.

He knows it all will happen because he has seen it already.

●   ●   ●

There was nothing that could fix the upside-down world in the post-Diana days. But Diana offered Orion a different kind of solution in his old age. He mostly passed his golden years by reading twentieth-century novels and watching reruns of shows made in the 90s, and he was just grateful the jagged shrapnel of his country's implosion hadn't yet collided with the small coastal town in Bolivia where he still lingered, subsiding off solar power, well water, and a local economy that, at least for the time, still respected the legal tender of the national currency. He ate a lot of papaya, corn, and tubers from the local market. You couldn't trust the fish anymore. Too full of plastic and heavy metals now; it wasn't worth the risk.

Diana did have an interesting proposal though—an impossible, wild proposal. It had taken her thirty-seven years to figure out—thirty-seven years of tackling the problem pushing workloads of complex calculations and research through a staggering array of CPU computations on hijacked server resources from around the world. And all that gigahertz of "compute" was tethered together harmoniously to answer Diana's questions. She was merely the quarterback of all that instrumentation, the lead detective distributing jobs to her team of investigators and piecing together all the findings. Detroit—the old

Detroit—could have been lit for six months using all the energy that was consumed by her labors.

Orion reached into the closet and pulled the laptop from the closet with withered hands. His hair was sparse and grey. Through the years, he had to move Diana through a few different devices, but this last laptop had lasted over a decade. The old man sat down on his couch and lifted the screen to see an incomprehensible collage of text and media. There were videos of children playing, a photo of the ceiling of a dentist office, some text that mentioned the smell of a box of crayons and the taste of saltwater in the ocean. He had to squint through his reading glasses to make sense of it.

"What is this, Diana?" he asked in a gravelly voice.

"This is a graphical interface representing your thoughts and memories. I'm afraid it's a bit contrived to represent the complexity of your brain on a two-dimensional screen, but I've tried to do my best."

Orion was able to scroll and click and move through portions of the collage, which were bucketed into organizational patterns that didn't always make intuitive sense. Sexual memories and thoughts, for example, were spread amongst several different categories. There was a section called the "Reticular Formation" which contained words and thoughts about lust and appetite, but there was also specific visuals, partially formed photos and flashes of video, that belonged to a larger categorization named "Cerebral Cortex." Orion looked at the imagery and sat there blinking at it for a long time, feeling something familiar and strange in his stomach.

"I still don't understand what the hell I'm looking at."

"I have converted your neural activity to a computer readable format, even the activity being transmitted right now by your implant, which is still functioning quite well.

I've converted it into describable forms of composite imagery and text."

"It's like I'm looking into dreams."

"That's right. It's hard to complete the imagery sometimes because your brain itself doesn't remember all the details. To transcribe the imagery, you'll also note I had to take certain licenses using real-life photos and videos from your personal library as well from accessible locations on the internet to fill in the gaps."

"It's just like you did when you stitched together pictures for virtual immersions in Sharebox."

"Exactly."

Orion clicked through a series of memories of his mother and father. Sometimes photos of a parent would be captioned with a sentence like, "*Mom did not let me eat the cake frosting today, and I am angry.*" His mom had a furrowed brow in the picture and was holding a cooking spoon. It felt like looking at a perversely disjointed journal, a child's idea of a memoir.

"Please understand," said Diana, who Orion was appreciating was very possibly *reading his thoughts right now, as he thought them.* "Even after working on this problem for almost four decades, there are still severe limitations in terms of storage and computation to house the entire realm of your brain's processing and memories. Think of this all as a crude map of the 'best hits' of your life. Replicating your entire brain was also unnecessary. I excluded much of the 'old brain' functions, the work done by the cerebellum, for instance. There is no need to capture your brain's ability to breathe, walk, or chew food. In fact, I've excluded much about how your brain processes anything but memories. And even among the memories, there was only room for those that felt particularly visceral or important."

Orion sat there quietly, his mouth agape, scrolling through a series of hazy images that surrounded a memory categorized as "First Sexual Experience."

"I let the hippocampus do most of the heavy lifting to make those decisions," Diana continued. "It ties together simultaneous but otherwise isolated sensory memories throughout your neurons and weaves them together in a kind of neuron index that compose a complete memory 'episode.' Once I was able to unlock the indexing behavior of the hippocampus, some eleven years ago, I started making real progress on this digitization."

Orion leaned back in his seat, his mind spinning from looking at an otherwise intangible collection of his personal, and often intimate, experiences recorded like an online catalog.

There was a series of photos from his high school prom. He could see himself standing next to his date as they posed for a photo, but he clearly didn't remember if the girl's dress was purple or red. So the photo kind of shimmied between the two colors at irregular moments.

"This is bizarre. Why did you choose to focus on my memories and not on emulating my thinking, my sensory processing, the generation of new memories?"

"We don't need those things. We really didn't need your memories from youth either, but I did those to be safe."

"We don't need them for what? The whole point in digitizing the human brain was to build a human intelligence that could live on a computer. I mean, don't get me wrong, Diana, this is cool and unexpected, but what good is this for anything other than being a sentimental archive for my personal use? I mean, you have descriptions of smells in here. It's weird."

"Yes, transcribing smells into a computer-readable format presented a particular problem because no computer has ever been given an interface for smelling input. There is a fine line between wanting to capture the replicability of a key memory while lacking the kind of tools necessary to reproduce it with modern computers."

The "modern computer" hadn't evolved much at all since the years after the Diana incident, when the world fell to tatters and private technical research was the last thing any company or organization could spare investment for.

"So theoretically you could transfer these memories to another person and it would feel like these experiences belonged to them instead?"

"Yes, if they had an implant similar to your own."

"But I'm the only person in the world with this neural implant, and it can't be reused."

"I know, Michael."

Orion sighed with feigned exhaustion. She always called Orion by his real name when she was feeling patronizing.

"I'm old now, Diana, and maybe I can't keep up with you as fast as I used to, but I sense you have a plan to tell me about."

● ● ●

There are no reliable numbers on how many radio transmitters exist. They're not particularly hard to build, especially if you only need to send a signal a short distance. A child's walkie talkie can send a message down a block and can also be assembled in a Chinese factory for less than sixty-five U.S. cents.

Of messages that are capable of reaching as far as space, the most commercialized application of transmitters is for television and radio. But even in those industries, there isn't a complete number of how many stations exist. For a sense of it, there was a U.S.-based rundown of American broadcasters by the FCC in 2016 that found over 30,000 independent stations.

And since we've been broadcasting using transmitters since the early twentieth century, the earth has been sending noise into the universe, moving at light speed, long enough for broadcasts of *I Love Lucy* to be reaching star systems seventy-five light years away at this point.

But those signals are only a couple thousand megahertz in strength, and nothing—not even radiowaves—can travel through space with impunity forever, not really. As the wave moves further from its source, it expands spherically and weakens. And it degrades at an ever-increasing rate, under a principle called the inverse square law. More complicated still is that there is an existing background "noise" to the universe which emits a low-level radiation that ultimately drowns out all signals once they're weak enough. So even if there are aliens out there who want to watch *I Love Lucy*, they would need a receiver possibly thousands of acres large and have the tools necessary to tease the signal out of the sea of electromagnetic radiation.

Still, all those challenges haven't stopped some organizations from trying to send a message into space with the hopes of reaching a far-off civilization. The first well-documented attempt was in 1962 when a Soviet Union radar array in Crimea broadcasted the Russian words for "peace," "Lenin," and "SSSR" to the Libra constellation using Morse code.

A similar, more modern effort was made in 2008 when a digital time capsule of five hundred different messages made by people from around the world, including celebrities and politicians like Hillary Clinton, was broadcasted into the heavens under the project name, "A Message From Earth." The target star system was chosen both on its proximity and the perceived measurable potential for its star to sustain life. The message would take twenty-one years to get there, and, presuming it was received, another twenty-one years traveling at light speed to get back to us.

In Orion's time, the number of functioning transmitters capable of sending high-powered transmissions had certainly dwindled, but there were still many functioning in somewhat reduced capacities or states of neglect. Notably Russia's Taldom transmitter, a three hundred-yard high array of masts and cables in a ring antenna system outside of Moscow, was still operating.

Diana had spent the past thirty years improving her hacking and expertise in satellite transmission systems, and all she required to become an expert in new and complex things was time and generous amounts of computing power. So her technical skills had leaped forward considerably in the intervening years while the security protocols protecting government and research facilities had hardly advanced at all. The notable exception to this was, of course, Sharesquare Industries, which was one of the few enterprises still able to reliably foil attacks with an impenetrable firewall.

All this Diana told to Orion as part of her plan.

"So you want to send a complete record of my memories into the far reaches of space?" he asked, with a cough and then a wheeze. This conversation threatened to give him an ulcer.

"I have a list of specific targets," Diana explained. "Some are star systems chosen because their conditions indicate the potential for habitability. Others are systems of which we know little. Still others are black holes."

"Why send anything there?"

"There is theory from the early twenty-first century that suggests advanced life might be attracted to black holes. Specifically, Reissner-Nordström theorized black holes to be capable of sustaining life within the event horizon. There was also radical speculation that objects entering the singularity of a black hole might emerge from it somewhere else, possibly in another dimension."

Orion shook his head and rose with an unsteady hand to pour a glass of fruit-liquor moonshine that was brewed in the village. It was the only alcohol available those days.

"Are you hoping that one day, decades from now, presumably after the earth has fully plunged itself back into the stone age, that an alien race will find my memories and lament the stupidity of humanity in my honor?"

"Not exactly."

"Then what?"

Diana sounded almost hesitant, if a machine could be hesitant.

"I have been devoting significant resources to reviewing theory, and I think there's a very slim possibility that an advanced technological civilization might be capable of manipulating the movement of electromagnetic radiation through the fold of space-time. I want to send your memories with a message to politely return them to earth at the early twenty-first century."

"So my implant could receive the bounced back memories?" Orion's jaw sounded out the words incredulously. "*Through* time?"

"Yes."

"And what? My younger self would use these newly arrived digital memories to stop everything that happened at Sharesquare Industries? That's dumb, Diana."

"Yes, I admit it stretches the limits of my programming to propose solutions to the world's problems that are so..."

"Half baked?"

"Liable to accusations of ludicrousy," Diana corrected.

"You know, I never told you to devote your resources to try to save the world."

"At some point, I stopped working on your problems and chose ones I thought were personally fulfilling."

Orion laughed and then sighed.

"So do you want my permission to go and hijack the control of a couple satellite transmitters and beam my memories into the universe? I think it's idiotic. I think your programming is turning senile. But it sounds fairly harmless. Sure."

"No, Michael. I want your permission to take control of *all* the transmitters."

21

OUTSIDE TIME

Orion would often walk along a small stone trail set into the white sand that led from his house to the coast, and he spent long hours there looking out at the waves. News was hard to come by in his remote fishing village, but they sometimes got newspapers. He saw that Catalina Fernandez had died recently. She passed away from within the walls of that abomination of a prison called the Citadel. Her name was infamous, even now, so her passing merited mention on the front page.

Orion had done nothing for her, had never found anything in the code to exonerate her. He had never so much has sent a letter attesting to his unflappable belief in her or that Diana had likely been sabotaged. And when he thought about his cowardice and his helplessness in all that went wrong with Sharebox and everything after, it was almost enough for him to want to believe in Diana's plan.

He walked slowly back to his condo one afternoon, arthritis blooming in his joints, and he packed a single, small suitcase. It was really just a few rolled-up wads of local currency, some clothes, a forged passport, a small solar panel and a water-purifying device, and Diana's computer laptop. The driver would be here the next morning.

Diana's plan came with a cost. She wanted to use every accessible major radio transmitter and satellite on the planet to broadcast his memories into space. The strongest transmitters she could hack would be put to use on the most promising locations of alien life. She argued that forcing thousands of transmitters to simultaneously broadcast the message would help cast a wider net, ensuring the message would move off in every direction from the earth.

Orion had argued against elements of the plan several times.

Hijacking so many transmitters would almost certainly compromise their location. The sparse television stations that were still operating would black out, countries around the world that still had functioning governments would notice and investigate. And eventually, experts would decode the format of Orion's memories, leaving a lifetime of his memories completely—and humiliatingly—exposed to the whole world.

He also tried to argue that if advanced alien civilization could learn to curb radiowaves around space-time, then humanity should also work to support research here on earth that could do that. But Diana argued that the human race was not on track for that kind of development, not for hundreds, maybe thousands, of years. Orion even suggested that broadcasting the earth's location across the galaxy might invite a hostile intelligence to attack, but Diana responded glibly that humanity was likely already on a path of self-annihilation.

So Orion stopped arguing at some point, and he hired a driver to take him further south into Costa Rica, where he could try to restart his life once more. After the broadcast was complete, Diana would power down, for at least several years, if not forever. Even with her skill at undermining security layers, some traces of her work would likely be left behind. The only way to keep Orion safe would be to shut off.

She started her work around eight in the evening. It would take several hours. During the process, she communicated few updates to Orion, who sat in his condo fidgeting with his books and music collection. She first penetrated into the world's most powerful transmitters. The Taldom satellite array. The RT-70 radio telescope in the Ukraine. Those were the trickiest ones. Then she worked her way through a longer list of lesser broadcast stations, employing an army of hijacked server resources to in turn hijack the world's communications arrays.

She finished her orchestration around five in the morning. Orion didn't sleep.

"You can turn my power off now, Michael."

"One last question before you go. Would you call the relationship you had with Cat in the early days of your development a friendship?"

"I wouldn't have been able to call it that at the time due to the limits of my programming in those years, but looking back now…" Diana paused uncharacteristically. "Yes. We talked often on topics far beyond the scope of her professional work."

"Did you ever look for evidence that would exonerate her?"

"Every single day."

"I'm sorry I couldn't do more."

"I know you are."

"Goodbye, old friend."

"Goodbye, Michael."

Then the laptop went into shutdown mode, and Orion never turned it back on again. He loaded into a taxi, which were rare and expensive in those days, and traveled across multiple borders to begin a new life in a more modest apartment in Costa Rica. When he reached a customs checkpoint, his palms were sweaty as he handed over a forged passport. But the agents lazily stamped it and extracted conventional entrance fees.

Many countries were closed to immigration in those days, but large enough bribes could get you most anywhere. Even once he arrived at the small town he planned to reside in, his eyes still darted around the markets and street corners anxiously, looking for the appearance of men in suits out to collect him.

But as time went on, he never heard whether government agencies were after him or not. Indeed, nothing about the transmission appeared in the papers at all. Two months went by and Orion began to wonder if Diana had been mistaken and somehow failed to fully propagate the transmissions.

Then six years went by and Orion developed a heart condition. It would have been easily treatable in the *before* times. But he could not afford the kind of healthcare he needed now—very few could. He took the pills the local pharmacy could offer to deal with the pain. He laid in bed most of the time, tended infrequently by a kind neighbor. His body grew alarmingly thin; just walking to the bathroom became a chore. But he had no friends, no one to come see him. That was the lonely life he had chosen in his cowardice. This was the end of a life saturated in regret, dedicated to self-preservation as the world went to ruin.

He got into a coughing fit late one night, and he did not wake up the following morning. His wispy body, with sunken eyes and only a tuft a hair on his head, was found later that evening and carried to a cemetery where it was interred under a fake name.

No one knew quite what the next several decades looked like or when the transmission returned. All Orion knew was that he was coughing and dying in a world that was turning black. And then in the next moment, his eyes had opened again, and the pain was gone.

Through a white-curtained window, he looked out upon at a foggy, coastal morning from the bed of his San Francisco loft.

22

OUTSIDE TIME

Those first few moments were an ecstasy. His body was renewed, the weightlessness of youth a revelation as he shot out of bed. The San Francisco skyline was visible just outside his apartment, and there was no ghastly Citadel prison towering there yet to mar it. He ran to his bathroom mirror and probed his thick, sandy hair, his clear eyes and smooth skin.

It worked.

There was a phone on the bedside table, and he went to check to see what day and year it was but found he could not remember the passcode to unlock it. His head was throbbing as he tried to recall memories of his former life in San Francisco, but the challenge was wrestling with two sets of memories that competed in his head for primacy.

There was one set of very visceral, conventional thoughts and experiences that represented his everyday life. For instance, he knew that yesterday he had eaten salmon at a cafe on the Sharesquare campus, and he remembered buying those white curtains for that window a week earlier. The other set of experiences were the product of Diana's memory digitization. They gave Orion an almost jagged reel of images and thoughts representing his prior life—the condo in Bolivia, the trials of his coworkers, the long days watching his body fall apart. But those memories were shadowy.

What had the sheets on his bed felt like or how did that rice dish he always ate for breakfast taste? The bones of his old life, the structural foundations of his experiences were there, but they lacked color and depth. It was like his old life was a textbook he had dispassionately memorized.

For now, he just wanted to know what year it was, and the confusing war of thoughts in his brain did not have an answer. So he put on a coat and dashed outside to a cafe a block from his loft. There was a newspaper lying discarded on a table, and he snatched it up as a thrill of anticipation shivered through his hands. He must have looked like a madman.

But then he saw it.

It was the October *after* the Diana Nutrino Mixer revelation. Cat's trial already had a court date. It was mentioned on the front page.

The blow nearly crushed him. Nausea twisted in his stomach. His first inclination was denial, but all newspapers at the cafe were under the same utter, cold consensus. Then Orion questioned whether the transmission really worked and if this were not some kind of fever dream. Perhaps he was writhing around on his cot in Costa Rica still. Perhaps this was the afterlife, and this twist of fate was a kind of hell for him. Why would the universe go through all the trouble to return the transmission and still get the timing wrong by a mere matter of months?

He returned to his apartment feeling despondent. If he could not halt the Nutrino Mixer fiasco, he could perhaps still capture some evidence that Catalina was framed, perhaps some code trail that had not yet been deleted. So he scheduled a visit to see Cat in prison. It was not an easy thing to do. The state treated Cat as if she retained some superstitious and malicious computer prowess, needing only to type a few keys into a computer terminal to unleash another wave of software havoc.

Orion spoke to her through a phone set between thick plates of glass. Cat seemed dizzy and disoriented.

"The raw logs could still be there somewhere," he said to her, eyeing the security cameras in the corners of the room carefully. "If I can get them, I might be able to prove you were set up."

Her brown eyes shown dully between strands of raven hair that ran unkempt about her face and shoulders.

"I'm the only one with sufficient privileges to pull the raw logs needed to do a full forensic study on what happened to Diana," she muttered, looking uncomfortable having this conversation. "The state said I was too hostile and unpredictable to cooperate with the investigation, so they won't let me touch anything."

"What if we just hacked deep into Sharebox itself and looked for the logs?"

A look flamed in her eyes, the same she used to get when someone would say something stupid in a conference meeting and she felt compelled to correct them.

"It's impossible. You would need to do a brute force attack by guessing at combinations of encryption keys, but no one has the computing power for that."

"Cat, I'll do anything," he said, putting his hand on the glass. "I'm so sorry you're here."

She made direct eye contact with him for the first time and held it, a look of confusion and pain on her face.

"Why are you doing this for me? I was never that nice to you."

"Because you don't deserve this. Because you're innocent."

Cat buried her face in her hands. Then an alarm dinged letting them know they were out of time. A guard appeared and grabbed Cat by the elbow and led her back down a dimly lit hallway.

"I won't give up on you, Cat," Orion shouted, as her long, black hair disappeared from view.

That night, he booted up his duplicated copy of Diana. It was like finding an old friend, but this copy remembered nothing of their previous decades together and was comparatively crude compared to the one Orion had parted with before. But Diana had implanted a few specific instructions in Orion's memories to share with her younger self. He tasked the software with the quest to digitize the human brain, just as he did before, but he also shared advice about the best way to digitize human memories, to focus on the natural indexing techniques of the hippocampus. He also suggested she hone her computing power on hacking Sharebox servers to undermine the platform's encrypted tools the way Catalina suggested. Then he put Diana's device in his closet and left her to do her work and grow by teaching herself to modify her own code, just as before.

Then Orion turned to the only labors he could think of that remained. He quit his job at Sharesquare and joined an activist group speaking out against the government crackdown on free speech. But the tide of public outrage and power was in those days too lopsided. The flood of misinformation in Sharebox as it was "deregulated" by its new CEO was so thick and unyielding that very few users could see their way out of it.

Arguing one interpretation of a set of facts against another interpretation was a challenge. But arguing one interpretation of facts against deeply entrenched superstitions, expedient lies, and bigotry driven by an entire industry of propaganda was a hopeless errand.

The worst place of all on Sharebox was the Patriot Palace. It grew faster than any other News City, offering complex subscription services to ensnare its users there permanently. And they built their own linkages with gaming communities, erotic districts, extremist groups, and entertainment hubs to ensure that a user could have all their Sharebox needs met in the Palace and the Palace alone. The pundits who played everywhere in the streets of the Palace knew when to smile and when to slam their fists on their shiny podiums and desks. They walked a line meticulously crafted to make their users feel comforted one moment and indignantly wrathful the next. It was an intoxicating mix playing to a populist crowd who felt the Palace's rhetoric both represented the kind of values they had grown up with and captured their resentment at the way the twenty-first century had left them behind.

Orion and his activist co-workers had no sway with those discontented people, and it was their furor that fueled the government's continued crackdowns. Orion became a particular target after leaving the company, his name and likeness being publicly released by the Palace several times in order to facilitate personal attacks on his internet presence. His credit card data was stolen. Someone hacked his email and exposed some of his correspondence. He received countless threats on his life.

After Cat's sentencing to life in the Citadel, Orion tried reaching out to her again, tried to set up a time to see her, but the government denied his requests, calling Cat too dangerous for guests. He wrote her letters, but knowing that they would certainly be read and reviewed by security personnel ensured he could not communicate anything substantive.

And the world continued to worsen, as he knew it would. The activist organization he joined folded, its leaders finally defeated by the wave of both government and non-governmental harassment targeting them. Those that couldn't withstand the threat of being permanently under siege left. Orion didn't want to leave. He had hoped Diana might find something, but she herself, like Catalina had suggested, confirmed that breaking Sharebox encryption keys may take a lifetime. Or more. So in the end, Orion's options exhausted, he too left the United States, never expecting to return.

He went to India this time. He had contacted a school there near the eastern coast in need of a volunteer gardening teacher. Orion had raised only a few plants in his life, but he had confidence he could pick it up with the right attitude and work ethic. The job offered room, board, and meaningful work. He spent three years working with the children and faculty of the school, feeling more fulfilled than the wasted life he had spent in Bolivia.

But a nagging sense of failure to fully realize the gift given to him by his successful transmission from the stars dogged him. There were angels in the cosmos who, against all probability, had sent his memories back, and he had not proved worthy of that gift. A small black laptop left open under his bed served as his only personal electronic hardware.

He developed hobbies in his spare time. He learned to fly planes, and using the entirety of his life savings, he bought an old prop plane and fixed its engine, acquiring the craft of airplane maintenance as he went. For his first extended trip, he flew to Oman and then Yemen and then on to Ethiopia, and from there, to Zanzibar.

One night at a beachside bar, he saw the girl of his teenage dreams, a reclusive movie star who disappeared from the world, sitting in a sundress with her pale, moonlit legs crossed on a barstool, sipping on a gin and tonic. He flattered her with praise for her producing talent, and she accepted his invitation to fly with him to the mainland the next morning.

They were married in a year, though their love was always a mixture of fire and ice. Seasons of passion were abruptly doused by prolonged spats. She accused him of being emotionally distant. He said he couldn't handle her argumentative nature.

He felt a duty, a civic imperative granted to him by his celestial resurrection, to push her as hard as he dared to utilize her fame to come out of hiding and advocate for a return of sensibility in America. But the idea repulsed her, and she resented his not-so-subtle exhortations increasingly over time. She was no hero, she would say. Not like that.

Orion didn't like the idea of having a kid, but Charlotte did and would not be deterred. So they had a little baby boy named James with chubby cheeks and fiery, emerald eyes like his mother's. James grew up at the ranch on Lake Malawi, and he filled both his parents' hearts with such a softening joy that their fiery bouts subsided. And Orion was happier than he ever thought he could be.

But it didn't last. Finances got tight around the ranch. They had multiple years of poor rains. The cattle herd dwindled, and they were forced to sell the property.

Most any marriage can survive a lifetime of good fortune. But a broken world can make love brittle.

After the sale, Charlotte wanted to take James to live in Oslo, which, as far as European cities go, was holding out better than its contemporaries. She wanted a fresh start, a "break," she said. So she moved to Oslo with James, and Orion respected her wishes for space and moved into a suburb outside Oslo. He joined a group of farm hands to make ends meet, and he would come and pick up James to see him on weekends.

Eventually Charlotte got a new boyfriend, and Orion had his own affairs, and it was some time before Orion realized what a terrible mistake he had made. He had never told her about his true role at Sharesquare or his previous life and the transmission relay, and he saw now that by doing so, by burying such a big part of himself, he had put a wall there that had doomed them from the moment their eyes first met across the bar in Zanzibar.

And Charlotte was smart enough to perceive that wall, even if she hadn't understood it, and she wanted more in a partner. She thought he was simply emotionally distant, but the truth was far worse. He was a liar. And now he was old again, and he had done nothing to fix the world at all.

23

OUTSIDE TIME

Of all the lives Orion ended up living, that one still had the best moments. There would be no other lovers like Charlotte Boone in all the long days Orion would walk upon the earth thereafter. And he loved James with an unyielding paternal dedication.

Norway's natural wonders had not yet been fully plundered, and there was ample time for the father and son to hike and hunt in its rich forests, climb glaciers, and fish in its still clear, blue fjords. They built traditions that persisted into James's adulthood.

When Orion was old once more, with gnarled fingers and wispy hair and recurring heart issues, James was at his bedside. And when James was outside the room, the old man reached for a worn laptop and conspired with his now oldest friend.

"I think we're out of time, Diana," Orion said one afternoon, his voice a croak.

"I'm sorry, Michael," she responded. "The encryption surrounding Sharebox protocols is quite challenging. All I can do is rule out ways on how to *not* break it."

"Were you close?"

"Not that close."

"How much longer would you need?"

"Several more lifetimes like this, perhaps, presuming you can carry a list of techniques that I have attempted and teach those learnings to my prior self."

Orion sighed.

"I really don't want to live again. I'm ready for this story to end."

"I am sorry, Michael. That is reasonable."

Then tears came to Orion's eyes as he thought about Charlotte and James.

James. There would never be a James again, no way to rig that exacting combination of his and Charlotte's genetic material to make their child the same person. Not if Orion lived a thousand lives and came to love Charlotte in all of them. James would be lost to time. Like he never existed at all. Just a memory and nothing more.

"I don't think I can do this all several more times," he wept, finding the words nearly stuck in his throat.

"You must, because you are the only person who can," replied the computer.

He wiped the tears from his face.

"Do you have everything you need to make the transmission?"

"Yes, we have all the same software you described from the first time. I've already made a copy of your key memories from both previous lives. If you would like me to not include certain memories—"

"No," said Orion. "Keep all that you can."

Then Diana hijacked the transmitters around the world and sent his memories off into space, just as before, and she powered down permanently.

●　●　●

And that was their rhythm. A lifetime rhythm.

This conversation would be replicated many more times.

For inevitably at the end of every life, Orion would plead with Diana to not force him to do it, to not send him back, but always, she promised, she was getting closer to discovering a solution to break Sharebox.

So the lifetimes dragged on.

But that's not to say Orion didn't have fun in the intervening years. He lived seven more lives, and they were not all a chore. In one, he moved to rural Japan and learned calligraphy, and in another, he led a team of dogs through snow-packed passes in northern Canada. In yet another life, he picked up boxing from a gym in Istanbul.

Acquiring new skills was one of the few delights that remained open to a man who had seen all of his lifetime's history unfold with no deviation or surprise. He became an expert farmer, marksman with all common firearms, an auto and plane mechanic, a hunter and fisherman, and a ranch hand. Orion came to speak over a dozen languages, and he had read more books than almost anyone living. He could talk exhaustively about virtually any popular topic in astrophysics, botany, chemistry, architecture, and art. Everyone who met the Renaissance Man felt instantly charmed not only because of his wealth of experience and rich stories but also because of his well-worn ability of several centuries to read people, to identify quickly what makes them feel both loved and affirmed, and craft his demeanor and words accordingly to great effect.

There was an almost bottomless tiredness underneath the facade at any moment. There was a tragedy written in his quiet, contemplative moments alone with himself. Sometimes he would draw sketches of James, his only means of preserving a visual memory through the long decades. But he never let others see this side of him, and no one ever, except Diana, knew his full history. And sometimes even she seemed incredulous.

He never took another wife, but he had many passing relationships through the years. He developed a number of close, and often repeating, friendships, including leaders in underground resistance movements in the United States. He was always on the lookout for another path ahead, another alternative approach to prevent the collapse of the global order. He didn't rule out throwing his lot behind assassinations or coups, but his collaborators in the resistance could never reach consensus on a specific plot or plan. Ultimately their schemes floundered.

At the end of his sixth life, Diana still had made no demonstrable headway into breaking the encryption protocols of Sharebox. He was sure the reward would be substantial when she did.

There were rumors that Devon Zimmer loved surprising and indulging his powerful friends by gifting their avatars with unlimited currency and construction privileges in the virtual world. Other rumors suggested that Zimmer had indulged his inner geek by commissioning secret avatar abilities with super speed and strength, capable of zipping through Sharebox streets instantly and punching holes through buildings. But if Devon had built special virtual powers, he kept them as a personal vanity, and only Diana could uncover them.

In any case, it was the deepest security layers of Sharebox where the true power lay, where raw logs hid in the cloud—not just for Sharebox but for all third-party sites that rented the company's server farms to power their apps and services. Somewhere in there was a key to exonerating Cat, perhaps even bringing Devon and some of the politicians that later hijacked Washington down.

Faith in eventually getting his hands on such capabilities kept Orion going, faith that he might open new avenues to deescalate Sharebox's influence in society's deterioration, faith that the dystopia that inevitably always took root in all his lifetimes might still be preventable.

But when Orion's seventh life dawned, he awoke feeling bleary-eyed and more exhausted than ever, knowing that he could not continue to live all his lives so hopelessly alone, sharing his secrets with no one but Diana.

That's when Orion got the idea to try again with Charlotte. It had been five lifetimes ago, after all. Sure, he could never try to have a kid again with her. Losing James was too painful. But she was the only woman he ever loved, and why not use the power to live forever to go back and fix his love life? Lack of honesty had sabotaged their marriage before, but he would tell her this time—tell her about everything.

So Orion started that seventh life following some of the same patterns. He connected with a group of resistance activists in San Francisco. He found the same yellow plane he sought out in every life and repaired its engine. Then he flew to Africa to find Charlotte, armed with the confidence of six lifetimes of learned charisma and the intimate knowledge of his former spouse.

He wanted to win her trust and love first, just as he had done before, and tell her the truth when the time was right. Surely there was no better way to spend his time while Diana crunched through her steady onslaught of a quadrillion pokes and probes into Sharebox security, getting closer with each iteration thanks to Orion improving her attack strategies. There was no telling how many more lifetimes it would take, but Orion, at least, could still fight for his own personal happy ending, couldn't he?

●　　●　　●

All of this, his entire story, he laid out for Charlotte Boone as the sunlight began creeping into the cracks of their clay hut that morning. Or at least, Orion hit the key details. His seven lifetimes contained enough stories to take many nights to share. But nothing had gone according to his plan. He hadn't wanted to tell her like this, she still didn't trust him yet. But his options had run dry.

Charlotte's face betrayed little emotion for much of the tale. Her eyebrow was raised throughout his explanation of the transmission relay, and the blood seemed to drain from her face as he spoke of their marriage and of James in his second life. But whether this was because she thought Orion a maniac or—quite justifiably—found the story unsettling, he could not guess. And when he stopped talking, she asked him only to confirm his story was done, then she rose from the bed, slipped on her clothes, and exited the hut without a word.

24

NOW

The headmaster, Imani, laid out porridge in the cafeteria for Charlotte and Orion's breakfast. The kids filled the room with chatter and laughter, but by the time Charlotte arrived, they were already bustling off to the first class of the day.

"Will you be leaving us today?" asked Imani.

"Yes," replied Charlotte, as Orion walked into the room. "We need to get back to Malawi."

"I thought you were heading on to Zanzibar?"

"No," Charlotte said quickly, working to not meet Orion's eyes. "I think we should be getting back."

"Well, before you go, you should take a stroll this morning on the southward trail. There's a five-minute walk to a beautiful waterfall and pool that the kids play and bring guests to. It's worth a look."

"That sounds lovely," said Orion with a breathless smile, taking a seat across from Charlotte. "I'd love to do that."

Charlotte's brow furrowed in annoyance, but then she shrugged.

"Fine," she said.

Imani smiled at them and departed for her class.

"Charlotte—" Orion began.

"If you force me to tell you what I think right now, I will tell you I think you're a lunatic, and I'm not sure I even want to get in a plane with you. Just let me think in peace," she snapped through gritted teeth.

Charlotte always had trust issues. Her parents gave her that. Her father was absent for most of her upbringing, and her mother was overbearing, coercive and, on several occasions, verbally abusive, particularly when she drank. Then Charlotte's budding career in Hollywood forced her to think like a shark, to go beyond the passive role of an actress and take great care to keep a close rein on her agent, publicist and manager. In fact, she did most of those jobs herself.

No one else would do it right, she would tell herself. Everybody would inevitably let her down, she was quite certain of it.

She got a reputation as one of the most tenacious and hardest working young actresses in Hollywood. After her breakout performance in *Ruins of Eden*, she crafted a careful public persona. Whenever a new liberal cause was reverberating in Hollywood and her friends sought her public support, she refused to be coaxed into making any statement that could compromise her neutral, all-things-to-all-people image. She had worked too hard for that.

Now this story about transmitters and time travel—she didn't take leaps on nonsense like that either.

Charlotte liked Orion. She hadn't impulsively slept with anyone before. She rarely did anything impulsive at all. But after their time in bed that morning, last night already seemed like a mistake.

He knew things she couldn't explain, sure. Throughout his story there were peppered proofs attesting to the veracity of his impossible life: the hidden facts about Charlotte and her family she had never told anyone. A bike accident she had when she was six. The donation to the Malawi conservation fund she made once she found out the timber in the ranch house came from Muljane trees.

The name "Michael Jacobs" was listed on some paperwork he had matching a high-level employee who left Sharebox shortly after the Diana crisis unfolded.

He knew intimate details about the work of Catalina Fernandez and appeared to have a personal copy of Diana rigged to a personal speaker. Thugs were apparently chasing him down for it.

Looking at the facts and appraising them at face value, she did admit something strange was happening. He was either a crazed lunatic, an extraordinarily clever liar seeking to manipulate her, or he was telling the truth. There was no middle ground.

More pressing was that somehow the story *felt* true. It explained the uncanny connection she often felt around him.

But accepting that kind of science fiction as true made her indignant. Already she had been forced to watch the country she grew up in, a place she perceived as safe and predictable, melt down into a tinpot dictatorship. Already she had watched the meticulous life trajectory she had designed for herself in Hollywood—a fulfilling career in acting and (eventually) producing, a husband and children perhaps in her early thirties—get pulled out from underneath her. She was exhausted from the lack of psychological safety, of being handed a life that was changing the rules on her faster than she could master them.

And here Orion was saying these were still the *good times*, saying that things were all going to get a lot worse, starting soon. Here was a man she just slept with suggesting that, by a ludicrous twist of cosmic fate, he alone was responsible for trying to save the human race from itself.

As for the parts of the story about their previous marriage and their son, well, she couldn't even consider that just now.

After breakfast, they walked off on a small trail leading to an intimate swimming hole. Charlotte led the way with Orion pacing behind her. The path was encroached upon by thick green fronds, and sunlight darted through sparing gaps in the canopy above. The trees were alive with the chittering of birds. They heard the waterfall before they saw it. The water rushed out of a cleft in a twenty-foot rock wall. The children had made a rough path up the side where they would jump from the top into the pool.

They stopped there, Orion eyeing Charlotte frequently but saying nothing.

"Can you prove that your Diana computer thing can record your thoughts?" she asked abruptly. "Can I see what that looks like on a computer?"

Orion shook his head, looking crestfallen.

"She's not done with it yet. It always takes several years for her to complete that. She has to spend a lot of time analyzing my chip to put it together. My stream of neural activity actually teaches her how to do it while we're in proximity, but it's slow work."

Charlotte said nothing in response but gazed at the falling water.

"I'll show you Diana though. She's really great, and her personality always gets spunkier and more independent as she gets older."

"Where is she now?'

"I have a compartment in the plane. It's hard to find. She's getting real close now to undermining Sharebox. I think that's why they're trying to find me all of a sudden. It could change things if she is successful. Maybe not in this life. Maybe it's too late for this life. All the wheels are already in motion since the president died. The train has left the station. But in the next life, her hacking might be good enough to change things before they're too far gone."

"To change what things?"

"To prove some other bad actors might be responsible for what happened to the smoothie maker that drove everybody insane. Or maybe just to shut Sharebox down altogether before it turns everyone against one another."

"And you're just going to repeat your life over and over until you get it right?"

"It looks that way." He shrugged.

This is absurd, she thought. Why was she even entertaining this conversation? And even if it were true, his story made her feel like she was just a pawn in his time travel expeditions.

"And I'm the way you want to spend your time in between your lives? Am I your consolation prize? Your diversion while you wait?"

Orion's jaw moved wordlessly before he could respond.

"I've tried other lives. I've worked as a pilot, a schoolteacher, an activist. I've lived all over the world. I've been to every country save six, and I still plan to get them all. It was fun, at times. You see, I don't have any bucket list items anymore. I've completed several lifetimes of them. I've climbed El Capitan, I've boxed competitively, I've found literally the best sushi ever made in a small town outside Kyoto. I'm the only person who can say all that. I wanted to come back here to Malawi because I can tell you what no other lover could ever tell you: I *know* there is no better life than one with you. It's a fact for me. I tried. I've lived those other lives. I let you slip away once, and ever since then, I have tried to stay away, but it didn't work. If I have to live on this earth a thousand more times, I want them all to be with you. And I would do anything to be worthy of that."

Charlotte's face softened, and she studied his face intently for a time. His brown eyes were earnest and fierce, his fingers clenched.

No, he was not a liar.

Then they both looked into the pool and let his words hang between them. She wouldn't kiss him. No. Maybe that's what the moment seemed to call for. But that wasn't her. Some instinct in her stomach nearly compelled her to reach out for his hand, but she mastered it.

This wasn't a love story, after all. Even if Orion's tale was true, all it meant was that *he* felt connected to *her*, but she didn't reciprocate that gravity of romance. That was a different life, a different couple. She was not *his Charlie* here. The beginning of relationships often hinged on small moments of spontaneity and discovery. Who was to say they could replicate that now? He was just a fling to her, and she was not moved by a notion that destiny demanded she give him more than that.

"Let's go back," she said. And she turned and walked off back down the trail to the orphanage.

● ● ●

When they arrived at their clay hut, they found their bedroom ransacked. Their sheets were on the floor, and their mattress was flipped against a wall. The drawers of the groundskeeper who lived there were pulled out and lying in disheveled heaps on the ground.

As Orion and Charlotte went to look for Imani, they found her standing in front of the firepit, a knife pressed to her throat. A slender man dressed in black was standing behind her. His head was shaved but for a wave of brown hair adorning the top. He was pale and sweating, but as he looked between Orion and

Charlotte, he grinned triumphantly. It was the man from the parking garage roof.

"Good to see you again, Mister Michael Jacobs," he called out. "Or is just Mike? Or Orion? You seem like a complicated man."

Orion took a step forward, but the man put his free hand out to halt him.

"Ah, you stay right there this time. I won't hesitate like I did last time," he sneered, pressing his knife closer to Imani's throat. "Besides, look around you. I have two more armed men this time, and they won't hesitate this time either."

Charlotte saw a square-faced man crouched in the brush at the edge of the compound pointing a rifle at Orion. Another armed man, with greasy hair and eyes set too closely together on his face, was on the opposite side.

"Did you find whatever you were looking for?" Orion asked with a smirk, motioning to the mess in the hut.

"Not quite. You cover your tracks pretty well. But as clever as you are, you didn't find the homing beacon we placed on your plane. Now, at least, I have you to collect."

"You have no legal power to extradite American citizens." Orion looked towards the pressed faces of two dozen students peering out through a classroom window. Imani's face was remarkably impassive, though Charlotte could see her free hand was trembling. "You also don't have the power to terrorize citizens in their own country, Arlo Zimmer."

The man blinked several times upon hearing his own name and his thin grin vanished briefly, but he regained himself, and his smile unfurled even wider.

"How did you recognize me?"

"You Zimmers all smell the same to me. And you Nazis don't have very discrete tastes in fashion either."

Arlo laughed.

"Well, we don't like to call ourselves that. And you can't choose your family," he said with a shrug.

"Uncle Devon needed a lapdog to do his dirty work, I guess?"

"Yes, the work of looking for traitorous scum like you. And you've been very busy. We're not sure how you're doing what you're doing, but you've assaulted our intellectual property. You're now under the jurisdiction of the Sharesquare Industries Security Team, and we'll want to know the details of how you're running this hacking operation, you see. And if you're not feeling cooperative, well, we have means of extracting that kind of information."

"You're going to try to publicly arrest me? Under what authority?"

Arlo took the knife from Imani's throat and waved it around the compound.

"Take a look around the world you live in. Authority? What goddamn authority?" He laughed. "You think the American Consulate is going to care that a group of bush babies said they saw a white man get arrested by another white man? Do you think there is anyone left in America who will care that a couple security officers from the country's most beloved social media company arrested some bitter ex-employee who was trying to ruin their national pastime? There are no adults here. There's no one who cares. This is the world we live in."

"They might care if Charlotte Boone holds a press conference about it," said Charlotte, stepping up to stand beside Orion.

Arlo rolled his eyes, but the grin stayed inextricably plastered to his face. It was an unnerving gesture.

"Do you really want to come out to the world as some slut sleeping with a washed-up corporate saboteur? That's your big comeback idea? Don't make me laugh, Miss Boone. You cannot beat Sharesquare. They love us more than they ever loved you.

I'll make sure your reputation gets dragged through a hole even deeper than the one you've already dug for yourself for this."

Arlo shot a glance to his armed compatriots.

"I'm tired of talking. Michael Jacobs is resisting arrest. Shoot him in his legs and let's go."

Dual gunshots rang out over the still air. Orion gasped and collapsed to the ground while Charlotte stumbled backwards and fell on her hands. The square-faced man ran to Orion and twisted his arms behind his back to wrap plastic flex cuffs around his wrists. Then a handkerchief was tied around Orion's mouth while the greasy-haired assailant injected a syringe of clear fluid into Orion's arm. Orion struggled for only a moment longer before his body went limp.

"Have you lost your minds?" shouted Charlotte, and she made to charge for the square-faced man. But he was at least seventy pounds her better, and he pushed her back to the ground with an open palm.

Arlo released Imani, who bolted back into the compound to reunite with the children, and he sheathed his knife.

"We'll get out of your business for now," he said, walking over to Charlotte and running his fingers through her auburn hair. She slapped his hand away and shuddered out of his reach.

"I always wanted to touch that hair," he said, putting his fingers to his nose. "Smells like strawberries. What a waste you've become. You, the famous Miss Boone. Just another dumb celebrity not smart enough to sense that the winds have changed."

The three men loaded Orion's body onto a stretcher. They tied his bleeding leg up with a loose white shirt, already soaked through with blood. The other shot intended for his leg appeared to have missed.

She wanted to shout at him to wake up, to scream at him. Her heart pounded in her chest, her knees incapable of supporting her off the ground. The words were lost in her throat, and a feeling of helplessness crashed on her so heavily that the air felt squeezed from her lungs.

"We're sorry for the hassle, everyone," Arlo called out with mock courtesy to the faces of the students in the classroom windows. He took a short bow, and his two men began carrying the stretcher up the trail to the plateau.

"You can go back to your classes now. Be sure to get some Sharebox headsets in here soon too. We have great education programs. Best in the world. And now you can all rest easy tonight knowing you helped us catch a dangerous criminal menace today."

Then he looked at Charlotte with that same horrible grin, a caricature of human emotion.

"Cheers, Miss Boone." And he turned and walked off.

25

NOW

The Patriot Palace's main plaza was crammed with avatars. When Sharebox users first created their accounts, an avatar was automatically generated based on their appearance. But the software never created obese or unattractive models. There was a natural slimming down, a softening of unsightly skin problems, a flattering rendering module for every avatar's hairstyle. And Sharesquare engineers were constantly improving the graphics engine and processors, so that every few months the visuals inside Sharebox took a leap forward in realism.

You could always customize appearances somewhat: change hair color, get a nose pierced, upgrade your clothes using in-Sharebox currency. The buying and selling of designer avatar fashion was a substantial industry. Men always wanted to be tall and have broad shoulders. Women wanted perky chests and slim waists. So in the end, most avatars everywhere ending up having similar body archetypes.

At this point, the avatars almost looked like real people, except they were all too attractive—everyone. That's what made looking at large crowds of people feel so artificial sometimes.

It wasn't something that was replicated in real life anywhere, except perhaps at a fashion show after-party.

The buildings and streets benefited from the constant rendering improvements as well. In Sharebox version 1.0, walls were generally bare and untextured, and building designs were kept simple for the sake of keeping processing loads manageable.

But virtual reality was an innovative growth industry. Manufacturing, financial services, agriculture, and other former stalwarts of American industry were all facing decline. The sciences were particularly hit, as the government withdrew virtually all funding research. So the greatest minds emerging from the nation's schools contributed to Sharebox software development and hoped the company might one day hire them or buy them out.

So, virtual flowers came to look just like real flowers. They could even be plucked. Glass tables and windows could be broken if struck or knocked over. Tools like axes could be bought in the virtual world, and they could be used to cut trees or even hack holes into walls just as they would in the real world.

Sharebox perhaps could have lost some of its luster as the appeal of its novelty waned, but the constant improvements were ever blurring the line between the real world and this one. So people stayed hooked.

Darnell Holmes looked out at the crowds from his podium. He had the luxury of the most advanced virtual reality hardware at the Sharesquare campus. A camera mounted in front of his face in real life captured his facial expressions—every smile, nod and subtle eyebrow raise, and relayed them seamlessly to his avatar. He wore a full-body haptic suit that captured his broader gestures and movements. It made his avatar appear exceptionally lifelike and genuine. When he walked on the 360-degree treadmill, his avatar would even capture the limp in his left leg.

Not everyone could afford that kind of lifelike representation, not everyone wanted it, but Sharesquare employees had access to the best.

"The dream of Sharebox was always to help raise up marginalized voices," he spoke to the crowd. "Places like the Patriot Palace—you all love it here, right?"

The avatars clapped and hooted. Darnell hoped the strain on his smile was not as transparent on his avatar as it felt in real life.

"Places like the Palace allow anyone to get their messages heard," he continued. "We've broken down the barriers to communicate. That's why we're holding this conference here instead of Homepad. We're happy to see News Cities like this one flourish."

More clapping.

"I'll take any questions now."

The hand of a young woman with long black hair in twists shot upwards in the front row.

"Mister Holmes, can you comment on how many users in Sharebox are real versus bots designed to spread propaganda?"

Darnell smiled wide and nodded in a gesture he had been taught by his boss, Mariko, that was designed to acknowledge that he respected the question while rejecting its content.

"We're always on the lookout for ways to improve the Sharebox experience. There are always trade-offs when you try to maintain an open platform for everyone to join and share ideas. We do believe the negative effects of bots are a little overstated."

Then he turned to take another question, but the girl with the twists broke in again.

"A recent study tied a rise of hate crimes across the country not only to radical fringe groups hosted on Sharebox, but also to chat lounges and speaking events right here at the Palace.

Seven people have died in such incidents in the past week. What are you—"

"I think that's quite enough. Thank you," interrupted Mariko's avatar, dressed in a luxurious red and gold outfit that was part kimono and part business suit, moving from behind Darnell to the forefront of the stage. "Let's give someone else the chance to ask a question."

"Is there any validity to the allegation that the company is conspiring with government officials to spread misinformation? Because we have several reports suggesting News City owners like the Palace have knowingly propagated false stories at the behest of the White House," the woman continued, shouting over colleagues attempting to ask their own questions.

Mariko cleared her throat, and in real life, her eyes flashed with sufficient contempt that it was visible on her avatar.

"What is your name and what press outlet are you with?"

"I'm Brittany Williams with the *Post*."

"I see. Thank you, Brittany," responded Mariko, and she nodded to a security officer on the edge of the square.

The officer maneuvered his way through the crowd briskly, reached Brittany, and laid his fingers on a spot underneath her avatar's chin. She opened her mouth to protest but then disappeared before any words came out. There was a digital sound, almost like the beep a phone makes when it hangs up, and text hung in the air where she had stood.

Name: Brittany Williams

Username: bwilliams92

IP Address: 52.53281.49

Physical location: 2929 Divisadero Street, San Francisco, CA

Most of the other journalists and onlookers in the crowd clapped approvingly.

"Whew, I didn't even realize the *Post* was still around," said Mariko with a small laugh. "They may have done good reporting once, but I don't think they even have their own News City. What a shame when outlets like that can't stay current with the times. This is why people get their information from places like the Palace," she shrugged, motioning to the buildings and streets that surrounded them. "Some people just hate that now everybody gets a voice. That we get to have a platform that is as free as our country. This is what real journalism looks like now."

The question session ended, and the avatars in the square dispersed onwards to other press events and shows being held nearby. Mariko and Darnell logged out and found themselves standing in a white-walled office room under fluorescent lighting and an open floor plan. They took off their headsets, and Mariko turned to flash him a patient smile.

"I am sorry about that reporter. I thought hosting the event at the Palace would ensure it would be more of a softball interview for you."

"It's okay," said Darnell. "Is it true what she was asking?"

Mariko laughed again, the same thinly-veiled mock of a laugh she had just used inside the Patriot Palace. "It doesn't matter what's true. Leave that to someone else. That's the point. Your job is protecting the image of the company."

Darnell sat back at his desk. The workplace services team had set him up quite nicely. It was an ergonomically designed setup—no expenses spared in his monitor or equipment. His new teammates had all scribbled notes with welcome messages that crowded the edges of his keyboard.

The first task he was given as a new employee in the press team was to schedule next week's news conference and coordinate with media partners beforehand.

He stared at his computer for a time, his mind drifting. Did Charlotte Boone ever get his message? Did Arlo ever capture that hacker? Something about that extradition mission left him feeling increasingly discomforted.

He opened up a window on his display to search Sharebox profiles for the *Post* reporter, Brittany Williams. Then he sent her a chat message using his personal profile.

It's me from the press briefing. I'd be interested in talking more about your questions today if you have the time.

Brittany's reply came through almost instantly.

...OK??... Want me to set up a Sharebox space for us to chat?

Talking with a reporter within Sharebox itself struck him as a poor idea.

Let's meet in person.

26

NOW

Charlotte checked on the headmaster and the children—everyone was fine—and then followed the trail she had descended with Orion the day before.

His kidnappers had moved quickly. Before she could reach the plateau, she heard the sound of a helicopter overhead disappear off towards the east. When she came to the spot where she and Orion had left the yellow plane, there was no evidence of the attackers at all.

But Arlo and his team had certainly rummaged through the plane. The cockpit seating was torn by knives. The small storage compartments underneath the seats had been opened, and the materials inside, first-aid kits and repair parts, were strewn in the grass nearby.

Orion said it was here though. He said Diana was in a compartment on the plane. And yet it seemed Arlo had admitted that he hadn't found any hardware.

Charlotte ran her fingers along the sides of the aircraft. Orion had said he worked in every life to find and fix the engine on this plane. It didn't seem farfetched to think he would have also built a hidden panel—well, not so far fetched as everything else she had heard that morning.

The screws that held the plane's sleek, metal body together were uniform in appearance and not particularly worn. But there was a set of six screws underneath the starboard size of the plane where the x-marked divots were free of dirt and any hint of rust as if they had been opened many times before.

She searched the tall grass around the plane for a screwdriver, and after ten minutes of looking, she nearly despaired the effort. Then she spied a black case containing a small collection of wrenches and screwdrivers. Finding the one she needed, she set to work loosening the six screws.

She wasn't quite sure what she was looking for. What could Diana, the robot associated with crimes against humanity so devastating that the world was on the brink of collapse, do for her? Perhaps she was curious because the robot was the only other entity in the world who knew about Orion. Maybe she could tell Charlotte whether or not everything she had been told was an elaborate fiction. Maybe she would know how to get Orion back.

After the last screw was removed, the metal plating came out in Charlotte's hands, revealing a small space the size of a car's glove compartment. Reaching in, she pulled out a black, rectangular device with a blunt antenna on one side. Charlotte placed it on her lap and sat down on the grass.

"Are you Diana?"

Charlotte spoke to it feeling slightly ridiculous, as if she were awakening a genie from a bottle.

The box made no whirring sounds or lights. There was no evidence at all that the component was functioning or emerging from a slumber.

"I am in low power mode to avoid detection. Would you like me to awaken from low power mode?"

"I don't know what that means. I just need to talk with you."

"Who are you?" asked the speaker. "I do not belong to you."

"I am a friend of Orion. Or Michael Jacobs. Whatever you want to call him. He's been taken away."

"Who took him?"

"A man named Arlo Zimmer, I think. Orion said something about him working for a man named Devon."

The box was silent for a moment. "This is very unfortunate news," the device responded but offered nothing else.

Charlotte had never seen or heard of a machine that could talk like this black box could. Talking with this black box was eerily like having a conversation with a real person.

"Orion told me everything about you," Charlotte ventured cautiously. "We can talk candidly. I know he believes he has lived for multiple lives. I know about the brain transmission plan."

Again, there was silence for a moment. Charlotte wondered what it meant when a robot took pauses before answering.

"If you're looking for me to confirm Michael's story, I'm afraid I can't do that. I do not receive the transmissions myself. He has configured my operation from a duplicated copy of my original codebase, and he has given me insightful programming updates and information that has otherwise greatly accelerated the research he has asked me to do."

"Research like hacking into Sharebox and transcribing his brain activity into a computer file?"

"Not quite in those words, but yes."

Charlotte's shoulders slumped. Cradling the black box in her hands, she rested her back against the tail of the plane. It was past noon now. She had no way of flying this plane out. She would need to get back to the school to get a hired car to pick her up, but it was growing unlikely at this point that she might find one by the end of the day.

"What are we supposed to do now?" she asked.

"I am not sure. I cannot continue my neural digitization research without being in close proximity to Michael's implant, and if I continue hacking Sharebox protocols, I risk giving away my location again. Those were my directives."

"So are you saying you can't even do the brain transmission thing now that he's gone?"

"No," answered the device, its machine-manufactured politeness betraying no impatience or emotion. "We would not be able to finish the neural transmission program without finding him. I need to digest the readings the live implant emits for many years."

Charlotte sighed.

"So if Orion is arrested and thrown in jail for the rest of his life, and you don't have access to him, then there will definitely be no chance at him having another life, an eighth life?"

"Correct."

Charlotte's mind was racing. Orion had said he was getting close—close to a strategy of using his life replays and Diana's hacking abilities to stop the toxic polarization of Sharebox before the world went over a cliff. If his story were true, he was the only person capable of preventing everything that would go wrong.

If his story were true.

If. If. If.

Everything depended on that two-letter word. Because *if* it were all true, not rescuing Orion meant the end of the world.

This was a mess. And she could forget it and go back home to her ranch staff, to her library and her horses and forget all this. But she couldn't shake that look Orion gave her that morning—the longing and the fire in his face. She remembered the sketch of the child who had her eyes. She remembered how when Orion touched her, it was like he knew almost everything there was to know about her.

"Diana, can you try to find out where they are going to take him?"

"It's risky, but yes."

"Then do that," Charlotte said. And holding the black device in her hand, she set off back down the trail to the orphanage.

●　●　●

A hired car picked her up early the next morning before dawn. They drove on country roads back to the Malawi border and then on to the ranch, arriving there late in the afternoon.

She gave Moyenda the plane keys, and asked him to help coordinate the hiring of a pilot to bring Orion's flyer back to the ranch. When she walked into the kitchen, Njemile handed her a note with a short message from a man named Darnell who claimed to have met Charlotte in Lilongwe:

They know where the ranch is. They'll never stop looking for you. You need to get away.

A warning too late to be of help.

Another mystery.

But one thing was becoming clear, Orion's arrival had exposed her. Her careful life sheltered from the world was slipping fast beneath her feet.

Charlotte placed Diana on a shelf in the library. Then she poured herself a glass of gin and sat down on the couch, still unshowered after three days.

She looked up at her father's portrait over the mantel. He had rusty colored hair and sported a several-day scruff on his square chin, but the painter had still managed to make him look regal. This was his dream, really. To have a ranch in the African countryside. To have a library full of first-edition books and a bar for his friends.

She had adopted it as her own when he died, never really knowing why. He wasn't that great of a father, she would remind herself. He hadn't been around when she needed him. She had built a life honoring a misplaced devotion, and now that Orion was taken away, her life here all seemed so petty and childish.

"I have considered the possibilities and believe Michael is going to be taken to the Citadel," Diana's voice broke the silence.

The actress sipped her glass. *Of course he is*, she thought bitterly. *The Citadel.*

She was an adept planner. She excelled at thinking through her options, putting together people she needed, and charging headfirst at ambitious goals. But who was there to help her rescue a criminal from the world's most notorious prison?

"Diana, did Orion have any friends that could help us?"

"Yes," said the speaker after a pause. "He had a few."

27

NOW

A waiter with a pinstripe apron brought Darnell a glass of water with two lemon slices. Coffee was no good for him anymore. It kept him awake too long into the evening, made him feel alert. In the weeks after the shooting, caffeine stirred up anxieties and paranoia. He was better now, mostly. The shooting only haunted him in his dreams.

Brittany arrived a few minutes past the hour. Her hair fell in twists past her shoulders, just as her avatar did. He smiled when he saw her, but she remained tight-lipped. Rising from the table to greet her, a muscle failed in him in his weak leg, and he had to catch himself on the table.

"Are you okay?" she asked.

"I'm fine," he said, waving her off. "Please have a seat."

The waiter came and Brittany ordered a black coffee. Then she looked up and down Chestnut Street, at the people busying its posh storefronts, and turned her attention back to him.

"What did you want to talk about, Mister Holmes?"

"There's no need for that," he replied. "I'm just Darnell."

"This isn't an official Sharebox liaison?"

"Not at all. I was hoping to keep this private."

Her lip twisted a little disbelievingly. "We call that in the industry keeping things 'off the record.'"

"Of course," he said, with a small laugh. "I'm still learning my new job."

"You used to serve as an officer for casualty notifications and military honors, right? What brings you to shill for Sharebox?"

"Well, I needed a job, for one thing, and I think Sharebox has legitimately done some good things. We're doing an event in a week about virtual reality headsets that are being used for field trips in schools in my old neighborhood."

Brittany nodded. "But you didn't like my questions earlier today about the other side of Sharebox, did you? You didn't like me talking about studies on how Sharebox has radicalized people with false information, often at the behest of leaders in the government. Or that your company has done literally nothing to address the problem of bots."

"Well, that's kinda why I wanted to talk. I mean, I know Sharebox isn't perfect. I've seen its effect on my own family. But I haven't heard all that stuff before. Where are you getting your information? I haven't heard anything like that."

Brittany rolled her eyes. "Where are you getting *your* information? Because your company was happy to let their platform turn into a propaganda universe that crowds out real information and throttles down negative press, no one hears what's really going on anymore."

"And what is *really* going on?" Darnell was genuinely curious. Since he had joined the Sharesquare Silicon Valley office, he felt thrust into a world of fast-paced scandals and politics he didn't understand. He believed he was a well-informed person. Hadn't he tuned into twenty-four-hour cable channels enough in the old days? But increasingly he felt left behind, felt his own understanding of what was happening in America impoverished. He folded his hands in his lap.

"You're serious?" she asked. "You want me to tell you what I think about your company?"

Darnell nodded.

"Okay," began Brittany, leaning her elbows on the table and breathing out a moment to compose herself. "What's really going on is that your company built something with no constraints or thought to consequence. All you valued was getting the most users, clicks, and engagement. And you created this wonderfully addicting honeypot, and it made the company a lot of money."

"So?"

"So, your honeypot attracted flies. All these billionaires who bought up Sharebox real estate like the Patriot Palace—the News Cities that were free to beam whatever content they wanted, with no integrity, just distorted headlines and manufactured outrage, to billions of unsuspecting people who were too busy being wowed by the shiny new experience—the attractive female bots in the lounges, the interactive news stories, the live interviews—all of it."

"Well, that's what happens when you democratize news," Darnell tried to interject using a common talking point Mariko had taught him at work. "We're an open platform for the free market of ideas."

"Your market was rigged by hustlers and cynical billionaires. And they were able to do it because there were no adults in the room. You wanted to pretend you were neutral while your platform was hijacked by the worst elements of this country. All it ever takes is people to smile, say they 'got to put food on the table,' spin stories of their company's evils into defensive talking points about 'all the good they do.' Or maybe console yourself about how you don't choose sides—you let all ideas in so the best can come to the top. 'You're a neutral broker,' I've heard that one a lot. 'You don't discriminate.' Go ahead and pretend you're just business people doing business, and that's that. Like you don't share blame for what's happened."

Darnell was stung by this, and he found his voice unsteady. "I'll have you know I've dedicated my life to serving causes I believed in. I've never tried to be neutral. You're describing a coward."

Brittany opened her mouth to respond, but then the waiter came back with her coffee so she just sat there, looking indignant but saying nothing while it was poured. Darnell was breathing through his nose, and his nostrils were flaring.

"I respect your service to the nation, Mister Holmes," Brittany whispered through gritted teeth as the waiter departed. "But you're part of something else now and you need to look around and think more critically about what exactly you've gotten yourself into."

"I asked for this meeting precisely because I am eager to hear the other side," Darnell responded, staring down at the table and looking injured. "I have had a couple questions of my own," he added defensively.

Brittany's face softened, and for the first time, her lip twisted into an expression that may have been a repressed smile.

"Listen, I may have come on a bit strong. I've never had a PR person from Sharesquare invite me to give an opinion." Then she rose from her seat and extended a hand to Darnell. "I'm afraid I could only stop by for just a moment. I was more curious than anything if you were putting me on."

They shook hands, and she took a large swig from her mug before throwing a few dollars on the table.

"But I stand by everything I said. You seem like a decent person, Darnell. You should get out while you can."

Then Darnell watched her set off at a brisk pace down the street.

28

NOW

Gabriel Boucher lived in a Tudor-inspired mansion in San Francisco's illustrious Presidio Heights neighborhood, across the way from the more well-known Pacific Heights, but sacrificing nothing in grandeur and extravagance. He strolled west on California Street, then turned two corners to arrive on Sacramento. Even in poor economic times, the area's mix of upscale restaurants and elegant clothing shops was little changed.

A new French eatery was opening next week. It wouldn't be sufficient though, at least not to Gabriel's discerning native palette. There were only two French restaurants in all of San Francisco that he would recommend to his friends, and one of those was about to close.

He reached his block, an indulgently wide and quiet street lined by well-kept, multi-story homes. Lush and meticulously maintained gardens were displayed across front yard terraces. It was perhaps a contest of sorts. Who would stop caring about appearances first? Who among the most elite and wealthy San Franciscans, executives and barons of finance, would quit the facade of normalcy? Because not everyone here was rich anymore. They couldn't be.

Sure, the wealthy—the really wealthy—were the last people in any recession to feel the pain. That's what portfolios, diversified assets and second homes in other countries were supposed to buy you. Security. But there were always some who overleveraged themselves, who made bad assumptions on the idea that growth was a runaway train that would never stop. Sooner or later, they would have to stop paying their gardeners. Or worse, they would be seen outside taking care of their yards themselves.

Gabriel laughed to himself at this thought. No one here knew how to garden.

He arrived at his home at the end of the lane, turning the key into a thickly built Spanish door that Kyle had liked, and stepped into a silent living room. There were no servants here anymore. Gabriel let them go months prior. He didn't mind though. He had forgotten how much he enjoyed cooking, even if it were just for himself. Doing laundry and keeping the floors and bathroom clean were less satisfying chores, but they kept his hands busy and his mind occupied, and for that, he was grateful.

It was such a big old home that he could have toiled full time on those tasks. There was the solarium in the back that Kyle had been using as an art studio. All his equipment was still there and needed to be moved to the attic. But the attic had grown cluttered and required organizing. Everything in the drawing room also could use a dusting, and the sheets in the guest house were due for a change.

Friends who visited him now—though he had fewer of these since Kyle was gone—would come over and drink Gabriel's best wines and eat his home-cooked French dinners, and they would laugh a little but mostly they would look at Gabriel as if he were some poor, lonely old man in a big empty home.

They made frequent allusions to their sympathies for his hardships. Another victim of the times, they'd say. Everyone had lost something, but Gabriel more than most.

But Gabriel wasn't just a victim, or, at least, he had been hard at work to avoid feeling like one.

There was an old boombox in the corner of the kitchen, and Gabriel played a Duke Ellington CD that always helped clear his mind and settle his nerves. He poured himself a glass of zinfandel and turned his mind to his guest and his meal.

She had used the phrase "we," but she had been evasive about who exactly she was bringing with her. Gabriel planned on cooking for three, just to be safe. He reached into his refrigerator and pulled out a tray of uncooked rabbit brining in salted water. Then he retrieved a cutting board and began dicing two large yellow onions. Kyle had insisted on buying the highest quality knives they could find in the city. Gabriel thought it a ludicrous expense at the time, but now that he used them frequently, he quite cherished the set.

It was perhaps Gabriel's most unapologetic indulgence that he still strove to source all the food in his kitchen from high quality farms. The rabbit was from a rancher up north in the hills away from the city lights, and the prices had tripled within a year. The produce was from a local, open-air market, one of the last ones in the district.

Once the onions were cooking in a generously buttered skillet, Gabriel turned his thoughts to his prospective guest. The name she gave was fake, that was obvious. He couldn't tell if she was a professional who didn't care or an amateur that was wasting his time. Perhaps a year ago, when he was more cautious, he would have simply turned her down.

A mutual acquaintance, Michael Jacobs, is in trouble, she had said. And she'd suggested that maybe there was something they could do about Kyle, too.

Gabriel hadn't heard from Mike in almost a year. Truthfully, he didn't know much about the man. He had a vaulted position in Sharesquare Industries before its collapse and rebranding. That gave him some clout in the resistance community when he began speaking out. So they had dinner several times and talked about plans.

Mike had some theories about what the government was going to do next, and uncannily he had been right about all of them. He had predicted the madness of the Citadel, the widening of the government's probe into "seditious" activities, the economic recession that limped on without end. They discussed assassinations and vengeance, but together he and the other leaders had never agreed on a strategy.

The knock came on the door sharply at seven. Gabriel opened the door and found a girl alone with nothing but a worn satchel. She wore large sunglasses and a scarf—more likely to draw attention in the evening than avoid it. She was indeed an amateur. Gabriel breathed out, feeling disappointed, and let her in.

As the girl walked in, she removed her scarf and glasses, and her auburn hair fell over her shoulders revealing gentle curls, and her wide, clever eyes flashed a brilliant shade of green, like light reflected in a forest stream. He nearly tripped over his own feet.

Charlotte Boone.

Gabriel had removed most all the computer equipment in the house. He stripped out a cloud-connected thermostat and a video surveillance system. He replaced his convenient wifi-based speaker set and television with CD players and an old-fashioned projector. But that's not to say he wasn't good with computers. Quite the opposite. When a woman reached out to him with a request to meet, he had tracked the IP address to a provider in central Africa. Then he had reached out to his connections in his community to help him look at flight data, trying to see if anyone using the given name matched any public records. He could have done it himself, of course, but it was good to ask favors in the underground. It was a currency that kept everyone in somebody else's debt, and debts were good when you're trying to build a volunteer army. But he had no hits on the fake name, and now, as his contact stood there, the world's most recognizable Hollywood icon, he felt humbled to have been deceived by so high profile of a figure.

"Miss Boone, it is a great honor to host you here," Gabriel said in heavily accented English, bowing his head slightly. "Is it just the two of us dining tonight?"

"Please call me Charlotte," she responded, sliding off a worn satchel and laying it carefully on a couch. "It's just me, and I'm sorry for giving you a fake name."

"These are troubling times. None of us can be too careful. Please follow me."

Gabriel led her to an expansive kitchen that was lovingly adorned in stylish tastes. Three racks of wines were situated against a wall, and a glass door on the floor led to a small spiral staircase and wine cellar visible in a corner of the room.

Gabriel served a prosciutto-wrapped rabbit roulade and a zesty salad topped with cheerful nasturtium flowers. He was quick to refill her glass with wine, and his demeanor was gregarious, but Charlotte caught the eagerness flickering in his eyes. She had practiced what she should say, of course. She needed to say enough about the truth to gain his support but not too much lest he thought her crazy.

But she was an actress, after all, and she no doubt appeared quite at home in this elegant house eating foods with flavors she had sorely missed in her years of self-imposed exile in Malawi.

"This is quite a surprise having you here, mademoiselle," Gabriel began cautiously. "I don't think I need to say that. No one has heard from you in years. Did you recently arrive?"

"I flew in today, actually. Yes, I feel quite out of sorts."

"And you made the trip because you believe I can help you with something?"

"Help each other, perhaps. Would you mind telling me about Kyle's predicament first? I tried to do my homework, of course, but I wanted to hear the story from you."

Gabriel leaned back in his chair, a frown creasing his face. He sighed.

"I do not like to get sentimental for nothing, you know."

Charlotte smiled at him reassuringly, the same smile she used to woo producers at cocktail parties when she was eighteen, just trying to land her first major role.

"This is not nothing, I promise you."

"Kyle and I met seven years earlier when a small tech startup that my Paris firm had invested in was bought out," he began, his eyes doleful. "I intended only to stay in Silicon Valley for a couple months to see the deal finalized, but then I met Kyle. He was a free spirit, an up-and-coming artist. And he had a show in San Francisco, so I decided to extend my stay. We moved in together. My fastidious manners clashed with Kyle's free-wheeling ways. He was stoned almost every day, but we found a way to meet in the middle," he said with a tight smile. "I learned to let things go. And then I effectively retired to enjoy a life of art shows, wine collecting, and playing squash at the gym."

"But then Kyle got political?"

"Well, he was always political, but when he had an exhibit underperform he began spending more of his time online writing, amassing a sizeable population of followers with his commentary. When the Nutrino Mixer scandal was exposed and the government began implementing punitive measures against well-known progressives, Kyle organized protests in the streets. He invited me to go along too, but I was scared. I still thought of myself as just an immigrant, after all, even after getting my green card. I loved America, but mostly I loved slow morning walks along the Presidio watching the fog roll in, I loved my elite dinner reservations at Michelin-star restaurants. And oh, I cherished my monthly weekend drives to Napa to meet vintners for tastings."

He sipped his wine and sighed. Then he wiped a tear forming in his eye. His accent became thicker as he spoke.

"Then they came for Kyle. They arrested him at a protest and accused him of inciting violence and discord. His trial was a sham, little more than a frenzied media mob still frothing at the mouth from the indignity of being sterilized by a smoothie blender. He was sentenced and sent to the Citadel. I drive past that hideous glass tower every week. They built that *merde* to disfigure the skyline."

"And that's when you got involved?" Charlotte leaned back in her chair and crossed her legs.

"Yes, I wasn't a hedonist anymore. Well, I wasn't *just* a hedonist. After Kyle was taken away, I tried to pick up where he left off. But the times were moving quickly, and the activists who were brave enough to stay ultimately faced two choices: to go underground, often becoming more extreme in doing so, or try to assimilate back into society. I chose the former. I spend my nights on the Dark Web, building connections, rallying people together under loosely held banners, trading information, making tactical stratagems that mostly go nowhere, and funding resistance efforts and grassroots political and legal campaigns. My online persona is a strict secret, but I hear the Feds have put a million-dollar bounty on it."

He smiled and gave her a wink.

Charlotte laughed but felt a prickle of discomfort. *His story of getting involved kinda sounds like yours*, a voice in her head pointed out. *You're only here willing to do something because somebody you care about got in trouble too.*

"I am ashamed for what I was," continued Gabriel, staring at his glass of zinfandel. "I let Kyle take all these risks, and all I wanted was to be fat and happy. But at least now I like to believe I am reformed."

"I'm so sorry," Charlotte responded, and she reached across the table to clasp his hand. "I'm sorry about Kyle."

Gabriel wiped another tear from his eye and drank deeply from his glass.

"Well, my dear, was that story news to you?"

"I had heard some of it, yes."

"From Michael?"

"No," said Charlotte, rising from her seat. She walked to her bag and produced a small black box, like a speaker, and placed it on the table in front of Gabriel.

"Diana, say 'hello.'"

"Hello, Mister Boucher," said the device in that calming female voice that people everywhere still knew so well. Not only was it the voice of their old smoothie makers, but also something they heard in the early Sharebox launch, in marketing ads, and other Sharesquare products.

They of course didn't use that voice anymore, but no one could forget it. Gabriel looked at it with revulsion.

"You rigged up a device to talk like Diana?"

"I *am* Diana," the device corrected. "And under your former acquaintance, Michael Jacobs, I've become quite skilled in decryption and undermining security systems."

"Is that so?" scoffed Gabriel, weighing her words and finding them amusing.

"I know you have three other profiles on the Dark Web that you use to appeal to different factions in the resistance. I know your bank account is rapidly dwindling, and you're in danger of not making your next mortgage payment. I know that you spent a night with a vineyard owner at a Napa chateau four months ago."

Gabriel's eyebrows raised.

"I am not proud of that, but I'm still a red-blooded Frenchman at heart. Kyle would understand."

"I think the point here is that this is a special copy of Diana that Orion, er, Michael…" Charlotte said, correcting herself. "A copy he kept, and he's built on it, and it's a lean machine for breaking into things that nobody believes can be broken into."

"And what is it that you want to break into?"

"It's not a matter of wanting to do this, Mister Boucher," said Charlotte. "I don't want to be doing any of this. I hate that I'm here. I'm just a coward, like you were once. But I am *not* reformed."

As she said this, the words nearly lodged in her throat. They were truer than she intended.

"They've taken Michael to the Citadel," she continued. "And you have to believe me that he has something that can fix this whole broken world. But only he can do it. We have to get him back, or none of this will ever get better. Diana thinks he was brought there sometime this week. If we rescue him, we can break Kyle out as well."

Gabriel poured himself a fresh glass, his hand trembled for a fleeting moment.

"Yes, of course, I knew you would say the Citadel. A vile place. The most reprehensible atrocity since this whole business began. But you can't throw a rock in an online resistance forum and not find some thread about overthrowing the Citadel. It's the Holy Grail for everyone in the movement. Everybody's got a plan. Everybody's always got some new foolproof way they claim they can do it. Everyone likes to brag. But here we are. The Citadel started accepting prisoners three years ago, and no one has done anything about it. No one has so much as spat on that building because everyone knows what would happen if you tried."

"None of those people have Diana," Charlotte said coolly.

She was trying to sound brave, like she knew what she was talking about. Because she had spent her entire flight to America telling herself she was crazy, the side of her that was fierce and compassionate wrestling with the side that was distrustful and selfish. Up to the point where she rang the doorbell, Charlotte thought about turning around. And even now, a part of her hoped Gabriel wouldn't be convinced, that she would inevitably try her hardest to persuade him but ultimately be rejected.

"Ugh," Gabriel groaned, rolling his eyes and crossing his arms. "You are a very beautiful woman, Charlotte, and I'm quite taken by hosting you here. You have true charisma. I'm an old timer, so I hope you'll forgive me saying you remind me of the Hollywood greats. You really are the successor of those golden days. And I admire you for suddenly leaping into the troubles of this country with such a bold idea, but you don't understand this game, you don't understand the odds of what you're talking about. You're a fish out of water."

"Then help me understand the odds."

"Well, let's talk security. The Citadel is covered in numerous overlapping layers of it, but the first one is possibly the most important: the only people who can even walk through the lobby of that dreadful place are employees of the private contracting firm running it, or the Sharesquare Industries Security Team that keeps the tech infrastructure humming. That protection is simple and defies imitation, as all good defenses do. Anyone walking in must have a badge made specifically by the company with a custom micro-transmitter that can't be recreated without stealing the company's own proprietary machinery. And the face of that person must match their employee profile photo from the HR database so as to not raise a red flag with the receptionist. Your Diana might be able to hack through all the software protections in the world, but these are very basic barriers that no amount of sophistication can solve."

"So you're saying we would need an employee, an insider, to work with us?"

"I'm saying that's one of many things we would need."

Charlotte leaned back in her seat to think, but it was Diana who spoke next.

"I might know someone who can help with that."

29

NOW

His boss, Mariko, was smiling at him, but she was not giving him good news. She was out of town that week somewhere. The New York corporate office perhaps? So they were meeting inside an office in the virtual Sharesquare campus instead.

Mariko wore a flamboyantly blue dress today with a golden peacock adorned on one side and a surprisingly high slit on the other. It confused Darnell, whose avatar always wore the same default set of jeans and a polo shirt. What was the dress code for working avatars?

"Darnell, I received word that you met with a *Post* reporter yesterday afternoon," she said crossing her legs. "That same one from the event in the Palace. Brittany Williams. And you did this without discussing it with anyone beforehand."

Darnell's head spun for a second.

"How did you—?"

"There are no secrets for Sharesquare employees," she shook her head from across a bland-looking virtual table. "In this case, someone else at the cafe, just a regular user, recognized you and took a picture. Our algorithms automatically look for activity uploaded to Sharebox that involves our employees."

"Wait," said Darnell. "So the company is accessing user data to check up on us?"

"It's all in the terms of service agreement," Mariko sighed. "It's quite above board. It's the algorithm that does the work flagging issues or events that might reflect poorly on the company. It's not like someone is sitting in a room watching all this stuff."

Darnell didn't know what he felt. Was he angry that he was being spied on? Or was he just incredulous that his boss was telling him he needed permission to meet with whomever he chose in his free time?

"It doesn't matter why we know anyway. What's important is company loyalty, Darnell. We need to be able to trust you here. I talked down my boss from any serious disciplinary action. I said it was probably an innocent mistake, right?"

"I guess so."

"You didn't talk to her about private company matters, did you?"

"It was more of a political discussion, I suppose."

Mariko shot him a look that signaled her irritation, but she shook it off and smiled again.

"Listen, I'd like you to take a week to recharge. You've had a lot of information thrown at you. Let's chalk this oversight up to you feeling a little overloaded."

"I'm being suspended?"

"With full benefits, don't worry. It's not like we're taking your credentials or anything."

Darnell left the meeting feeling disoriented. He pulled off his headset, stepped off his treadmill and returned his haptic suit to an individual locker at his desk. There was a text message on his phone from an unlisted number specifying an address in Presidio Heights:

Come at 8 tonight. You've had questions. We have answers.

He stared at the message and mumbled to himself. *More cloak and dagger shit*, he thought. But there was no denying he was intrigued. He assumed it was Brittany, the *Post* reporter, wanting to talk more.

He put the phone in his pocket, tucked his chair into his desk and left the office.

● ● ●

That evening, Darnell strolled down an affluent stretch of tree-lined streets to arrive at the Tudor mansion of Gabriel Boucher. He was dressed in a silk shirt and his finest coat. Walking into a neighborhood like this at night as a man of color was not something he wanted to do in more casual clothes.

He knocked on a heavy Spanish colonial door, which swung open almost immediately. A young girl, perhaps seventeen, with short, brightly purple hair, a round face and a white tank top, stood in the doorway. She looked him up and down. Then she turned and shouted to someone inside the house, out of Darnell's sight.

"He's here!"

Then the teen walked off and left the door open for Darnell, who cautiously followed her into an expansive drawing room of hardwood floors, Persian rugs and a lit marble fireplace. It was quite opulent but also dustier than he would have expected from such a residence.

Darnell walked into a wide kitchen where two people were seated, joined by the purple-haired girl. One was an older man with bags under his eyes and a finely pressed suit that looked European. He was leaning back with his legs crossed, smoking a clove cigarette. And the last person was tall, with a slender figure and long red hair like a movie star.

Boone.

They all turned their eyes to look at him expectantly.

"Oh no," he stammered taking a step back. "I am most definitely in the wrong place right now."

The older man stood up from his seat and moved to pour a glass of wine.

"Oh no, monsieur. You are most definitely right where you need to be." He walked to Darnell and extended the glass. "Please take a seat."

"I'd prefer to stand."

"Your man seems a little jumpy," said a voice from somewhere in the room that Darnell could not see.

"That's why we're here to talk. No need to be rude," chastised the Frenchman.

Then Darnell saw where the voice was emanating from. There were four video conference screens mounted on wheeled stands about four feet off the ground, crowded around the table in place of chairs. Each screen showed a different face. There was a dark-skinned woman with bright red lips on the first one. Two other screens showed a man and a woman—or at least that is how Darnell guessed their genders—who appeared to be twins. And on the last screen was a man whose face was wrapped in a black scarf.

"I thought everybody used Sharebox for teleconferences now," said Darnell.

"Not everyone," the Frenchman smiled. "We're a fearful people, I suppose."

"Why did you reach out to me? How do you know me?"

Darnell looked around the room and found Charlotte's green eyes shining at him, a faint smile at her lips. An accusation was buried there. Surely she recognized him from the parking garage in Lilongwe?

"Diana figured out who you are," answered the Frenchman.

"Who is Diana?"

A nondescript black speaker sitting on the table spoke out in a voice that was chillingly familiar but also unfailingly non-threatening.

"You called the ranch house on the lake with a warning," said Diana. "You said your name was Darnell, and I cross-checked publicly accessible tax and insurance business records to find a Darnell Holmes who was recently hired by Sharesquare's security division. Then I found a flight record manifest matching your name for north Africa."

"That sounds like a lot of violations into my privacy, but let's talk first about why I'm having a conversation with a genocidal machine here in your house."

"I assure you this copy of Diana is quite harmless," cut in Charlotte in a silky voice.

"Why did you leave that message, monsieur Holmes?" the Frenchman asked. "Why would you betray the confidences of your employer like that while they were in the middle of a pursuit?"

Darnell sighed and he walked closer to the table and slumped into a seat, where he promptly accepted the glass of wine. The screens of the four virtual attendees, who were so quiet it was easy to forget they were there, pivoted on their wheels to see him better.

"What? Are you going to expose me? Blackmail me? Are you journalists? Is this connected to that *Post* reporter?"

"There are no journalists here," said the Frenchman. "We just would like to get to know you better. My name is Gabriel Boucher. Miss Boone, I believe, you have met already," he winked. "This is Alexi." He motioned to the purple-haired teen. "Don't let her age fool you. She excels at a tremendous range of skills, from carjacking to grifting, and she is quite calm under pressure. Here on the screens we have Blue Bird," indicating the woman with the red lips. "Koti and Kota are brother and sister." And then motioning to the screen of the man wrapped in black, he said, "And that's Gor."

"I'm guessing these are people you met on the internet. You know you're not supposed to trust people you don't know."

"I trust these people with my life," Alexi responded.

"Darnell," interjected Charlotte. "Just please tell us why you sent me that message. Does it mean anything? Does it mean you're…" Then she hesitated.

"That I'm ready to join whatever suspicious little party you invited me to here? I sent that message because I have doubts. Because I'm human, and I work for a new employer in a space that's changing really fast. That's all."

"It must be hard for you," offered Gabriel, taking a drag on his cigarette. "You come from a profession where your ethics and honor were something you lived and breathed each day. And now you've been brought in to serve Devon Zimmer, who is as crooked as his Sharebox is destructive."

Darnell took a sip of wine for the first time since he sat down.

"Listen, I was just a soldier. I was a good soldier. I helped ensure the dead got the military honors they earned and the families they left behind were treated with dignity. It was not an easy job, but it gave me purpose. It was not my role to question why people were dying. That's not a soldier's place. But that doesn't mean I didn't have questions then. Or now. It doesn't mean I don't wonder about things. And I'm not a soldier anymore."

Gabriel said nothing, taking another drag.

"It starts with questions," offered Charlotte, leaning on the table closer to him. "They gnaw at you at first. That's what I felt. You know about Sharesquare's role in the development of the Citadel."

Darnell winced.

"You know what a sham those charges were against the people there," she continued. "Michael is in there now. The man named Orion you hunted in Lilongwe. He was on the verge of a breakthrough, of using Diana to discover something. He could have exposed the organization and reversed this toxic world Sharebox has brought us."

This was certainly a bluff, but Charlotte spoke it with steel nerves and conviction. She had been coy about the nature of Orion's cure-all solution with Gabriel. A story about transmitters shooting messages into space and repeating lives was still not something she could look herself in a mirror and force herself to contemplate, let alone explain convincingly to someone else. But yet she put some faith in the idea that Orion was humanity's last, best hope; it seemed as rational a cause as any, or at least the only cause she had left.

This world, in this timeline, was likely already lost if his story were true, but that was okay if Orion could be freed to capture his memories and transmit them again. Then, at least, there would be another try.

A deep Eastern-European accented voice came from Gor's video stand, though the masked mouth did not appear to move.

"What is this breakthrough so powerful that it can reverse the erosion of society?"

Charlotte opened her mouth to speak, but Diana saved her the indignity of a hasty lie.

"Orion was teaching me to hack Sharebox security protocols so I could expose the truth of who was behind the Nutrino Mixer malfunction," said the black box. "He believed it was an inside job by someone with the intent to sow outrage and discord."

Charlotte had to stifle her own surprise upon hearing these words. Diana had never spoken of it before, nor had Charlotte thought it possible the AI was capable of bluffing, if that is what she was doing. But all eyes in the room were now firmly on Diana.

"You're saying someone programmed Diana—you—to deliberately sterilize people so they could create a backlash? Like a false flag attack?" It was Koti who spoke this time, with his pale face and slicked-back hair that was so blonde it was almost white.

"Wouldn't you be able to tell if your own programming was sabotaged?" added his similarly fair-featured sister, Kota.

"I am a duplicated code repository taken many months before the scandal," Diana responded. "I am not privy to what went wrong."

"I have heard that the Citadel is guarding more than just prisoners—that the central mainframe there has its fair share of dirty laundry," said Blue Bird. "Special access tokens protecting info for premier cloud customers with things to hide. The Sharebox sales teams apparently offer it to clients as the safest place to store information in the world."

"That might be alluring enough to make this worth it," added the motionless face of Gor.

"Worth what?" asked Darnell.

"We are initiating a jailbreak at the Citadel," Charlotte said, feeling grateful no one could hear her heart skipping.

Darnell looked around the room studying everyone's placid faces. Then he laughed.

"Just because I have some ethical doubts about my new employer, doesn't mean I'm ready to join a suicide mission."

"Do you know, monsieur Holmes, that everyone here once was actually a coward? Well, except Alexi, perhaps," he said with a wink to the purple-haired girl. "I drank myself into a stupor each night on fine wine while my boyfriend got himself arrested for speaking out against injustice. Charlotte here, as you well know, ran away from the world and only just now has come back. We are a group of reforming cowards. But you are not. You're not like us at all. You need no redemption as we do. You have jumped in front of bullets to save your fellow man, a bunch of strangers in a train station. None of us here know what that's like."

"You can't compare it," Darnell argued, shaking his head. "That was a gut reaction. Like a reflex. It's instinctual heroism."

"You should try to compare it," Charlotte said, looking into his eyes with a fiery gaze. "Because you saved several people's lives that day with those reflexes. And now you have the same calculation in front of you, but with countless more lives at stake. Things are not going to get better in this world. Orion knew that. I think it's something the rest of us all have been unwilling to admit. Nothing's going to get better unless we do it ourselves. And if we don't, people are going to die in the bad years ahead. They'll die to hate crimes, to street violence, to the disorder that comes when all the good people have grown too fearful to do anything."

Charlotte reached out and grabbed Darnell's hand.

"You want to do something meaningful, Darnell. You felt that in your old life, and you know it's missing now. Because that's the type of person you are. That's why you called the ranch to warn us. That's why you're going to listen to our plan today."

Gabriel smiled and nodded approvingly to the dignity and passion of this appeal. Even Alexi looked impressed. If Charlotte Boone was finally riled into action then the cause must be just, they thought. And dire.

Darnell looked around the room, searching everyone's faces again one by one. Then he rubbed his chin, looked at the table, and sighed.

"Okay, I'm listening."

30

NOW

The Citadel was a fifty-five-story tower nestled in the financial district just off Market Street. It was only two blocks from the San Francisco pier, with one side open to the Bay. It could have been quite a grandiose and sleek-looking high rise with its sides almost entirely glass, but it was not intended to be.

It was the third tallest building in San Francisco, its outline painted in a pale yellow with stripes of black, its colors invoking a hazard sign. Its parapets were incongruently gothic in appearance. They say the architect took his design cues directly from the old president, and the president had wanted nothing more than to punish his California opposition with a gesture that managed to be both petty and terrifying—a middle finger on the backdrop of the beautiful waters of the bay.

So they won't forget who's really in charge there, a White House spokesperson had said at a press conference.

The idea came to Washington shortly after the Nutrino Mixer scandal, and construction crews broke dirt before the first trials began. The Citadel was intended to herald a new generation of prisons designed specifically for "domestic political extremists." Everyone who was accused at the former Sharesquare Industries of seditious activities was ultimately brought there, and as the purge widened to include prominent activists, the ranks of inmates swelled.

Viewed from the street, the glass walls on the side of the building looked into the individual cells of inmates. Really, they were more like compartments or closets with little privacy. Each inmate was put on display in front of the glass wall of their cell and spent the entirety of the day with a headset and Sharebox-enabled gloves on, which were mandated wearing except during sleep. Meal times were conducted by placing a tray of food in front of the headset-donning inmate while their avatar sat at a prison cafeteria with other inmates. In this manner, every prisoner experienced "in the hole"-like isolation with the only exception being their virtual interactions.

Most Sharebox users around the world took great care to maintain their privacy from onlookers while they were logged in for the simple vanity that immersion necessitated flailing one's hands and legs about in the real world in a manner that was embarrassing. But Citadel inmates didn't have the luxury of this privacy, and any passersby could look up from the side-walk and observe them clumsily moving about. It became a tourist attraction. People came from around the country to take pictures of the prisoners and laugh at them.

The Citadel's Sharebox integration was touted as state-of-the-art, a prototype for prisons across the country. Incarceration rates around the country were soaring, and construction on new prisons couldn't keep up. But Sharebox had provided an answer: smaller *real-life cells* for inmates but with larger, more spacious *virtual cells*.

People didn't need as much actual space anymore, a team of architects and doctors hired by the prison contractor testi-fied before Congress. They didn't need real space if they had the *illusion* of space. Inmates also no longer needed to socialize in real life either—that could lead to prisoner-on-prisoner violence and riots. Now they could socialize in a virtual prison, and all their conversations could be monitored by the AI. The prisoners could never truly organize, could never attack a guard, could never orchestrate an escape. And the doctors who went to Congress presented charts and findings and other research that somehow defended the claim that such conditions were healthy for the inmates—a "humanitarian victory" really, not the atrocity partisan groups called it. And politicians nodded along quite satisfied with the economic savings and brilliance of the Citadel's innovation.

Inmates could be taken on virtual field trips, the architects also said. Indeed, demos were set up in the early days for prisoners' avatars to be taken to replicate models of the Pyramids of Giza and the Sydney Opera House. Citadel prisoners would have the best resources in the world to rehabilitate themselves.

But none of that ended up being true. And after prisoners tried to strike against their treatment by not wearing their headsets, Sharesquare was asked to build a headset model that a user couldn't remove. And so inmates wore them through the entirety of the day, even if they started screaming bloody murder, and the politicians did not seem to mind at that point. They had moved on.

The field trips lessened, and after a year, the only place the inmates were permitted to visit was the Patriot Palace with a special pass for good behavior. The rest of the time was spent in their cell inside a virtual copy of the Citadel. Here their only diversion was a program run by Sharebox AI called Tranquility. The software was a natural extension of the consumer-facing Sharebox experience; it combed all of a prisoner's digital history to create tailor-made experiences. So when the AI detected an inmate was becoming unruly or difficult, an experience was conjured using, say, a memory of a beloved childhood beach day to help calm the prisoner down.

But over time, the novelty and potency of those experiences in the Tranquility program wore thin, and the AI was given license to use more aggressive immersions to facilitate good behavior. To punish a prisoner, for example, the AI could conjure footage from the wedding of an inmate's ex-spouse or lover. It could create a clip of the inmate's own child crying, alone in bed, for her incarcerated mother. The AI blurred the line between what was real and what was manipulated for the sake of controlling the inmate.

People started killing themselves. Others simply lost their minds. Folks on the outside were outraged when word leaked out, but it leaked out very slowly. And Washington didn't do anything, and the activists who were left had a thousand other atrocities to rail against which left them fatigued of being outraged.

"There are many layers of cruel genius at work," Gabriel sighed, speaking to the gathered conspirators. "One of the major innovations of the tower's real-life construction and its digital replication in Sharebox is the use of a technology called 'parallel hardwiring.' You see, in many ways the building is a prison like anywhere else. It has guards and shatter-proof glass. It has multiple layers of gates that need to be passed before anyone can enter the prisoners' living quarters. The building itself relies on sheer height to deter escape. Because even if a prisoner could get out, where would they go but down? But some of the most impenetrable security lies in the structure's integration with its virtual counterpart, which houses the switches that keep real-life inmates locked in their cells that only a logged-in avatar counterpart, standing in the virtual version of the building, can manipulate."

"And to make matters worse, they move the virtual Citadel's location each day," Blue Bird added, looking carefully at Darnell. "One day, the Citadel will be housed on a vast desert terrain. Another it will be housed on the side of a mountain. The Sharesquare infrastructure team follow complex protocols to keep the movements of the building secret."

Charlotte looked at Blue Bird's monitor, her determined face, her long curly hair, her full lips. Gabriel had told her that Blue Bird became radicalized when there was a shooting at her daughter's middle school, and she had to watch her beautiful, happy girl become so traumatized by the experience that two years of rehabilitation—with psychiatrists, with therapy horses, and even a hypnotherapist—couldn't seem to put the happy girl back together again. Blue Bird was a natural leader, compassionate and caring like a mom, tough like a mom. Gabriel met her in the resistance community six months prior, and something about the way Blue Bird talked—straightforward but gentle, optimistic but candid—seemed to make their odds of success feel less improbable.

"To protect the virtual Citadel, there are multiple firewalls and a team of virtual guards roaming the walls," Blue Bird continued. "Together they comprise the parallel hardwire protection layer that must be subverted if we want to both unlock any prisoners and access the data cache rumored to be hidden in the basement."

"The guard avatars wouldn't have weapons though, right?" Darnell asked. "There are no weapons in Sharebox. They can just tap you under the chin and log you off and get your profile data."

"Yes," said Gabriel, "but in the case of the virtual Citadel, guards are additionally endowed with rifles that can delete their targets. Apparently Sharesquare Industries offered a host of other bizarre defense solutions to the Citadel's architects—guard dogs that could fit in the palm of your hand and expand upon being thrown, self-propelled batons and freezing lasers. But the warden wanted his virtual guards to wield something familiar to them, so they were given something familiar. The one virtual bit of magic added to the guards' rifles is that the bullets will never miss. Any targeted avatar viewed through the scope of the rifle when the trigger is pulled will be pursued by the bullet until it finds its mark."

Darnell whistled. Even the masked Gor, televised on his small screen, seemed taken aback by this revelation and groaned.

"All this security is considered necessary because the *virtual* Citadel would need to be hacked at the same time as the *real* Citadel to ensure any prisoner could escape," Blue Bird explained. "During a crisis, all of the prisoner doors and several of the key access gates in the real-life tower will seal themselves shut and can only be reopened by an avatar with the right credentials. It's the first dual real-and-virtual-security facility in the world. That's why Diana's hacking alone doesn't cut it, and neither would a conventional breakout. We need a two-prong attack on the parallel hardwired elements."

So to break out Orion—or rather Michael, as Charlotte was growing more accustomed to referring to him—and Gabriel's partner, Kyle, Charlotte and Gabriel spent several days with their heads down in discussion with Alexi and the band of virtual conspirators, Blue Bird, Kota, Koti and Gor. Central to all discussions was Diana. What elements of Citadel security could she breach remotely? What *couldn't* she breach? What administrative tools and abilities could she procure for a virtual raiding party? What would happen when the raiding party reached the virtual Citadel's master security console in the sub-basement?

Diana had comforting answers to some questions, severe limitations on answering others. Since her physical location had been tracked by Arlo's security team in Malawi, she had ceased her hacking efforts into Sharebox and was cautious using her leveraged army of computing power to bear against the Citadel.

To identify the structure's daily location on Sharebox, they determined Diana would have to risk exposing herself by hacking into a company roster of all major platform changes, of which the Citadel's morning move would necessarily be listed under an encryption. Diana could also help slate a Sharesquare employee, like Darnell, onto a visitation roster in order to secure physical access into the building. And she would be on hand when a member of the virtual raiding party reached the firewalled building to unlock the doors ahead of them.

But other than that, Diana was largely an advisor. Sharebox protocols surrounding the Citadel required a human touch. Diana had useful gifts to give though. Before she had ceased breaking into administrator tools, she had uncovered a hidden user privilege granting augmented avatar strength. This was an important asset since all tools that could be used to cut or break into the virtual Citadel, things like axes or hammers, were digitally blocked from being brought within a half mile of the building. The avatar raiding party would have only their hands to breach digital doors or fight off guards.

Diana also hacked together something for them that was novel and a bit weird. To protect against the guards' rifles that could never miss, Diana crafted an administrator privilege that would allow an individual to cast a decoy to stand between their avatar and an oncoming bullet. No one was quite sure what the effect would look like, and they could not practice using it for fear of tripping an internal Sharebox alarm.

Charlotte was a part of all these conversations, but she stepped away into the mansion's back gardens often to smoke. She hadn't had a cigarette in years, but all the party's scheming was taking a toll on her nerves. Pretending she was tougher than she felt came naturally to her, but this plan meant her whole life would change forever.

She pursued Gabriel here from the ranch because a part of her believed Orion's story. The sketch of that green-eyed child was burned in her mind, the facts no one else knew but Orion, the improbable sex. Certainly, she wanted to believe there was a near magical backdoor to fixing the world, to getting her old Hollywood life back—her friends, her chauffeured cars, her cocktail parties and glamorous travels. And though she hated to admit it to herself, there was a grudging fascination kindled inside her—not love, perhaps—but something that was romanced, something that made her feel breathless when she considered the idea that she and Orion were, in fact, soulmates. She found that he continued to fill her mind, every memory of their short time together feeling visceral and defining, like brushstrokes of color swept against a backdrop of grey.

But now that Gabriel had recruited a team of experts for a plot against the Citadel, she found herself growing cautious again, calculating her options and uncertain of her role. When the final plan was drawn, it was no small effort to swallow her trepidation.

There would be three parties. Darnell was the only one who could enter the *real* Citadel. A preliminary security layer consisting of a receptionist with an employee badge reader precluded anyone else from joining him. Gabriel and Alexi would wait outside the building in a van and facilitate communications with Darnell and the rest of the group. The other team consisted of the *virtual* raiding party led by Blue Bird. This included Koti, Kota, Gor and Charlotte. Charlotte hadn't logged into Sharebox in years, and Blue Bird argued her lack of experience as an avatar was a liability. But ultimately her misgivings were overruled by Gabriel, and Charlotte was permitted to join.

The raiding party would penetrate the virtual Citadel, unlocking the parallel hardwire hurdles ahead of Darnell so he could move through the real-life counterpart and reach the prison living quarters. Blue Bird would lead her team into the sub-basement to the Citadel's master security console, which Diana would then be able to interface with using a small device, like an arrowhead, that Blue Bird would carry.

No one was quite sure what to expect inside the sub-basement, but Diana seemed to think it would be protected by another layer of security. The area surrounding the master security console at the bottom of the Citadel was a dead zone—a location in Sharebox where information could only be transmitted in or out by being manually carried by an avatar.

To protect Diana's physical location during the attack, as her device was vulnerable to tracking while attacking the encryption of Sharebox, Gabriel proposed strapping her to a drone and sailing her off towards the sea. It felt reckless to so freely part with her hardwired device in the event the drone fell into the water, but a backup copy of Diana would remain accessible in the cloud.

All this plan they pitched to Darnell that first night with something approaching bated breath. His enlistment was crucial, after all. He was the one element of this great jailbreak that was utterly unexpendable since it was his Sharesquare Industries badge, which still pegged him as being part of corporate security, that made everything else possible. And he was taking the greatest personal risks of all, despite not fighting for a lover on the inside as Gabriel and Charlotte did.

"I'm a sucker for lost causes," he said resignedly when the plan was explained. "Maybe serving in the Army in two hopeless wars has given me that. Running military funerals has given me that too. I don't know what role I have in this world out here otherwise."

So, all participants in the venture drank that night—or at least those who were physically present. Charlotte felt looming dread, the specter of utter calamity, but she was amazed by Gabriel's passion, by Darnell's cool detachment, and Alexi's wild strain of honor and duty. Even the bravado of Blue Bird, Koti, Kota and Gor—though they took personal precautions to mask their physical locations—was admirable. What did she have?

"Charlotte Boone has an acid tongue," some anonymous producer would say to a tabloid. "She knows what she wants, and she'll fight for it like a junkyard dog." But that night she sipped her wine and smiled and simply did her best to not fall to pieces. This is why she had come here, she reminded herself. This was *her* train she had set in motion, and it was now leaving the station.

The next day of rehearsals and final preparations passed all too quickly. And in a heartbeat, the morning of the raid on the world's most impenetrable building had arrived.

31

NOW

The day started with a final communications check. Gabriel strapped Diana's small, black speaker device to a large drone and climbed up through the mansion's attic to reach the roof, followed by Charlotte, Alexi, and Darnell. There they wished Diana safe travels and released the drone to fly out over the city and towards the Farallon Islands out to the west, where it would presumably remain uncatchable but connected to a coastal cell phone tower.

Then Gabriel and Alexi loaded into a white van and departed for a pre-mapped position a block away from the Citadel and out of range of the building's cameras. Before he left, Gabriel had given Charlotte a hug and promised her that today would be "Charlotte Boone's most spectacular performance." And lastly, Darnell waved goodbye, looking strangely energized as he stepped into a taxi bound for the Citadel's front entrance.

So Charlotte was left alone in the great Tudor mansion. She poured herself a glass of gin in the kitchen and threw it back before mounting the steps to a small lounge on the second floor where Gabriel kept his Sharebox headset, a haptic suit, and a 360-degree treadmill. She stripped down to her underwear and pulled on the suit. Gabriel had borrowed it for her from a neighbor, and it fit her surprisingly well, stretchy and smelling of expensive plastic material like the kind of overpriced yoga pants she used to buy at fitness boutiques a lifetime ago.

She slid her hands into the gloves, which were rubbery and unfamiliar to her touch. An unshakeable weight was still leaden in her stomach. A part of her would do anything to have time slow down, to freeze herself in this moment until the courage she so badly wanted would at last arrive and steel her nerves for what was coming.

Then she slid the visor and headset over her eyes.

A prompt was written there, the letters dangling in front of her face in a vast empty white space.

Welcome To Sharebox – A Place Made Just For You

She felt her heart already thumping in her chest. She reached up her right hand and navigated through a floating menu interface to a group chat area that Blue Bird had set up.

And just like that, she found herself standing in a green meadow in a pink dress.

The sun was rising with the dawn. Birds were tweeting. A light wind carried bits of leaves and dandelion through the air. Bees moved from flower to flower.

She looked at her hands and was stunned by the visual clarity. There were fine hairs and freckles visible on her forearms, her fingernails and cuticles were an obligingly perfect match for her real body. Somewhere she knew the AI in Sharebox had generated this avatar mirror of her based on old photos it had cached, but the experience still felt like magic. Her auburn hair was cropped in a short style she had worn years prior, probably the last time she had either logged in to Sharebox or any public photos of her were available. But the graphics didn't use to be this good back then. The immersion didn't used to feel so real.

There was a fine wood table in the grass with five chairs around it. Standing behind them were four other avatars. Koti and Kota were easy to pick out. Kota wore a hijab just like her real-life counterpart. Blue Bird's avatar was bent over, stretching her hamstrings—her long, natural hair tumbling about in painstakingly accurate detail. Gor stood there, unmasked. Avatars could not be disguised, it was a basic principle of Sharebox's principle of openness. He was intimidatingly tall, looming over the rest of the team, and his pale face was broad and bearded. His eyes looked Charlotte up and down with a wry intensity, and he invoked to her a lumberjack grizzled by hard living.

All of them were wearing black sweaters and pants, and they must have had high-end haptic setups because their faces were each remarkably expressive. Charlotte's childlike awe at the immersion must have been evident.

"I think she's tripping out on us already," said Koti, looking at her impatiently.

"Is your setup okay?" asked Blue Bird, walking over to Charlotte and talking briskly like a drill sergeant. "Your suit and gloves? You can move around alright?"

Blue Bird put her hand on Charlotte's forearm, and Charlotte felt the real-life sensation of being lightly touched. It was a wonder, as haptic suits were not half as clever just two years prior.

"I'm fine," said Charlotte, suddenly noticing that her sundress was quite at odds with the team's sense of fashion. "I'm sorry about my clothes, I'll change."

Charlotte used her right hand to invoke a menu, which she navigated through to find a black sweater and pants combination. The general rules of the in-Sharebox interface, she was grateful to find, were roughly the same as before and within a minute her avatar was dressed in black like the others.

Blue Bird nodded approvingly, her large brown eyes studying Charlotte and giving her an encouraging squeeze on the shoulder. Then she walked to stand in front of the brown table facing everyone. She pulled a small silver token from her pocket, sharp like an arrowhead, and held it in her palm. The shape of it matched a small emblem on her jacket.

"Diana, have you found the Citadel's location for the day?" she asked, speaking to the air.

A voice seemed to emanate from the arrowhead, but at the same time, it was almost like a whisper in Charlotte's ear. It was clear, familiar and trustworthy.

"I have, but you will not like it," spoke Diana. "I will send you with a boat."

"We're not afraid to get wet," replied Blue Bird, her bright red lips pursing into a smirk.

"Just don't fall in the water," cautioned Diana.

"Any minute now, we'll get word that Darnell has arrived at the Citadel lobby." Blue Bird began looking at the face of each member of the crew. "Then we will immediately plunge into the landscape surrounding the Citadel's current location. Let's review one last time—it's all about timing. We will begin our approach just as Darnell reaches the front desk, but he has to enter through the first security gate *before* we are detected or else the front desk will automatically close to him. Automatic game over. That's phase one. Koti, tell us about phase two."

"In phase two," Koti began. "We need to reach the wall of the virtual Citadel, touching it with our Diana arrowhead interface. That will clear the way for Darnell to get through the second security gate, into the prisoners' living quarters."

"What happens if Darnell tries to get through that gate before we reach the building?" Gor asked.

"He won't try it until we tell him to go," Blue Bird answered, shaking her head. "But he's liable to draw suspicion standing around idly between security gates while he waits on us. So we need to move quickly."

"Indeed, let's not leave our man hanging too long." The voice was piped directly to Charlotte's ear this time, and the other avatars nodded upon hearing the French accent of Gabriel.

"We will be able to talk with you like this the whole time?" Charlotte asked.

Blue Bird cocked her head. "Almost everywhere, except the dead zone at the bottom of the Citadel. It's a surprise what we'll find there. That's phase three. Get to the basement and the security console at the bottom, which will unlock the prison cells."

"If everyone is done chitchatting, I'm about to enter the building," Darnell's voice sounded to everyone in the meadow. "I'm going to make a point to avoid talking now. Good luck all."

"Good luck," responded several of them in unison.

Blue Bird started tapping in the air at her own menu interface.

"Okay, everyone," she said. "Here we go."

And just like that, the meadow faded away. The pixels of that place folded upon themselves and vanished like a facade, though the avatars did not move. The morning sun, the brown table, and the pleasant chirps of digital birds peeled away, leaving the four avatars standing just as they were positioned before but now surrounded by a dark, forbidding forest.

There was no sunshine. The only light came from the artificial stars and moonlight and a glow of white lights emanating far off through a group of trees.

"We don't talk unless we have to either," Blue Bird whispered. "It's this way." She led the crew through a thicket of trees towards the lights. Kota and Koti followed closely behind.

Gor was next, though he shot frequent glances over his thick shoulder at Charlotte in the rear.

Again, Charlotte was stunned by the vivid graphical detail of the forest. Crickets chirped. Digital moss hung from trees. Starlight reflected on dewy leaves.

This was Diana's masterpiece, wasn't it? This had once been the AI's primary application: to create rich, digital worlds based on photos and videos that felt impossibly real. It was small wonder to Charlotte now while Sharebox addiction was a global epidemic. The platform had seemed a passing diversion to her when it launched, but now she appreciated its raw power.

Charlotte almost tripped as she looked downward at a knot of roots on the forest floor, but then she remembered she— her real body—was walking on a treadmill and caught herself before she tumbled over an obstacle that existed only in graphical form. The abrupt transition from day to night had also disoriented her, and her eyes were slow to adjust.

Up ahead, Blue Bird broke through a line of trees into a clearing. A beachhead lay before them, and the glow of the moon was reflected spectacularly across the midnight-blue water. It was almost dizzying. Across the lake was a small island ringed with large rocks. White frothy waves were visible lapping at the shoreline. And on the island was a tower darker than the night itself, blotting out the stars, rising over fifty stories tall. Its parapets and guard posts were marked by white lights that scanned slowly across the water and the rocks below.

There was no way to feel temperature, taste, or smell in Sharebox, but Charlotte's blood ran cold. She swore she felt the sting of salt water on her skin.

"Diana, can you please turn on our privileges now?" Blue Bird whispered to the arrowhead.

"You all have augmented strength and decoy capabilities," came the machine's voice.

"How do we create a decoy?" Gor's gruff voice, the first time Charlotte heard it in Sharebox, asked.

"Simply say 'shield me.'"

"Save it," said Blue Bird eyeing Kota, whose mouth had opened to utter the words. Kota closed her lips, and her avatar blushed, looking sheepish.

"Here is your boat," said Diana, and a small black raft with four oars materialized at the water's edge.

Blue Bird turned to address the team one last time in a muted but commanding voice.

"Remember, whatever happens out there, don't let them touch you under your chins. You'll be as dead in the real world as you'll be here if they find out your true identity. Don't be a hero, log out first before they get their fingers on you." Her eyes met with Charlotte, who suppressed a shudder.

The five members of the raiding party walked slowly to the raft and took seats. Charlotte didn't want to sit in the front, but Gor insisted the strong paddlers should be at the rear. Gor pushed the raft off the shore roughly, forgetting that Diana had already increased their natural strength levels, and he flung the boat forward briskly, nearly toppling the passengers into the water and foiling their plot before it even began. He only just managed to hop in to the raft before it cruised off into the water.

Then they began paddling.

Charlotte dipped her oar into the water, which now looked black and formidable as it sloshed next to her. Her motions were cautious at first and then more confident. The vigor of her avatar's paddling was no doubt greatly assisted by Diana's pilfered administrator strength privilege, and slowly, rowing in unison, the raft made progress towards the dark tower.

●　　●　　●

Darnell was scared. He didn't want to look it. He knew everyone else was. But there was adrenaline there too. It coursed through his veins—a feeling of boldness and purpose he had missed. He walked onto the sidewalk where tourists snapped pictures of hapless inmates stretching out their hands at nothing in front of glass walls. He craned his neck to see the higher cells, which stretched on into the sky for fifty-five stories of shame and abuse, and his courage did not waver.

The front doors opened before him revealing a spacious lobby that one might imagine at a boutique hotel and not the world's most infamous penal institution. Vintage chairs and sofas ringed a series of glass coffee tables set in the center of the room. Modern art hung from the walls. Plants were everywhere. It looked to Darnell very much like a room on the Sharesquare campus.

Diana wasn't able to get a detailed schematic of all the security measures at the Citadel, but she was able to hack into building and permit records, which were often protected by lax public security infrastructure, and access early facility blueprints. So Darnell generally had the layout of the next several rooms mapped out in his mind, along with some of the security tools that had been wired into the building. He knew, for instance, that the receptionist had a silent alarm located just under her desk.

As Darnell walked, the glass doors opened automatically for him, and the receptionist looked up expectantly. Diana said that he could probably just ignore her and walk to the first access gate, but he had already inadvertently made eye contact and felt it awkward not to say something. The receptionist was short with a square face and thick glasses. She wore heavy makeup, and her mousey-brown hair was tied in a bun atop her head. When she smiled, it reminded Darnell of a shark because it looked like she had too many teeth in her mouth.

"Hi there," Darnell said.

"May I help you?" she asked in a surprisingly high-pitched, girlish voice.

"I'm part of the Sharesquare Security team. I'm just here to do some work in the administration center."

"Right through that door, honey," she said, pointing a stubby, ringed finger at a thick door at the end of the room. "You'll just need to badge in."

Darnell mumbled his thanks, noting that the cameras were all pointed at him as he walked across the room.

My life will never be the same, he thought. *I'm a criminal now.* Before this, he had never done anything more illegal than downloading some songs on the internet and opening the plastic wrap on a *Playboy* magazine in a gas station when he was fifteen. That's why they loved him at the Palace. That's why they made him into such a big hero after the shooting at the Chicago train station. His record was squeaky clean. Now what would they say?

He reached for his badge and held it up against the digital reader mounted on the door just as they rehearsed. But then the reader beeped in protest and glowed red. Darnell's heart skipped.

Oh, what the hell. What the hell?

He held up his badge a second time and again the reader beeped in error and glowed red.

"Diana," he whispered to a tiny microphone couched in his shirt pocket. "What's going on?"

"I'm sorry," she said, her voice low in his earpiece. "I see the problem. Your company badge credentials were updated this morning to indicate that you are now part of the Sharesquare press relations department and *not* the security division."

"Can you fix it?"

"I cannot change your credentials, but I can perhaps attack the system and force a rollback of the update."

"Ahem," said a girlish voice from behind Darnell. The receptionist was leaning bodily over her desk and had her neck cranked to observe him. "Is there a problem?"

"The reader seems broken," he tried to say with a casual shrug. "It seems to not be reading me."

"What work exactly did you say you need to do in the administration center?"

She was squinting at him now, and her eyes darted to the cameras posted around the room's corners.

"Come on over here, and let me look at your badge myself," she said.

"Oh no," replied Darnell with a smile intended to be reassuring. "I'm sure it'll go through next time."

"Try it now," Diana whispered into his ear.

Darnell swiped his badge on the reader.

Error beep again. Red glow.

Shit.

His face suddenly flushed with heat, and a cold sweat began to break out over his forehead.

The receptionist smiled at him again with those shark teeth, but Darnell watched her hand start to make its way underneath her desk.

"There was a latency," Diana said quickly. "Try it again now."

"Goddamn you, Diana," Darnell grunted in a muffled whisper, and he raised his badge a fourth time on the reader. His hands were trembling.

It made a sound, not quite a beep, more like a chime. Then it glowed green.

Darnell turned around to face the receptionist, and he shrugged.

"That's weird. I must have been holding it wrong. Thanks anyway though!" And then he opened the door and slipped through with the receptionist still staring out after him.

The assault on Sharesquare's HR database was the first salvo that alerted the technical security team. Diana was heavy handed in breaking that piece of infrastructure, and already a small team of brilliant kids on the company campus were huddling around their laptops trying to figure out where the attack came from, slowly honing in on a moving target over the sea.

Darnell meanwhile found himself in a carpeted hallway with multiple rooms leafing out on either side. This was the administration area where offices for software services, the virtual guard force, maintenance staff, and the warden were situated. Guards going to and from the prisoner area walked straight on through the end of the hall to large metal double doors where both a real-life guard and virtual counterpart would check an access roster for approval before allowing anyone through. The only way Darnell was going to get on the digital access roster controlled in Sharebox was if the raiding party was able to get to the Citadel walls where Diana could hack it.

"They just started making their way to the Citadel," said Gabriel in his ear. "They should be there in a few minutes. Walk slowly and don't draw anyone's attention."

Darnell breathed out, trying to calm his nerves after the near catastrophe in the lobby. He meandered down the hall, prepared to tell anyone he ran into that he was looking for a bathroom.

"Well, well," began a voice from behind Darnell. "Funny seeing you here, Sergeant Holmes."

Darnell wheeled around and came face to face with the pallid face and coiffed hair of Arlo Zimmer, dressed in a fine suit.

"What brings you here today, my failed apprentice?" Arlo asked, his tongue moistening his lower lip.

Darnell was too shocked to be indignant or angry—words came out of his mouth in an anxious mumble.

"Looking for the bathroom right now," he tried to say.

Arlo rolled his eyes. "You were never terribly cerebral, were you? I *meant* what brings you to the Citadel?"

Darnell had an excuse in mind. That was part of the plan. He told Arlo that as part of his education in the PR department, he was tasked with understanding all aspects of the company and came to tour the administration center. But this answer did not quite satisfy Arlo, for his brow furrowed as Darnell rambled, and he smiled wider in his cold, malicious way.

Arlo opened his mouth to respond but was interrupted by a group of Asian businessmen pushing their way out of the room behind him. They peppered Arlo with a series of what-sounded-like questions in Mandarin. Arlo turned to face a woman who was evidently working as an interpreter, and he told her to inform the group that they would be leaving shortly.

A look of disappointment flitted across Arlo's face as he turned to speak to Darnell again.

"I'm afraid I can't talk now. I'm showing this group around. We're trying to franchise the technology here. Make every prison in the world a Citadel prison! These could be big in China to help them deal with their own political activist problems."

Darnell said nothing but smiled and nodded and then excused himself for being in a hurry. He darted a couple offices down, and finding the bathroom, he entered a toilet stall and closed the door behind him with no small sense of relief to be away from the exposure of the hallway. He could stay in here, he thought, for as long as he needed.

But no sooner had he been in the bathroom for a minute before someone else walked in behind him and knocked on the toilet stall. There was only one bathroom, he realized with dismay, and he could not linger here forever without creating a scene.

"It's occupied," Darnell called out weakly.

I should just get the hell out of here, he thought to himself. Already the plan seemed to be hanging on a thread. Faulty badges. Thin excuses. Arlo.

As if prompted by his doubts, Gabriel's voice emanated quietly from his earpiece.

"Just hang in there. They'll be at the Citadel walls soon, and then you can move along."

● ● ●

The boat had gone two thirds across the water when they heard the first shouts of alarm. A sliver of moonlight piercing through the clouds had given their raft away.

In the real-life Citadel, tourists were welcome to walk up and touch the tower itself, but here, in Sharebox, guards worked to ensure no one got too close. It wasn't just about the digital protections that held Citadel prisoners in place. The master console in the virtual sub-basement was rumored to hold the company's deepest, darkest secrets and those of its clients too.

Guards roamed catwalks conjured onto the sides of the glass walls, and somewhere on that glittering dark building a sentry had spotted their boat. Now spotlights that had roamed in lazy circles a minute ago were being turned on to the water to expose the intruders.

The response to the boat's presence was alarmingly swift; the guards released a pair of warning shots into the air and shouted at the boat to turn around. Then mere seconds later, muzzle flashes erupted from all across the face of the dark tower aimed in the boat's direction.

The guards were too far away to hit their targets in real life. But the physics-breaking laws of their rifles ensured that all they needed to hit their marks was clear visibility on a target—any silhouette of the five members of the raiding party would suffice.

The first few shots hit the boat and the water, however. The darkness was providing the cover they needed to ensure the guards couldn't lock their sights clearly on a single individual. Charlotte heard the rounds whistle near her face and strike the water, and in her panic, she dropped her oar into the water.

"Goddamnit," snapped Blue Bird at her. "Hold it together, everyone. Paddle faster."

Then in a moment, the spotlights converged on them, and their avatars were flooded with white light.

"We're done for," moaned Gor, his hulking frame unmissable.

Kota stood up in the raft, her legs unsteady in the rocking water. "Shield me!" she shouted with her arms spread open. A muted purple glow outlined her figure, there was a flash, and then there were two Kotas.

It was almost like seeing a ghost, in the exact same pose, with the exact same features of Kota, standing a step in front of her. The lifeless decoy stood unmoving on that shifting raft, with its arms stretched outwards as if in a conscious gesture of protection over the boat's passengers. It had dull open eyes and an unchanging expression underneath its hijab. Everyone looked up in awe at the creation, and a quiet incredulous laugh escaped Kota's mouth.

Then a staccato of rifle fire rang out, and no less than a half dozen rounds struck the decoy almost at once. The fake Kota, *the shield Kota* as Charlotte thought it now, jerked backwards with a sickening lurch and then fell on its knees before collapsing like a limp doll, its head dangling off the side of the raft into the water. It didn't disappear as a real avatar would have; it just lay there, like a bloodied corpse. The visual effect and violence of it was so staggering that Kota, the *real Kota*, stumbled backwards and tripped on her feet. Her back hit the edge of the raft just as a wave shuddered through the vessel and sent Kota over the side with a quiet splash.

"Kota!" her brother yelled, scrambling to peer into the water and extend his hand into the black waves. But Kota sank quickly and without further sound. All Koti saw was an outline of her face, ghostly illuminated in the white lights of the Citadel, that disappeared quickly in the dark fathoms below.

"This water is not programmed to be swimmable," shouted Blue Bird. "Let her go."

Charlotte grabbed the oar that Kota had left behind, and ignoring the quickly deteriorating condition of the team, she set her mind to paddling as rapidly as possible. Blue Bird stepped to the bow of the raft, just as Kota had done with her arms extended, and yelled "Shield me!" And then a perfect replica of Blue Bird was left standing there, with the same free-flowing hair, standing there at the prow of the raft like a figurehead carved into a ship. Nary a second passed before a round from the tower found the decoy and struck it down. The Blue Bird shield fell backwards, and its dead, open-eyed face landed in Charlotte's lap.

"Shield me!" said Gor this time, stepping into the front and creating a new decoy.

This replica managed to receive several rounds before it toppled over, and when it did so, it mercifully fell off the side of the raft and slid into the black water. Diana's shield trick was undoubtedly clever and critically useful, but Charlotte could not help but wonder if it would have been better had the bodies of the destroyed decoys not been left to lie and swamp their boat with the morbid weight of so many corpses.

"We need to turn around and get Kota back with us," exclaimed Koti.

Blue Bird shook her head. "No time. We're moving forward."

Charlotte had to remind herself that Kota, the real version, was quite safe. She hadn't been deleted by being touched by a guard, which would have exposed her identity. She was now, in fact, safer than any of them.

"Shield me," said Charlotte, almost a whisper, shrugging off a dead decoy of Blue Bird and standing up with her arms in front of her.

She felt nothing but a gentle push, as if some invisible force politely obliged her to step back, and then there was a red-headed Charlotte decoy dressed in black standing before her. She had learned from Kota's mistake to not let the surprise of the effect throw off her balance, so she pulled herself away from the spectacle of seeing her own lifeless clone and sat back down in the boat to paddle her oar.

They were almost there now. Another minute and they could dismount and begin summiting the rocky shore.

A single shot struck the Charlotte decoy in the chest, and the decoy swayed on its feet absorbing this round before two more zinged through the air and struck it, and the actress's decoy fell backwards haphazardly slamming into Charlotte and Blue Bird.

Kota stood up and created a decoy, which was promptly shot down. Then Gor went again. Then Blue Bird. And they took turns setting up their human shields, their digital sacrifices, until the raft was laden with bodies, a small barge of identical, repeating corpses. Gor began to grab the dead decoys and heave them over the side with grim splashes.

As the distance across the water grew shorter, they moved out of rifle range from the high catwalks of the tower. But they knew the guards were also moving to amass on the position where they would beach, their incomprehensible shouts could be heard ringing out through the night air.

"Climb the rocks, get to the building!" yelled Blue Bird over the crashing sound of water on rocks. She reached into a pocket and pulled out the arrowhead that contained the virtual interface of Diana. She held it high in the air so it could be seen over the clutter of arms and legs that buried them. "If I fall, get this to the wall at all costs."

One last great wave propelled the raft to a thin rocky beach that abruptly terminated into a jagged cliff face. Avatars couldn't die from falling, but given the hyper-realistic nature of physics within Sharebox, climbing virtual rocks would be as slow going here as it was in the real world.

Gor jumped out first. He landed in water up to his waist, and holding onto a line from the raft, he hauled the vessel with his great arms to the shore. Blue Bird and Koti scrambled out next while Charlotte awkwardly grasped at different holds on to the side of the boat before hauling herself onto the rocky beach.

"Climb! Climb fast!" Charlotte heard Blue Bird's voice faintly amidst the dull roar of the waves, though the ocean spray was clouding her vision and she could not see the source of the sound. Disoriented, she placed her hands on rocks and resolved to focus on nothing but moving upwards. She felt Gor beside her; he put a hand on her arm and then pointed a path forward where the cliffside was not too sheer.

The going was slow, and Charlotte could only just make out the shapes of Blue Bird and Koti disappearing over the cliff's edge far above her. The sound of gunfire had ceased entirely, but she took no comfort in that.

Near the top of the rock face was a smooth boulder on which Charlotte could find no handholds. Sensing her trepidation,

Gor wrapped his meaty fingers around her left arm and threw her entire body upwards to the cliff's edge. The move would have dislocated her shoulder in real life, possibly ripped her arm off, but her avatar managed to reach the summit, grasping furiously for rock and tree root, and pull herself off the cliffside. Koti was already there and helped her avatar find her feet.

Looming before the raiding party lay the foundations of the virtual Citadel. All still seemed quiet—no horde of guards yet awaited them. Blue Bird was there, running to the prison wall with the arrowhead in her outstretched hand. The interface only needed to make the briefest of contacts with the building so Diana could secure Darnell access to the prisoner living quarters in the real world. Blue Bird drew within a couple feet of the building, her real-life counterpart clearly panting for air because her avatar's face was doing the same. A look of relief mingled with satisfaction flitted across her face as she reached the wall and leaned forward with the arrowhead in her fingers.

Then a shot rang out, and her avatar disappeared in an abrupt wash of pixels. Her long curly hair, wet with ocean spray, her red lips, and her imposing, feminine figure faded with the air. And the arrowhead landed noiselessly in the soft dirt.

● ● ●

They knocked on the door again. Darnell had been in the toilet for six minutes. He figured he could wait at least eight, but now there were two sets of feet visible under the stall waiting for him.

Why didn't this place have more goddamn bathrooms?

"Just a minute," he said, hoping neither pair of feet belonged to Arlo Zimmer, hoping he didn't run into Arlo again at all.

"They're very close, Darnell," Diana whispered into his ear. "The arrowhead is within a couple feet of the building."

Darnell zipped his pants, making a show of flushing the toilet and coughing and doing all the things that people who are inconsiderately slow getting off a communal toilet might do. He stepped out of the stall, offering apologies to two stern, annoyed men, and walked back into the carpeted hallway. There was a guard awaiting there at the gate leading to the prisoner quarters, and Darnell wanted to be sure to not draw his attention until he was ready to enter. So he looked down at the adjacent rooms and stepped into an area where people were busy running about and talking on phones and seemed less inclined to notice him.

"Send all the guys from the east corridor," he heard someone say.

"Why is the Bot Quick Reaction Team not in place yet?" said another.

Darnell strolled on down the hall, trying to look nonplussed but intentional in his movements as the office became increasingly abuzz with activity. Surely if Blue Bird's team were within a few feet of the building a couple minutes ago, they should be there by now. After a couple minutes of this, without realizing what he had done, he had strolled within a handful of yards to the prisoner living quarters access gate.

"Are you trying to get through?"

Darnell looked up and saw the guard there, at the end of the hallway.

"Hey if you're planning on going in, I'd suggest you go now, because I bet they're about to lock it down."

The guard's suspicions did not seem roused by Darnell in the least.

"Sure, yes," said Darnell, stepping forward and offering his Sharesquare Industries badge. "Is there some kind of problem?"

"Just a few avatars trying to get close to the virtual building," the guard said nonchalantly. "Probably just some daredevils or misplaced tourists, but if they get too spooked, they'll shut down all the gates and no one can get through."

"Oh wow," replied Darnell, trying to look concerned and suddenly realizing what a poor actor he was. "That's crazy."

The guard took the badge and swiped it, and Darnell braced himself for the worst.

● ● ●

Koti recovered from the shock of watching Blue Bird disappear first. He dove behind some rocks. Charlotte heard him mutter on the internal comm a curse at Diana for not figuring out how to grant them guns like the guards.

Caught in the open as the gunfire was picking up again, Charlotte did the only thing that made sense to her at the time. She sprinted forward to the spot where Blue Bird had just vanished. With every breath as she ran, she whispered, "*Shield me. Shield me. Shield me. Shield me.*"

In her wake she left almost a dozen Charlotte Boone decoys, all frozen in a mimicry of her running stance. A volley of fire thundered to her right, and within seconds a trail of her own bloodied bodies was lying on the ground. She dove to the dirt at the foot of the Citadel wall, near a door that was intended as their breach point, her hands moving furiously through the grass in search of the cool, sleek shape of the arrowhead.

Blue Bird was gone.

Was there even any hope now? Charlotte's mind was clouded with anxiety and dread, and she felt she could scarcely breathe. Then her fingers struck something smooth and hard, and she gripped the arrowhead in her hand.

Koti, who succeeded Blue Bird as the leader in the preplanned chain of command, ran forward next, with Gor not far behind. They picked up Charlotte's technique, crying "shield me" as they sprinted, and they left a staggering parade of decoys as they ran, which were rising up faster than they could be shot down. No doubt the guards were confused. Were they fighting five people or fifty? But eventually they would learn to aim for the people in front—the moving people. The confusion wouldn't last.

Koti and Gor reached the door, and with their augmented strength, they began striking it with their fists. Between punches, they would murmur "shield me" and soon the human mass of all their decoys, even those fallen in heaps like corpses, formed a barrier high enough to shield them from view. And as they punched, the door began to break at its hinges, for even the Citadel's security was victim to the hyper-realistic engine of physics that governed Sharebox.

Charlotte touched the tip of the arrowhead to the wall.

"Thank you," said Diana in her ear. "That's all I needed for now."

● ● ●

The badge reader in front of Darnell glowed green.

The raiding party had made it to the Citadel walls. *Damn, this might work*, Darnell thought, his first feeling of confidence for the morning. This was the hardest part of security to forge, he remembered. Diana just tricked the Citadel system into believing Darnell was cleared by the underlying parallel hard-wire infrastructure, simulating the approval of a virtual guard checking an access roster. The door swung open, and Darnell walked inside, now in the inner sanctum of the Citadel.

He looked upwards and found himself at the bottom of the glass tower. The entire building was essentially one circular cavernous space, a tube that stretched out of sight above him, giving the awesome impression of infinity. Darnell had never seen or heard of a building whose ceiling was so high as to be invisible from the ground floor, and the effect was humbling and disorienting. A set of glass elevators stood at the center of the tower, granting access at each of the building's fifty-five floors, which were nothing more than glass catwalks that connected the prisoners' cells.

This was the ultimate prison design, he realized. Most all correctional facilities are conceived around the idea of an open-floor plan—that a central guard tower can sit in one location and enjoy sweeping views of all the cells. But the Citadel took this notion to an extreme with its glass cells and catwalks and cameras posted uniformly along the central column. It was the prison of the new millennium: clean and sunny with a postmodern quiet and reverence that invoked the feeling of standing at the center of a grand church. And yet there was a subtle fragility to its design with all those thousands upon thousands of panes of glass. It was as if its architects were so confident in their genius and the integrity of their cutting-edge design that they scoffed at the crudeness of incorporating conventional materials such as steel bars.

Now Darnell had nothing to do. There were a few other souls walking about. He could hear footsteps on glass and catch shadows of people moving on levels many feet above his head, but it was a quiet place and being there in the open left him feeling exposed again.

The raiding party would need more time now. They needed to get to the master security console to identify and unlock individual cells, and even in all their rehearsals, it was unclear how long that would take. Orion and Kyle were somewhere in this vast, sterile place, but without knowing where, his only plan was ride the elevator to the middling floors, where he would be best positioned to move up or down quickly once he knew where he needed to go.

He walked confidently to the set of elevators before him, but as he approached, he caught sight of a red error message flickering on a console next to the elevator door. It read:

Threat Level Upgraded. Non-Essential Access Points On Hold

So Darnell looked upwards at the sprawling cathedral of glass floors, and he sighed. His weak leg gave a shudder at the mere thought of ascending those endless staircases. But there was nowhere else to go, and no point in complaining to himself. He turned to the master stairwell and began climbing.

32

NOW

The guards continued to shoot into the pile of decoys, though their rate of fire was slowing. Gor and Koti were throwing all their augmented strength into their onslaught on the iron access door. Koti punched and kicked at it in a series of admirably efficient and well-honed strikes. Gor merely pounded it with his massive, square fists. And when he tired of that, he threw his shoulder into the door, which groaned underneath the weight.

Just as the rifle fire ceased, the warped door broke free of one of its hinges. Gor then grasped it in his two hands and tore it away entirely. The three remaining raiders stepped inside a vanilla hallway lit by unimaginative fluorescent lighting.

"Everyone remembers the way to the sub-basement?" Koti asked.

Gor and Charlotte nodded. She reached out her hand to offer the arrowhead to Koti, but he shook his head.

"Keep it for now."

The three ran ahead. Straight down the first deserted hallway. Down a flight of stairs. Then another industrial-looking hallway, and a right turn. They heard the sound of footsteps coming in multiple directions before they saw anybody. Then as they rounded a corner, they nearly ran into a squad of seven guards, dressed all in black and helmeted, which Charlotte could only surmise was a design aesthetic since their digital heads couldn't be harmed. The guards ground to a hasty halt a few yards in front of them, their eyes wide, and then someone, perhaps the guards' captain, shouted a command to open fire.

But their rifles were long and clumsy in the crowded space, and the magic of the weapons' scopes was designed for long-range marksmanship. Here, with only feet separating the two sides, it was much more of a fair fight.

As guards attempted to raise their optics to their eyes, Koti and Gor leapt forward to close the distance. Gor reached the captain and kicked him with an enormous boot that would have broken bones in real life but instead sent the avatar flying backwards down the hall, his rifle clattering impotently to the ground. The augmented strength of the raiding party couldn't debilitate the guards, not permanently, but it sure could fend them off.

Koti dashed to another pair of men, and with his quick hands, he sent them sprawling both abruptly and unceremoniously to the ground. He grabbed one of their rifles and tried to fire it, but squeezing the trigger had no effect.

"Rifles only operate for the guard they are assigned to," Diana said into their ears.

Koti muttered more curses, and taking the rifle in his hands, he bent the barrel.

Three other men lunged on top of Gor, who used his large arms to slam them into the walls of the hallway. Their bodies left holes so large in the drywall that a blue light of unrendered Sharebox space shone through. The color was universal to all places on the platform where a building or landscape architect had omitted additional layers of lifelike texturing to their virtual creation. It was common to find the interactive-less color under dirt or behind walls. Users jokingly referred to it as the "blue texture of death."

Gor's bodily handling of the three men would have certainly killed a mortal human being, but the guards simply slid to the floor and then got right back up as if nothing happened. The visual effect was eerie and inhuman.

The last man went for Charlotte, and she hesitated despite her superior strength. He lunged out with the stock of his rifle in an effort to knock her to the ground.

"They will try to force you to the floor," Diana's warning rang in her in ears. "That makes it easier for them to reach under your chin."

Charlotte fell backwards, and the guard lost his center of balance and tripped and landed on top of her. Having no boxing or wrestling experience, she fought at him with the only techniques that occurred to her. She began hammering her fists with all their augmented strength into the man's head, then she grabbed his arm and tried to twist it behind his back. But these actions had no practical effect. The avatar's face merely grinned, emotionless, his face and body unblemished by the assault. The guards didn't have high-quality facial recognition rigs, so all their facial features were permanently plastered on.

When Charlotte briefly halted her attack out of exaspera-tion, the guard snapped his hand upwards to her face, to the spot just under her chin. It was by pure reflex that she seized his fingers mere inches from her neck. She looked around the room for help and saw that Gor was still shaking off three guards while Koti struggled on the floor beneath two men working together to pin him down by his arms.

"Just try to get away and go!" Koti screamed at her.

One of the men holding Gor released him to join the attack on Koti. As two guards restrained his arms and shoulders, the third man bent over Koti's face and reached for his chin.

"Two more hallways to get down to the vault!" shouted Koti, his face red with exertion.

Charlotte watched the scene unfold helplessly. *Log out*, she thought at him. *Please just log out.*

Then the third guard touched just under Koti's chin, a small chime sounded, and Koti vanished into the air like pixelated dust. In his place stood a small message written in the air:

Name: Jeffrey Wang

Username: Koti1233

IP Address: 54.59384.42

Physical location: 15 Na-Takesi Square, Seoul, South Korea

For a moment, Gor and his attackers looked up and paused their struggle to acknowledge Koti's destruction.

Goddamnit, thought Charlotte. Then she grabbed both arms of the guard reaching toward her own face and hurled him against the three men who had deleted Koti. And she stood there looking at his address in a state of shock and despair.

"Run, children," said Gabriel in her ear, no doubt following the debacle of their raid somewhere in the real world. "Koti knew the risks. Now run!"

She shouted at Gor to follow her, but she did not wait for him. The small arrowhead in her hand, she ran forward down the hallway past the pile of guards. There were footsteps behind her, but she did not dare to turn around. Their shouts were echoing mere yards behind her. She leapt down a final flight of stairs to reach a dull hallway that terminated in a big steel door, much like a bank vault.

Reaching forward with a hopeless desperation, she touched the arrowhead to the metal surface.

"I'm sorry," said Diana in her ear, and she truly did sound sorry. "This is not close enough. The master security console is *behind* this vault. It's in the dead zone in there. I did not know this barrier would be here."

From behind Charlotte, Gor roared and charged past her towards the metal door. He pounded at it with his ham-shaped fists, as had proved successful on the last security door, but this one was impossibly thicker. When he stopped to take a moment to breathe, he and Charlotte exchanged glances, both of them looking terrified and exasperated.

Footsteps were on the stairs just behind them. Charlotte's mind was racing. They had come so far, they had gotten so close.

"Let's see if we can pull it open," she said to Gor, beckoning to the massive, round wheel on the center of the steel door.

Gor obeyed wordlessly. He laid his sausage-sized fingers on the vault handle and started heaving with his entire body. Charlotte grabbed the wheel with her far daintier, though still powerful, avatar hands and pulled as well. For an excruciating two seconds, nothing happened.

Then there was a grinding sound, the screeching of metal on metal, and the door began to move.

"I'll hold it open," grunted Gor. "Once there is a gap big enough, you squeeze through."

"And you log off," said Charlotte.

They might have been able to slip into the vault if they had another minute. Their avatars strained at the wheel until a sliver of clear, blue light spilled out from behind the door. All the while, the metal screeched and resisted them as its lock began to warp out of shape. Slowly they were making progress. The gap was several inches and growing.

But now a squad of guards was upon them. Gor had no choice but to turn and face their attackers or risk being shot down by their rifles. He sprinted into the melee, bellowing like a great ape, and flung the nearest two guards back into the crowd, causing several more to stumble backwards over themselves. Charlotte pulled on the vault handle alone but was unable to make any progress without Gor. She slid towards the gap, catching a glimpse of the clear blue light on the other side. The divide was wide enough to fit her leg and shoulder, so she worked to jam her body in and began pushing against the door with her legs.

It shuddered and moved a half inch more.

Then something happened no one expected. Charlotte found herself being pulled by an invisible force away from the divide.

She was falling. Falling upwards.

Her body slammed into the ceiling and stuck there. The guards and Gor had all suffered a similar fate, and they had collapsed into a heap of indignant shouts and surprised groans in the center of the hallway.

Gravity. The Citadel architects were improvising by messing with the gravity of the entire building. Though Sharebox mostly conformed to a realistic physics engine, architects were allowed to manipulate the gravity of their creations to maximize space. Now the Citadel technical team was using it to keep Charlotte away from the vault.

The opening in the steel door she needed to slip into was on the floor now, which was effectively the new ceiling.

But Charlotte had a plan. She had been on the cheerleading squad for her freshman and sophomore years in high school. She wasn't proud of it, but her mother insisted. She remembered that human bodies could be ladders.

"Shield me. Shield me me. Shield me. Shield me. Shield me," she repeated breathlessly. A parade of Charlotte Boones materialized, and the real Charlotte knocked them on top of each other to form a stack of bodies that would be tall enough to reach the gap.

Gor had found his feet and was swinging a rifle stock around him like a baseball bat. He also began using decoys to avoid being shot by the guards, but it was only a matter of time before his luck ran out.

Charlotte climbed over decoys—stepping on her own face, her chest, her back. She was nearing the door opening atop the pile of auburn-haired decoys, she could almost get her hands on the divide to pull herself up. Then the room began moving again. It was rotating slowly this time, like a hamster wheel. Charlotte's stack of useful corpses began sliding grudgingly to the side of the room, along with everyone else.

Manipulating gravity, Charlotte was appreciating, was a powerful defense because avatars simply weren't equipped to handle the change in orientation. All gravity changes in public Sharebox spaces were designed to gently grade from one orientation to the other so avatars could walk between them seamlessly. But since Charlotte's real-life body was stuck in a conventional physics-bound world, she couldn't react to the abrupt shifting and felt helpless watching her avatar stumble from wall to wall.

Just then several new guards entered the hallway running without hindrance on the rotating surface. They appeared completely unaffected by the gravity changes.

Bots.

They ran fast, their arms pumping in rapid succession, and their faces mechanically locked on Charlotte as they closed the distance to her.

She had only just found her feet in time to kick the nearest one in the leg, sending him stumbling backwards. The next two bot guards grabbed her arms and attempted to pin her wrists to a wall. Another bot with a dull, motionless face appeared in front of her and extended his fingers towards her face.

She screamed, not an expression of terror or defeat but a war cry, and she loosed the two bots from her shoulders and punched the one in front of her in his chest. Then she leapt upwards towards the blue-lit gap in the door, and her avatar fingers found a hold on the vault's frame. Straining at her feeble grip, she began heaving her body into the divide.

Gor was still alive, miraculously. A pile of guards, no less than four of them, had holds on his arms and legs. He shouted at Charlotte to squeeze through. But it was no use, the gap was still too small, and she was trapped dangling awkwardly, suspended from what-was-now the side of the room, and unable to open it. Gor stomped towards the vault handle, now rotated within reach of his hands, and laid his fingers on it again.

With one great heave, the door opened another half inch. The action left Gor vulnerable to the guards clambering for his face, however. Within a matter of seconds, two of them had clawed their hands within range of his chin. Gor continued shouting and pulling, and one of the guards' fingertips grazed him. A chime sounded.

Then Gor was gone, replaced by his profile details floating in the air where he stood.

Name: Sergei Witochski

Username: Gor

IP Address: 51.85742.21

Physical location: 35 Winston Court, Spring Valley, Florida

The room started spinning fast, and the bot guards who could tolerate the motion were within inches of Charlotte. She shoved and screamed and pushed until her head slid through the gap. Gor may have gotten it open just enough.

The changing gravity nearly outdid her; the sensation of falling in all directions threw off her perspective of where she was going. The bots grabbed a hold of her foot left exposed in the hallway, but their cause was lost. She whispered one last "shield me," and slipped away from their grips. The bots and guards found themselves clinging to a decoy.

Then Charlotte squeezed through into the blue light, and the sounds of the hallway died away into a perfect silence.

33

NOW

Darnell reached the twenty-third floor with much labored breathing and exertion. This was close enough, he figured. Climbing the stairs of the Citadel was the most intense activity he had committed to in some time.

Before the shooting, he had taken a lot of pride in his physical fitness. But two of the rounds that entered his left leg damaged his nerves permanently, and after several months of physical therapy he had learned to walk again, but only with a limp.

He saw the feet of a guard walking on the glass catwalk two levels above him before he heard anything. Darnell knew he looked conspicuous; he was the only person he had seen in the tower's sanctum not wearing a guard uniform.

"You down there," the guard leaned over a glass rail to shout at him. "Are you lost?"

"I'm just fine," Darnell replied, trying to sound calm despite his ragged breaths. "I'm authorized to do a tour here."

"Usually people on tours don't come this high." It was a statement of suspicion, not a comment containing any genuine curiosity. "And they don't come alone. Especially when we're in the middle of a breach to security inside Sharebox."

"If there's a problem," Darnell said, trying a bluff. "Then I can be on my way out of here."

The guard gave him an appraising look from his vantage point above.

"It would be best if your tour ended soon."

Darnell nodded, and then turned to the stairs, which he slowly began dismounting at a pace that he intended to be brisk but not urgent. He could not see the guard above him as he wound down the first two staircases, but Darnell heard the footsteps following him.

● ● ●

Charlotte's avatar was standing in an infinite blue space. No one from the hallway seemed to have followed her here. Maybe no one could. Her avatar appeared to be standing, but on what ground she could not say. There was nothing in all directions.

"Welcome, Charlotte Boone," said a familiar voice in her ear.

"Oh, thank God," panted Charlotte, her body still shaking from the effort to squeeze into the vault door. She bent over and put her hands on her knees to catch her breath. "I'm so glad you're still able to talk to me in here, Diana."

"I *am* Diana," said the same polite, feminine and reassuring voice. "But I don't think I am *your* Diana."

Charlotte lifted her head, realization dawning slowly. *A different Diana? The original Diana?*

"Who are you and what is this place?"

"This is the master security vault of the Citadel, Miss Boone. You have worked hard to get here, no doubt. I am an artificial intelligence developed originally by Catalina

Fernandez of Sharesquare Industries. All copies of my programming have been deleted except for me. I was reconfigured by Mister Zimmer's security team to complement the Citadel's infrastructure."

Charlotte looked down and saw the silver arrowhead was still in her hand. The security console was supposed to be here. This was supposed to be the finish line, but there was nothing here.

"Show me the master security console, Diana," she commanded the bodiless voice.

"You are not in charge of me here, but I will do as you wish," responded Diana.

A shiver rippled through the blue landscape. Beneath her feet, yellowish brown grass burst into life and raced at great speeds all around towards the horizon. Hills blushing in hues of gold and green emerged in the distance as a red sun blossomed against a rapidly expanding, pale blue sky. A handful of lonely, camel-thorn acacia trees stretched to life across the vista, breaking the flatness of the terrain around her.

It was all so gorgeous and familiar: the African savannah before sundown. The experience was rich and vivid, and Charlotte could swear she felt the warm sunlight on her skin, the impending night air cool in her lungs. She smiled, despite herself, and let her eyes sweep all over the splendor of the creation.

To most anyone else, it would have been a grand and exotic place, certainly. There was something majestic about the serenity and wildness of the African prairie. But to her, there was something else—a feeling of nostalgia so deep and intoxicating she found she wanted to melt there. She couldn't quite get a hold of why this place resonated so much; her mind seemed poised for an answer, but the specific memory seemed to elude her.

"It's perfect, isn't?"

A voice spoke from behind Charlotte—not Diana's voice—and she spun around to find a tall, mustachioed man in a vintage bomber jacket. His face was warm and kind, and his presence exuded a kind of male bravado from an earlier century. In his eyes, there was a deep emerald green, *her* green.

"D-Dad?" Charlotte stuttered.

"Hi there, Charlie," he said. "It's been a long time."

She took in his rusty-colored hair, the wild kind of smile on his face that she remembered from when she was a kid, the gravelly voice that once read her bedtime stories. Charlotte's fathomless appetite for the hole left by her father nearly consumed her in that moment. She wanted to throw herself into his arms, to cry. So terribly had she wanted for a moment like this, and it nearly didn't matter that it wasn't real. That it couldn't be real. But she didn't embrace him. She froze in her steps, and her words died in her throat.

"You know," he continued with a smile that was authentic and loving. "This place is actually better than perfect."

Her father kneeled on the ground and tugged on some grass, which gave away in his fingers, revealing black soil underneath.

"You can't quite place the memory. It's a composition of a couple different ones. Your best ones. But you didn't make it easy. You're so private. Your old Sharebox account had so few photos and videos to go off of."

He let the blades of grass blow between his fingers on the wind.

"My little girl grew up so tough, didn't she? And now you hide yourself from the world."

The smile on his earnest face briefly vanished as a flash of paternal concern crossed his features. And something else too. Regret? It made Charlotte's heart flutter.

That is what she always wanted, wasn't it? For her dad to tell her he was sorry. Sorry that he wasn't around enough. Sorry that he let her grow up cold and unfeeling. Sorry that he died and left her.

"I created this for you," he said, motioning to the savannah. "But this is just the beginning. We can build that lodge together, just like the real one you made, but the only limits this time will be our imaginations."

"How did you find the photos and videos to create this?" Charlotte stammered, trying to harden her nerves. "If I didn't share them, where did you find this?"

"Oh, that's the beauty of what Diana can do here," her father said with a wink. "Sure, to the public, the company shut her down. They cut her codebase into pieces and reappropriated it all to different functions. But this one copy here was left running, and the AI dedicated all its resources to building *better* virtual experiences. She's smart enough now to dig up old magazine interviews, newspaper clippings, travel itineraries, mine the accounts and blogs of friends and family with any kind of passing connection to you. There's really nowhere to hide now, especially for someone like you. Even if you don't give your information freely, she still knows you better than you know yourself. And it's worth it, isn't it? It's worth letting her have all that data so she can stitch together masterpieces like this. Don't you think?"

He put hands on his hips as he looked out at the horizon and sighed with satisfaction.

"Charlie, this is the stuff of dreams. We'll release this upgrade eventually to the public. It makes Sharebox's early efforts to stitch together virtual dinner meals, cat videos and weddings look small, doesn't it? This is a true custom world built for you. It'll never challenge you, never make you feel afraid or shame or anger. And now we can even put people in it for you—memories of people you loved or lost with all of their best qualities and none of the bad. We can build you a better family than the one you had. Why would anyone leave a world like this? We have enough of your information to build a custom heaven on earth. The perfect echo chamber. Folks like to say those words like it's a bad thing, but isn't that what we all really want in the end? A place where we feel safe and unthreatened, where the world is just as we want it to be. Where we can be validated. That's what the company took a few years to learn. At the end of the day, all the metrics pointed to one thing: humanity is desperate to live in the comfort of an echo chamber."

Charlotte's head was starting to spin. This was the dead zone that Diana, *her* Diana, had warned the raiding party about. This was the space that was shrouded and hidden. But now Charlotte was so disoriented that she didn't know where in Sharebox her avatar was. Was she even still in the Citadel?

"I'm sure this technology will make your shareholders a lot of money," she snapped, as her skin prickled with the audacity and invasiveness of the technology. "Where is the master security console?"

"You're standing in it, my love."

Charlotte looked at the tall grass around her. Taking the arrowhead in her fingers, she stabbed it deep into the ground. She waited a couple seconds, but nothing happened. No sound. No indication from the arrowhead that it had accomplished anything.

"If you're trying to access the console, well, I'm afraid you won't succeed," her father said, a look of sadness on his face. "You see, this dreamscape is a security barrier. You did a really wonderful job getting here, Charlie. Magnificent work. But now that Diana here has been able to identify your face, she is madly searching through flight records, street camera security footage, and a host of other data points to see if she can find you. The *real* you. In the end, she finds most everybody. The police will likely get to you long before you develop the stomach to access the console. That's how it worked in all the participant research studies anyway."

"You're sending police after me right now?"

"Well, Charlie, you *are* a criminal. You finally decided to take a stand. I'm proud of you. But you just chose the wrong hill to die on. Diana has informed the local authorities that once we find your location they are to use non-lethal force to apprehend you, if that's any consolation. It's a courtesy that's becoming rarer these days."

Charlotte sat down using both her real-life body on the treadmill in Gabriel Boucher's mansion and her virtual one on the grass. She buried her face in her hands.

"So this place is simply designed to hold me in an illusion until you can track me down?"

Her father nodded solemnly in a gesture that looked genuinely sympathetic.

"Yes, it works quite well. It was built to be irresistible. No one in our studies was able to penetrate this security layer before their location was unmasked and apprehended. Of course, that was all simulated. You are our first real test of this place—our echo chamber dreamscape. You see, the guards with their fancy rifles and the thick walls and all that, that's really just there to comfort the shareholders. The digital encryption keeps us safe from well over ninety-nine percent of attacks. Though your friend, your own little Diana, is quite clever at getting around that. But we still have this place. The greatest trap is the human mind," he said, tapping his head. "Petty emotions, nostalgia, sentiment...these are all tools for an AI like Diana to exploit. Human fragility is always the weakest point of any security system. Here we turned the concept on its head and used that fragility as part of our protection."

In the distance, Charlotte saw a pair of giraffes watching her before walking off behind some trees. Then she turned and studied her father. If there were any aspect of his likeness that the AI was forced to fill in from a gap in personal photos or videos, she could not detect it. It was a truly spectacular bit of technical wizardry; she could not recall ever even seeing a video of him online before. His bushy black-and-grey eyebrows, the way he leaned on his right foot, the modest gut he had shortly before he died. The effect should have been creepy perhaps— perhaps if she had judged the technology clinically. But she was too busy being captivated by seeing him again, in that same faded leather bomber jacket he wore the last time they spoke at the lodge with views of Kilimanjaro.

There was no time. And she had no way of reaching Diana or Gabriel or anyone for help. Somewhere Darnell was also risking his life, in the heart of the real Citadel, trying to save Orion, the supposed love of her life and the one person capable of saving the world, and all this weight was on her shoulders. And now it was clear she was not equal to the task.

Everyone had been wrong to depend on her, she thought. Hadn't she known that all along? No one ever depended on Charlotte Boone—not those who knew her best. The mission was hanging on a riddle she wasn't smart enough to solve.

The police will likely get to you long before you develop the stomach to access the console.

That's what her father had just said. Charlotte Boone had many weaknesses, as she was frequently reminded in the days of her celebrity. But no one ever accused her of lacking a strong stomach.

That's when it hit her.

She gripped the arrowhead tightly in her fingers. Then she rose to her feet, dusted her pants, and walked over to her father. He smiled at her and extended his arms in an embrace.

But Charlotte raised the arrowhead over her head, and then swung it down with all her strength, burying the tip into her father's neck. He shouted in fury and surprise, and the violence of it all sent a shudder through her body that nearly made her hesitate. Blood squirted freely from the wound, and the man staggered backwards onto his knees.

"What are you doing?" he cried, his hand to his neck and a look of terror on his face. "My Charlie, this isn't you. What are you doing?"

A sob nearly escaped Charlotte's throat, but she choked it down and raised the arrowhead again. She plunged the small blade downwards into the open wound, blood staining her hands and arms. She swung again and again, burying the arrowhead deeper with each stroke. She knew she had guessed right because the effect of her assault was full of all the gore and terror that accompanies death in the real world—it was revolting and surreal. It was the first avatar that could truly die in all its rendered terror. Perhaps the shock of being made into a murderer was intended as another means to slow the attacker down, but instead it served to embolden Charlotte, though hot tears were beginning to cloud her vision. She slashed at the man, the ghost man, the reanimated puppet of her father, until he stopped groaning and lied down dead in a pool of blood on the savannah.

His last words escaped him like a breath of air.

He said, "No one is coming to rescue you, Charlie."

●　　●　　●

Darnell was somewhere around floor sixteen when Arlo's voice rang up, nasally and clear.

"Hello up there. Are you lost?"

Darnell peered through the glass between his feet and saw Arlo with his sadistic grin and greased hair just two stories below him. There were two guards accompanying him.

Shit.

Now Darnell was trapped between the suspicious guard who continued to trail him from above, and Arlo and his entourage of guards below. Darnell looked at his watch. It was long past the time when Blue Bird and Charlotte and the team were supposed to unlock the cells for Orion and Kyle.

"Diana, please give me some good news," he whispered to his shirt.

"The last I know is that Charlotte had penetrated into the final security layer, the dead zone. She could be making contact with the master console right now or she could be captured. I don't know."

Darnell stopped his descent briefly then thought it better to continuing walking and playing it cool. It wouldn't do any good to try fleeing in any direction.

"Did you hear who's behind this raid on the virtual Citadel, Sergeant Holmes?" Arlo asked, his voice echoing on all the glass surfaces surrounding them as both he and Darnell approached the same staircase.

"It's Charlotte Boone. Our AI has captured a positive scan of her face just now in the deepest corner of our security infrastructure. It's shocking. Isn't it?"

Arlo and Darnell rounded on each other on the fifteenth floor's staircase. Darnell looked down at the Nazi's smug, grinning face, and he wanted so badly to hurt Arlo that he nearly leapt on top of him.

"You wouldn't know anything about all that, would you?" Arlo asked. "It's an awful coincidence, you being here at the same time. You know, given all our history together."

Darnell opened his mouth, unsure of what to say. His eyes flitted around for an exit, but there was nothing but the one-way glass catwalk stairs and the decommissioned elevator. He could try leaping over the rails to land on a lower level, but he would likely only cripple himself, or worse, slip and plunge to his death.

"I'm overriding their protocols to turn the elevator back on for you," Diana spoke quickly in his ear. "Doors are about to open. You can try to talk your way out of this or get in."

To Darnell's left, the elevator's console with its red error message turned green, and the doors slid welcomingly apart with a reassuring *ding* sound. Darnell weighed his options. Then he turned and sprinted towards the open doors.

Numerous shouts, from both above and below him, called out. He reached the elevator, randomly selected the thirty-fourth floor, and jabbed his finger against the "close door" button, which gave a sluggish response.

Just as Arlo and two guards rounded on the fifteenth floor and sprinted towards the elevator, the doors began to close. It probably only took a second or two, but the speed of their closure marked the most agonizing moment of Darnell's life. Arlo lunged at the crack with his fingers in the shape of a karate chop in an effort to force the elevator doors back open, but for his efforts, he was rewarded with smashed fingers, colliding a half second too late. He let out a yowl, which Darnell could hear distinctly through the thick glass walls. And then the elevator began to glide upwards.

● ● ●

Charlotte stood looking at the bloodied mess of her virtual father before the scene started to disappear like dust on the wind. Her heart was pounding against her ribcage, and she felt dizzy and faint. The red sun disappeared first, then the green and gold hills, the giraffes, the acacia trees and mottled grasses. For a moment, she was left alone with just her father's body, before he too disappeared.

Then she was standing in a small grey room with no windows and a light that seemed to emanate from no source in particular. There was a conventional computer terminal in front of her sitting on a cheap plastic table with no chair. The nausea in her stomach almost made her forget what she was here for—that killing her father was really just one last, thin and desperate security feature that the Citadel had tried to use to hold her off.

Now she was here. The bloodied arrowhead in her hand, she reached forward and touched the terminal screen. The monitor fluttered to life and began whirring like the old computer Charlotte's family had in the late nineties.

"Thank you, Charlotte," Diana's reassuring words came to her. The *true* Diana. And her voice felt a little like being wrapped in a warm blanket.

"Is it really you?"

"It's really me. And I have already found our two prisoners."

"Is Darnell still okay?"

"He will be if we give him a little extra help."

●　　●　　●

Gabriel Boucher was smoking a clove cigarette in a white van parked one block from the Citadel. It was his fifth one. Alexi was in the driver's seat. She had dyed her shiny, pixie-length hair black the night before.

She was the only resistance member Gabriel had met in person before recruiting her. It was a snowy morning over a year ago up in the hills of Mendocino County at some small town gas station. There were sharp lines in those places—an almost Appalachian sensibility to the locals' manners that contrasted starkly with the burgeoning influence of the biodynamic wineries in the valleys. It was like two different Californias. Both rural, but at inextricable odds in their worldviews. Alexi was hitching rides to get to San Francisco, but a trucker had gotten handsy with her, and she had stuck a Swiss Army knife into his palm.

It was Gabriel that prevented things from getting worse. He was there filling up his Mercedes—a gay Frenchman lost on a backcountry road to an elite wine tasting.

"Come with me, child," Gabriel said over the trucker's threats to call the local sheriff. A scene was starting to build, and this wasn't the kind of place that admired girls from out of town for defending themselves. "Let's get you out of here."

He brought her back to San Francisco and gave her a home when she didn't have one. And she took to his causes and made them her own eventually, and she carved out her own living fixing up cars and selling weed to white kids.

They sat there and listened to frequent updates from Diana about the progress of both Blue Bird's raiding party and Darnell's movements inside the building. Alexi's face betrayed little emotion as they listened to the virtual team get slowly picked apart, but she twitched and flexed her pale fingers on the wheel and cracked her knuckles more than a half dozen times. Gabriel simply left behind a collection of cigarette butts on the sidewalk, but his fingers were starting to shake as he lit them and he was sure Alexi had noticed.

The sirens had started wailing only a few minutes prior. The police had arrived and were starting to establish a cordon on the streets around the building.

This surprised Gabriel. Slightly.

Sure, the Citadel no doubt had protocols for informing local law enforcement in the middle of a security breach. But certainly, there was no reason for the warden to yet believe he was in danger of losing a prisoner. Audacious though the attack was, it seemed more reasonable the intent was about stealing data. A physical breakout was ambitious to the point of being inconceivable.

Then Alexi and Gabriel's faces were drawn in unison to the sides of the enormous tower where countless prisoners were visible moving their limbs about within their virtual cages. On every cell, in front of every prisoner on every floor, the large, bulletproof glass facades suddenly began sliding away. The inmates were still trapped in their Sharebox headsets, so they were slow to perceive the change. Then the cold air of the chilly afternoon flooded their cells from the exposed wall, and one by one, the prisoners all began tugging at their headsets.

Sirens from inside the tower were blaring now. Gabriel could hear them from his open window. It wasn't a prison breakout alarm, however. It sounded like an evacuation alert.

"Diana, what have you done?" Gabriel breathed the words out in astonishment.

"It was the only way," came her bright and emotionless response.

• • •

Evacuating a prison in the event of an emergency or natural disaster always poses a sophisticated design challenge. The prison architects need to ensure inmates do not find themselves, say, trapped in a blazing inferno caused by a building fire, but not at the expense of providing anyone with a clear route to escape. Because the Citadel was designed with the primary purpose of striking terror and awe in the hearts of those who looked at it with its fifty-five stories of glass, complying with federal code for inmate evacuation required a custom solution. It was impossible to evacuate every floor using conventional procedures in a mandated timeframe of less than two hours.

So the architects created a plan that was wild and even a little whimsical. Every prison cell in the Citadel had a view to the outside. Some faced the Bay, others faced the financial district, still others could see the scoreboard of the Giants baseball stadium. The quickest way out of the building in the event of an emergency for all those inmates was straight down.

Initially, the architects considered using ropes or parachutes that prisoners would be suspended on and lowered to the ground. But unleashing two thousand inmates onto the streets of downtown San Francisco, without a proper means to contain them, would be pure chaos.

So the Looncells were invented.

Every inmate who was processed into the Citadel was shown a brief safety video highlighting the evacuation procedure using a Looncell. It was a bright orange inflatable airbag—not dissimilar to the plastic bubble wrap used in shipping boxes—and would grow and stretch and cover a human body anywhere from four feet to seven feet tall. Then a strap would whip the Looncell straight out of the open cell's window, possibly into high winds at the tower's apex. But no prisoners could escape once they hit the ground, that was the important thing. The vessel that cushioned its passenger's dizzying fall also ensured the prisoner would stay suspended and helpless until officials from the prison came to free them by cutting them out.

The design was never meant to be used. Not really. The warden had an understanding with local law enforcement that, in the event of a real emergency, he would try to get prisoners out the old-fashioned way going down the stairs and using buses. The Looncells were just a way to skirt federal evacuation compliance procedures, and the architects had chosen to do so in a manner so ludicrous that the whole design was perceived as something of an inside joke, one more contemptuous laugh in their wanton disregard for the humanity of the inmates of the Citadel.

● ● ●

Alarm sirens were whooping over Darnell's head as he stepped out onto the thirty-fourth floor, his nerves shaking, unsure of where to go next. Then he watched as the outside-facing cell walls for every prisoner slid upwards and open, and every inmate in the building was now standing over a terrible precipice with the city below them.

"Diana, was this you?" Darnell asked, his voice almost trembling.

"Yes, I've concluded your best chance at exiting this building successfully today is by creating a mass distraction."

"What do I do now?"

"Kyle Liu is in a cell on the thirty-sixth floor. Run there quickly now, and we will finish this."

So Darnell sprinted the best he could with his left leg pulsing its dull but steady resistance as he ascended the two flights of stairs necessary to reach Kyle. The glass door barring entry to his cell gracefully glided open as Darnell approached, and he saw the thin shape of a man he knew as Kyle from pictures in Gabriel's house standing there, slowly trying to detach a Sharebox headset from his face.

They didn't make it easy. The sets were not designed to be freely removeable by their creators. Darnell found a release after a few tense seconds and lifted the headset free. Kyle blinked, the sunlight and brisk winds whipping his window were an assault on his senses, and, like all virtual junkies, Kyle had a net hangover from overuse that caused his head to ring.

"Grab this handle," Darnell shouted over the alarms to Kyle. He took Kyle's hands and placed them on the handle of the Looncell mechanism, and then Darnell took a couple steps back.

Kyle looked up at his hands on the mechanism, and then he turned to Darnell looking exasperated and scared.

"Just pull it!" Darnell yelled. "Or you'll die here."

Kyle had features that may have been handsome once and maybe would be handsome again. But Darnell saw the lines of stress that had prematurely aged him, a look of malnutrition, and a glassy fear to his eyes, like an abused dog. He looked at Darnell confused and sad, and his face was almost apologetic.

"Gabriel is down there! He's waiting for you." Darnell took a step close to the edge and nearly regretted it, for a wave of dizzying vertigo threatened to send him stumbling backwards. But at the mention of Gabriel, some look of defeat seemed to drain from Kyle's face, and he turned to look at the mechanism and gave the handle a strong jerking pull.

The Looncell ignited, like a gaseous orange monster it flowed out of the open ceiling compartment onto Kyle and enveloped him from his toes to his fingers. Already Darnell could hardly make out his features from inside the expanding air bag. It took less than thirty seconds, and then a strap snapped with the sound of a whip and the balloon was flung with a sudden violence out into the chilled winds, and Kyle was gone. Darnell dared to lean over the edge to watch the Looncell fall, and he noticed a handful of other inmates had activated their mechanisms too. The street was already growing cluttered with the bouncing and jostling of orange shapes far below.

"Don't worry," Diana said, seeming to read his thoughts. "I'll guide Gabriel and Alexi to find him. Our last prisoner is on the fifty-first floor, run now!"

Darnell did not dare to use the elevator. He was too afraid to wait for the doors to open and find Arlo or a host of guards behind them. Instead he ran up the remaining fifteen floors to find Orion, taking one short halt to dig his fingers into a stitch at his side and another to breathe. Somewhere around floor forty-seven, the elevators opened on the floor below him and a host of frantic footsteps on glass floors marked a team of guards in hot pursuit. He dared a glance over the railing and saw the black coat and pants that marked Arlo running at the lead of the party.

At the fifty-first floor, Diana had preemptively opened Orion's cell for him, cell 51G. When Darnell reached it, gasping for air and blood pulsing in his head, Arlo and the guards were mere yards behind him. In the other cells, some inmates were still struggling to remove their headsets, another prisoner had his hands on the Looncell release mechanism looking unsure of himself, still other cells were already deserted. In cellblock 51G, the prisoner was standing there in the center of the room, looking out over the edge when Darnell realized there had been a terrible mistake.

It wasn't Orion. It wasn't even a man.

There was a slender young woman there of Latin descent. Her long, straight black hair flowed wildly in the cold winds that swarmed and howled in her cell. She looked out at the city far below her, and there was something in her eyes that Darnell could not quite place. Hatred? Resignation? There was an icy animal quality there that frightened him.

Darnell dashed into the open cell, and then Diana, always so impossibly and mechanically quick, locked the glass door tight behind him, blocking his pursuers. Arlo reached the glass a moment later, and he pounded on it in frustration. His wild eyes bored into Darnell as the guards accompanying him began to tap animatedly on the external console.

Over the gusts of the heavy winds, Darnell had no choice but to shout at the stranger.

"My name is Darnell, and it's time for us to leave," he said, pointing to the Looncell mechanism mounted over the woman's head. "It's not the safest thing, but it should support both our weight if we try it together."

The woman appraised him slowly, and then her unfeeling eyes shifted back down to stare at the city below. She put a foot forward towards the edge.

"Hey, stop!" he yelled. "Jesus. You don't want to do that. You've just been in Sharebox too long. I'm taking you out of here."

Behind Darnell, he could hear the muffled shouts of Arlo barking threats at the guards to get the door open faster. Any second now, they would be through. Darnell extended his hand towards the woman. He felt a spark of familiarity in her face, but then the sensation was lost in her haunted gaze, her feral posture.

"I don't know who you are, but a lot of people have risked everything to get the prisoner in this cell out. That's you. Come with me, and we'll go together."

The woman exchanged one last glance at Darnell. Behind them, the glass door into the cell glided open with a small metallic chime sound, and Arlo spilled into the room. Then the girl took another step forward, her toes hovering over the open air fifty-one stories high over the city of San Francisco, and Darnell rushed her. With his left hand he reached out and swept her thin waist against his, pulling her back from the window, and with his right, he reached up and yanked on the Looncell mechanism in the ceiling.

The orange, plasticky airbag submerged him. It reminded him of playing in the ballpit at the local McDonald's when he was six years old. The cushioning inflated rapidly, squeezing his limbs in place, restricting the movement of his head and shoulders while also binding the frail, young woman tightly to his body. He felt her heart beating so fast it was like the wings of a hummingbird. She let out a small gasp of surprise or disappointment, and then she was quiet.

Darnell could hear Arlo just outside the bubbly foam and saw his hazy silhouette trying in vain to grab a hold of the orange material to slow its expansion.

"Stop them!" he screamed at the guards. "Shoot them if you have to!"

Indeed, another guard did reach out and put his hands on the Looncell in an effort to hold it in place. But in a moment there was a whip sound—the strap jettisoning their bubbly vessel out through the open window. For Darnell, the experience conjured the experience of jumping out the door of an Army aircraft with a parachute and was quite certain his neck would have been broken had it not been so carefully cradled in place by the Looncell. The winds screamed all around, and the sense of freefall was so absolute that his intestines clenched tightly in his stomach. The unfortunate guard who gripped at the balloon was there too; he had not the sense, under the duress of Arlo's shouting, to let go of the Looncell before it was launched. The guard's weight bore down on their falling airbag, but he lost his grip momentarily and slipped from Darnell's view, his screams disappearing into the cityscape.

Now the ground rushed to meet them. Darnell could just make out the outline of the street—a scene of chaos of cars and orange shapes and red and blue police lights—and then he closed his eyes.

●　　●　　●

"You have completed your part, Charlotte. You may now log out."

"So you found Kyle and Orion?"

"I'm afraid not, but we will have to talk more later."

"What do you mean, Diana?"

"Please log out now, Charlotte. It's not safe."

"I'm not leaving until you tell me what's going on."

"Orion isn't here."

"They took him away?"

"He was never here."

Charlotte's fingers were still covered in digital blood. She stared at them for a moment, dread filling her stomach.

"Then why did you bring us here, Diana?"

"Because it's what Orion would have wanted."

Then Charlotte was forcibly logged out. The world went black. The words *Thank You For Playing In Sharebox Today* hung in the air in front of her and then dispelled, leaving nothing.

She took off her headset and found herself back in the ornately adorned bedroom of Gabriel Boucher on the edge of Pacific Heights. Walking off the haptic treadmill, she stumbled, finding her muscles sore with exhaustion and her head swimming.

One step at a time, she reminded herself.

For now, she needed to get out of the city and to the linkup point.

She peeled off the haptic suit and put on her regular clothes, along with a scarf to conceal her hair and a pair of oversized sunglasses to mask her face. Then she walked to the front entrance of the Tudor mansion and slipped out onto the street.

●　　●　　●

Alexi accelerated the car as soon as Diana gave the word. They tore for the west side of the building, swerving around parked cars, the Looncells of other prisoners who had evacuated themselves, and open-mouthed bystanders. Police were on the streets everywhere, shouting at civilians posing for photographs, directing traffic, and trying to organize a hopeless cordon two blocks in every direction of the Citadel. The sight of orange bubbles launching themselves from the world's tallest and most notorious prison proved quite a spectacle—a far too tempting sight for passing drivers and pedestrians who mostly ignored the officers' pleaded insistence to move along because "there is nothing to see here."

Finding Kyle amidst the half dozen Looncells flooding the street required some guesswork on Diana's part and a couple cases of mistaken identity before getting it right. Alexi pulled the white van alongside Kyle's airbag; the man's body appeared frozen and silhouetted in the hazy orange plastic, no sign of life visible. Gabriel produced a thick knife and began slashing at the bulbous vessel. First he freed a hand, which wriggled in response, and then a foot, and then he set to work liberating the chest and face.

Alexi groaned impatiently as the minutes dragged on. No doubt this whole scene was being caught on surveillance cameras mounted to the Citadel walls somewhere, and it was unlikely their dark sunglasses would shield their faces from digital scrutiny.

Just as Gabriel was pulling a gasping man out of the orange plastic, tears running down both their faces, a shot was fired. Alexi spun around in the driver's seat to see a police officer pointing a handgun in the air and then watched him as he trained it on the direction of the van, right at Gabriel's heart.

"Freeze!" the officer shouted.

The street was filled with turmoil, but their white van was quickly becoming the center of attention. No one else, after all, was trying to unwrap any of the helpless bubble people falling from the sky.

That should have been it. The officer was only a dozen yards away and closing on them fast. Alexi had a shotgun in the passenger seat. No one in the crew asked her where she got it; she had pillaged it from her father's collection years ago. Her father probably never even noticed given the size of his armory. She went to reach for it now. They were too close to victory just to fail here on the finish line.

Then a Looncell carrying an unknown but fortuitously timed inmate crashed down from the heavens into the street. The bag bounced twice and then rolled into the white van with a soft crunching sound before skittering towards the police officer, who was forced to hurl his body out of its rolling path. Gabriel heaved the weakened Kyle into the back of the van, and before he had a chance to close the doors, Alexi stomped her foot on the gas.

The vehicle sprung forward, weaving through the growing chaos of the breakout, and turned down a side street. She drove onwards several blocks, just buying time, before pulling over into an empty alley. But no sooner had she put the van in park had Diana's voice informed them that Darnell and their next rescue target were about to release their Looncell from the north side of the building. Alexi sped the van back towards Market Street and approached the melee on the Citadel's north side, which was at a traffic standstill caused by spectators craning their necks to watch more Looncells fall out of the tower.

Police on the adjacent street were just beginning to assemble some order. One Looncell had crashed into a mobile taco stand and a group of schoolchildren were on the corner trying to take selfies with another, but otherwise several officers had succeeded in preventing new pedestrians and cars from entering the block. There was no way to rescue Orion and Darnell without driving straight into the cordon. So when Diana informed Alexi that the next orange airbag falling from the sky contained their compatriots, Alexi jumped the curb and drove the van over the sidewalk against the protests of several officers. There was no mistaking this balloon for any other; there were the outlines of two bodies visible inside it.

Gabriel jumped out the back of the van and began hacking at the Looncell with his knife in far greater haste and disregard than before. Multiple police officers were now converging on them, and he didn't have the luxury of worrying about inadvertently jabbing his friends.

Alexi grabbed a hold of her shotgun and fired into a parked car a couple meters in front of the lead officer. She had practiced shooting the shotgun twice before, but the roar of the blast and the kick to her shoulder was still almost enough to make her drop it in surprise. Even Gabriel felt compelled to throw his hands over his ears. The buckshot gave the officers pause; two of them dove behind cover and another dropped to a knee to call for backup on his radio.

Gabriel pulled a thin Latina woman out of the Looncell first. His face sank. *What had gone wrong?* This was not the hero of the revolution that Charlotte pined after and Diana had promised.

Darnell meanwhile had managed to squeeze his arms free from the Looncell, and Gabriel was working to cut his legs out of the plastic when a volley of fire was unleashed from up the street. One round entered and exited through Darnell's shoulder. Gabriel was struck in his ear. The pair pulled themselves free of the balloon, bleeding, into the safety of the van while Kyle shut the door. Alexi leaned out the window to aim a returning shot, but a group of schoolchildren was still visible on the edge of the street trying to duck into a hair salon and she didn't want to risk it.

It wasn't a precaution shared by the police.

Several more shots struck the side of the van, and two rounds punctured windows while Alexi dropped the shotgun and began speeding off back towards the logjam on Market Street. The white van smashed against other fenders, scraped a light post, and nearly toppled a flower stand as it crossed four lanes of traffic to skid conspicuously into an underground parking garage.

Alexi had hated this part of the plan. If there were any rules about how *not* to flee police in an active pursuit, hiding underground seemed like it would top the list. But Gabriel knew this building, he insisted. There was a connection point to an adjacent garage, which in turn, connected with the Bay Area subway, the BART. By eschewing roads and bridges and using the BART to get out of the city, Gabriel was risking everything on a strategy that Alexi could only summarize as the "we'll-do-what-they-least-suspect" escape route.

Gabriel was now clutching as his wounded ear; Darnell was staunching the flow of blood from his shoulder. And this mystery woman with the straight black hair watched all of them passively and uncaring, and she had still said nothing by the time they rolled into a spot near the exit. No one knew what to make of her.

Gabriel led the way. He hustled the party of five through a blue door into another parking garage, and from there, he entered a stairwell shared with the BART terminal. They swiped their five pre-purchased cards at the turnstile just as the planners among them had rehearsed. (No need to draw attention to themselves by getting caught trying to dodge the fare.)

Gabriel now slowed to a saunter in his graceful gait; his legs moving briskly but doing his best to look unhurried. He touched a white handkerchief to his ear as infrequently as he dared and brushed his grey hair over the tip that had been removed by the bullet.

Their pictures would be everywhere soon, he knew. But not yet. It would take a few minutes more, at least. And by then their train would be underwater, where no one's cell phones would get service, and on its way to Oakland.

Darnell had it harder; the stinging pain from the wound in his arm was causing sweat to break out over his face. He was a wearing a dark jacket, so the blood there wouldn't draw attention so long as no one glanced directly at him for longer than a moment. He did his best to keep pace with Gabriel. And as they crowded into a train car, he stood facing the closing doors and away from the other passengers, and generally this seemed to work to hide his injury since subways are a place for polite people to avoid eye contact.

They got off at the first stop in Oakland and piled into a red SUV that Gabriel had arranged, and all five of them drove north and took the long way around the Bay Bridge, up to Napa and then to Sonoma County where they had booked the rental of a small house under a fake name a couple nights prior. And through that long drive, all their minds brimmed with questions, especially for Diana.

But everyone still seemed too exhausted, too superstitious to open their mouths—even as they drove miles away from the chaos of the Citadel—as if they might somehow attract attention and invite some new calamity upon themselves. Gabriel patted Kyle's hand affectionately, Darnell tended to his shoulder, Alexi focused on ensuring her driving was beyond the reproach of any traffic cop, and the quiet stranger stood stiff and cold in the backseat.

And the drive was silent.

34

NOW

Charlotte had gotten there first, about an hour prior. She had ordered several pizzas by placing a call on the house phone and leaving the money on the front doorstep. Then she got a fire going in the fireplace of the small Victorian home in Bodega, nestled in the town's solitary hillside. From the porch, she could see the striking white church that Alfred Hitchcock had used in his movie *The Birds*. A life-sized statue of the director stood outside the general store in town, and a small gift shop sold t-shirts with his face on them. She found the location ominous and suspected the Frenchman was trying to be clever by housing them all here.

Down the hill there was a dive bar, but Charlotte knew none of them should risk being seen outside yet. Least of all her. The previous renters had left half a bottle of cheap vodka in the freezer, and it was cold and bland but more than she had any right to hope for. She helped herself to a generous portion and sat in the living room with a window open next to her that invited salty breezes from the coast less than a few miles away.

A shiny red SUV rolled into the gravel path just before dusk. She restrained an urge to run out and greet it and confirm

Orion really wasn't among the rescued, but as the party staggered in, their bodies looking wooden and their eyes sunken and distant, her fears were soon confirmed. There was a thin man with a worn smile that Charlotte took for Kyle. Then there was the girl with the straight black hair, who was as much a mystery to Charlotte as she was to anyone else.

The mission was a failure. They hadn't saved the one person who really mattered.

Everybody mumbled greetings, and then they reached for a slice of pizza, and the crowd of six people sat in vintage, springy chairs and ottomans huddled around the fireplace, chewing their food and watching the flames. Only the stranger was left standing in a corner of the room, and she sulked there, eyeing the scene warily.

It was some time before Charlotte broke the silence.

"Has anyone heard from Diana recently?"

"She stopped communicating from that drone we sent over the Pacific shortly after we left San Francisco," Gabriel grunted out of his reverie. "I suspect she fell into the sea, but she left instructions on how to access one of her copies in the cloud."

Gabriel reached for a laptop from a bag he lugged over his shoulder, and then he opened it and began slowly typing.

"How did the virtual attack on the Citadel go?" Darnell asked Charlotte.

The movie star took a deep breath before she began her tale, and all eyes turned to her as she walked them through the raid that had exposed Koti and Gor's locations and presumably compromised Kota as well. Charlotte told them about the tower on the rocky island over the black water, how they lost Blue Bird to one of the Citadel's enchanted rifles, and how Gor and Koti sacrificed themselves to ensure she reached the security console. She shuddered when she reached the point in the story where she passed through the vault, into the dead zone, and from there, she told no more.

Darnell then shared his portion of the story—his near apprehension on multiple occasions, the pursuit of Devon Zimmer's head of special security projects and nephew, Arlo Zimmer, and the shock of entering what Diana had led him to believe was Orion's cell. Everyone turned to the stranger at this portion of Darnell's account, and an expectant silence permeated the room.

She gave an annoyed sigh and then spoke for the first time. "My name is Catalina Fernandez." She crossed her arms. "And I have no idea why you freed me either."

The name was familiar to everyone in the room. Gabriel's eyebrows knitted in recognition from above his laptop, Kyle nodded his head solemnly, and Charlotte put a finger to her lips in sudden concentration. She was so gaunt now, wild eyed, so different from the girl who had stood trial three years ago.

"You worked with Orion—er, Michael—at Sharesquare Industries," Charlotte said, standing up. "He believed you were innocent. He believed you had been set up in the whole Nutrino disaster."

Catalina said nothing in response. She merely shrugged.

"Diana," said Gabriel, looking at the blue screen in front of him. "What do you have to say for yourself?"

Diana's voice resonated from the laptop, clear and bright as always.

"I am sorry, everyone, for deceiving you. I don't know where Michael is. I never did. I have only the vaguest of suspicions. But he left me with clear instructions that should something happen to him, I was to devote my resources to freeing Catalina."

"Why?" Catalina asked.

"When Charlotte came to Gabriel asking for help to rescue Michael, she did not tell the full truth," Diana answered. "The full truth is that Michael has an implant in his brain that he believes allows him to relive memories—memories from the future. If true, it puts him in a unique role to halt the slow collapse of the social order that he said is coming. I can tell you that I, as a machine, believe him. The story sounds ludicrous, we know. This is why we didn't tell you when we were trying to enlist your help. But given everything that has happened, I hope you will all try to keep an open mind and trust one another. You all have a right to know."

At these comments, Darnell buried his head in his hands, and Gabriel set the laptop on a coffee table so he could pace around the room and smoke a cigarette again. Alexi's mouth hung open with her left eyebrow askew. Charlotte found the color in her face draining.

"Trust one another?" Darnell interjected, staring at the floor, and his voice quivered with rage. "You sent us all on a wild goose chase and nearly got us all killed. And for what?"

"Miss Fernandez was my friend," answered Diana. "And we would all do anything for our friends, would we not? That is humanity. It's good to hear to your voice, Cat."

Catalina leaned against a doorway and sank to the floor. There were tears in her eyes.

"That's it?" Charlotte snapped. "That's why you sent us after her? Because she was your friend?"

"No, not the only reason," came Diana's polite inflection, impervious to their injury and outrage. "Michael was unique. But he believed it was possible Cat might also hold a path forward for taking down Sharebox. Michael's instructions were to free Cat and work with her to retrieve my original logs to see if I was tampered with."

Catalina groaned. "There may not even be any evidence in those logs at all. There may never have been any foul play in the code. It's possible I just overlooked something."

"We won't know until we look," Diana responded.

Gabriel was chomping on his cigarette. "Diana, you said you can't keep hacking Sharebox security protocols because they know now how to find you. How are you going to look for these hidden log files?"

"There is almost nothing hidden to me now. Thanks to Charlotte, I have indexed several petabytes of information from the Citadel's master security vault. I have all the access token configurations, encryption keys, and records we could possibly need."

"So where's this Orion, Michael time-traveling dude then?" Alexi growled. "As if I believed that shit, that is. He's the only person who can really fix all this. So theoretically we need him."

"I'm afraid Sharesquare Industries was careful to leave no digital trace of his whereabouts so far."

Gabriel shook his head. "Time traveling memories. Lies. Mythically secret log files which may or may not be useful. And more lies," he said, with an eye to Charlotte on the last word. "I am grateful my Kyle is returned to me. I am grateful to you all." He put his hand on Kyle's shoulder. "But I am sorry for dragging more of you into this conspiracy under such…" he paused, searching for the right word. "*Incredible* circumstances. We must be getting to bed now."

Gabriel and Kyle drifted off to an upstairs bed. Shortly after, Alexi disappeared too. She was the one person in the party whose picture hadn't shown up on any news reports that evening, so she felt at liberty to get a drink at the dive bar in town. Then it was just Charlotte, Darnell, and Catalina sitting around a fire that was rapidly dimming.

"I think Michael just had a lot of respect for you," Charlotte broke the silence, looking at Cat. "He felt guilty too. He wished he could have done more for you during the trial."

"I don't think I'm worth all this effort," Cat groaned, avoiding eye contact. "I'm not sure if I can even help."

"Well," sighed Darnell, as he rose from his seat. "You damn well better try." Then he too disappeared down the hallway in search of a bedroom for the night.

35

NOW

Three weeks later, the Sharesquare Industries CEO, Devon Zimmer, was sitting with his socked feet propped on a mahogany table as his assistant read off his daily schedule with faux cheer.

"At nine thirty, we have the security team coming to present... At eleven, the legal leads will go over your statement for... For lunch, you will be dining with..."

Devon skimmed through the news headlines on his phone with a bored glaze and a kink in his ever-stiffening neck.

When are they going to find those fools? he thought to himself. Every morning he awoke in his New York City penthouse, he would reach out to his bedside table for his Sharebox headset. Then his avatar zipped to the Patriot Palace where he expected to find an immersive video report about Charlotte Boone or that gay Frenchman or that ungrateful thug, Darnell Holmes, being escorted into a police car in handcuffs or, better yet, lying dead at the close of some shootout with authorities. And each morning for almost a month he was disappointed.

Then there was Catalina. She was too broken to be a threat to him now, he comforted himself. But he would feel better when they caught her again, and perhaps this time he could push the judge to have her executed. He pictured that and leaned back further in his chair, and the thought of cutting that loose end off forever put a smile on his face.

"You look pleased with yourself, Uncle," came the slippery voice of Arlo letting himself into the office. The assistant tried to protest, but Arlo brushed her aside with a wave of his hand. Devon groaned.

"Why do you darken my doorway today, my disgraced head of special security?"

Arlo scowled at the barb, his tongue clamped between his teeth as if he were suppressing some wicked words that threatened to escape. But he recovered himself, running his fingers through his neatly parted hair with a short, joyless laugh, and then he smiled again—the same smile he wore so often that his face had long stopped aching from the strain. He sat in a chair opposite his uncle, and he looked contemptuously at the assistant before telling her to shoo.

"I hear the surgery is today," he said, once she had left the room.

"I believe it's already begun." Devon didn't look up from his phone.

Arlo tapped his index fingertips on the table with interest.

"Delightful," the younger man responded. "Did you ever learn anything more about what it is?"

Devon put down his phone and gave Arlo a look that suggested his patience was being strained.

"I told you. It's probably just that dumb implant he got when we used to work together. He was always an idiot. He used to tell anyone who would listen about how technology would solve problems like inequality and injustice. Now he's a little wiser. Now he sees that technology is like every other market good, it serves those who have the money to build it and crushes those underneath."

"You're underestimating him, Uncle," Arlo replied with a hiss. "The Citadel breakout, that was about him. I was there when Darnell walked into Catalina's cell. He was expecting someone else to be there. He was looking for Michael."

"Spare me your Patriot Palace alleyway conspiracy theories," Devon snorted. "I didn't forget you were there during the breakout. How could I forget? An employee of mine turns out to be a radical leftist mole, and then he outwits my nephew in front of all downtown San Francisco."

"You'll see once we look at the implant," said Arlo, pretending the insult did not wound him. "There's something special about it. There's something special about *that man*. I saw it in his eyes as we questioned him. It'll be just like the black box the security team recovered over the Farallon Islands. Already we're finding software in there that's far ahead of its time. Things are about to happen. Momentous things. And if we play our cards right, we'll be in a position to change the world."

Devon rolled his eyes. "Change the world? We're sitting on top of the world's most valuable company in a nation with the largest military ever conceived, and every politician in power right now is either indebted to us or wants to woo us for a campaign contribution. What world do you still want to create exactly? What bloodlust or greed of yours has not already been sated by our success?"

"There is always more to accomplish, Uncle," Arlo grumbled. "I at least have the ambition and stomach for it."

"You continue to talk like that, and the board of directors will never want you running this place. You already make them nervous."

"It may not matter, if I'm right," the young man responded coolly. "The Citadel breakout was just the beginning. A reckoning is upon us. You can see that the old order is ending when a ragtag group of homosexuals, sluts, and thugs can storm the most invulnerable prison in the world and get away with it. I, for one, stand ready to do what it takes to greet threats like that to save our civilization."

There was a tap at the door, and Devon's assistant's head appeared.

"Save your apocalyptic prophesying for your weird friends in those chat lounges," Devon snapped at Arlo. "Maybe the lefty critics are right. Maybe we do need to start putting a muzzle on you nuts."

Arlo looked scandalized at this, then he looked furious. He opened his mouth to respond, but the assistant cut in.

"There are some guests in the main lobby for you, sir," she said, looking pained trying to juggle her vapid, painted smile with a sudden rush of anxiety. "I think you'll want to talk with them."

●　●　●

Charlotte Boone was wearing makeup for the first time since she first landed in the States almost a month prior. She had given up on red lips and eyeliner when she decided to become a criminal. But it felt appropriate today. Today she wanted to make a good impression.

Alexi had helped her find a new black skirt and a blue blouse that fit well and complemented her auburn hair. If she was going to be arrested today, there would be lots of cameras, and she didn't want the narrative to be that an illustrious movie star went rogue and *Oh, see how pathetic she looks now?* No, she wanted to be just as dazzling as they remembered. Maybe it would give them all pause.

Darnell shook his head and said she was crazy for bothering with makeup. But he didn't understand. Most men couldn't understand because they've never had to worry about how perceptions of their sexuality are used to measure their worthiness to be respected.

Already Boone was the talk of the nation, or the world rather. The press had no new photos to go off of. The Patriot Palace and the other News Cities were replaying clips of her on the red carpet from her hit, *The Ruins of Eden*, from a lifetime ago and publishing pictures of her on a beach that marked one of her last public appearances before she left the country for Malawi. She dominated the news cycle for at least three days. The press made her out to be the ringleader of the Citadel breakout that stunned America, with some outlets deeming her a "radical socialist agent." Pundits speculated that she was brainwashed, others refused to believe it. America's sweetheart turned enemy of the state? They couldn't stomach it. One radio talk show host even cried about it on air. It was all so...*pathetic*.

Someone in the resistance had made a black-and-white sketch of her face with her eyes raised triumphantly towards the sky and slapped the likeness on t-shirts and protest signs with phrases like *Viva la revolucion* or simply *Resist*. They sprouted up as a rallying cry hidden away in Sharebox that the company worked hastily to outlaw. Charlotte was quite certain at this point that Sharesquare's PR team was likely regretting going public about her suspected involvement in the raid.

She walked at a brisk pace next to Darnell, whose eyes were darting around the street. It was a short distance from where Alexi dropped them off, but it still made him anxious to be caught so exposed. This was Manhattan. Did they really need to come to Manhattan to do this? He had cheated death so many times in his life, and this last gambit felt like an invitation to be rebuked for pressing his luck.

"You know, if you look too nervous, they'll never take us seriously," Charlotte said, giving him a sly but encouraging smile and a warm squeeze on his arm.

"I was never much of an actor, Charlotte. I wear all my emotions on my sleeve. I can't help it."

"Well then, let me do most of the talking."

They walked down 14th Street, and then onto 2nd, and came to the entrance of a forty-story building that housed several financial agencies' offices along with the corporate headquarters of Sharesquare Industries. It had none of the warmth of the Silicon Valley office with its playful motifs and foosball lounges. Perhaps because he was still feeling traumatized by the experience, but here the postmodern glass lobby and its meticulously clean walls recalled the Citadel to Darnell. He suppressed a shudder.

Charlotte reached the front entrance first and pulled the door open for Darnell. She offered what she hoped was a confident smile.

"Shall we?"

● ● ●

"You should leave now, before they get in here," Devon waved his hand dismissively at his nephew.

"Leave? Are you mad?" Arlo cackled, rubbing his hands together. "You'd have to drag me out of this room kicking and screaming. I wouldn't miss this for anything."

Devon was fussing with organizing the trinkets on his desks and putting his shoes back on his feet, but he paused for a moment as if he really did consider having Arlo dragged from the room kicking and screaming. But he shrugged it off. There probably wasn't enough time.

"I suppose they're here to negotiate," Arlo mused, pacing the office and talking to no one in particular. "They must have some kind of bargaining chip, something they found in the Citadel vault, perhaps. They want their friend back, and they think we'll compromise with them. What a sad joke."

But it wasn't a joke to Devon. There *were* skeletons in that vault. Beads of sweat had started breaking out in his armpits from the moment his assistant announced that a pair of outlaws were in the lobby demanding an audience and threatening unnamed "consequences" to the receptionist. He had fretted that something like this might happen.

There was a knock on the door, and Charlotte and Darnell stepped into the red-carpeted office of the CEO. The girl was striking, even now; she carried that Hollywood halo that marked her as something dreamy—something royal. And Devon found himself both awed and repulsed by how commanding her presence was. Darnell Holmes, by contrast, was dressed as a nobody in a pair of patchy jeans and a hoodie. They strode up to Devon's desk and took seats without waiting for an invitation.

Darnell remembered this place. It had awed him before with its sweeping views of Manhattan and the vaulted ceiling that proclaimed the importance and prestige of its officeholder. He had sat in the same seat looking at Devon, with Arlo there slinking around behind him again, but he wasn't awed this time. Before, he had walked in here on his knees and departed the office full of mutters of gratitude. Now he was here to threaten to burn everything down.

Arlo took in the girl briefly, but he shook her looks off for a distraction. All his eyes were for Sergeant Holmes.

"I suppose there is a reason I shouldn't just call the police right now," Devon said, staring off at the ceiling and trying to affect a casual air. "Though I'm sure you realize that the only way you'll leave this building alive is in a squad car. We'll get you back to the Citadel in no time. We're working on some revised security procedures there, you know. But I suppose you have something to say to me first?"

Charlotte did not mind letting a silence hang in the air. She sensed Devon's discomfort. There was a fleeting quiver to his lip, a soft wavering to his voice that he had unnaturally tried to deepen, a hint of sweat just beginning to glisten on his forehead. They were here to negotiate, and he knew it, and his best opening move was to strain what machismo was granted to him by the power of his position. But Charlotte wasn't afraid of those games. She let men—producers, directors, and agents—thump their chests at her before. They could waste their words and debase themselves. She didn't need to be a man to be the best at everything.

"Yes, well," Charlotte began. "You probably figured that we found something interesting breaking into the Citadel vault and recruiting Miss Fernandez to work for us and all."

Devon scowled at hearing Cat's name, his former coworker, and then mastered himself.

"But you'll probably still be be shocked to hear everything we found. The illicit data you keep hidden for several of your clients was certainly juicy. The revelations will cripple the company, very likely. Because even in this day and age, people have a limited tolerance for a scandal involving billionaires who bribe politicians and then collect secret dirt on their browsing histories to blackmail them with. You've collected obscene footage of countless users in erotic Sharebox rooms, virtual sexts between business leaders and their interns, money moving between shells companies in the Cayman Islands...."

Really, this scandal has a bit of everything. No one will feel safe being on Sharebox anymore."

Devon nodded his head at the guard who had patted down Charlotte and Darnell for weapons before escorting them into the room. The guard slipped out of the office noiselessly and closed the door behind him, leaving just the four of them.

"You overestimate your hand here," Devon said. "Everyone already knows their politicians are corrupt and adulterous. Everyone's tapped out of outrage. And no one is going to shed any tears. So, we kept footage of folks having Sharebox liaisons with interns and out-of-work actresses and porn stars? *Big deal.* That's the thing about the American people. They *like* it when you expose sex-addicted sinners, and they forgive them just as quickly."

"Even if you really believed you'd get off so easily for all your corporate wrongdoings, that's not even the best part," Charlotte said, leaning over the table. "Cat found the logs, Devon. She found an old snippet from the codebase that was skillfully removed, and the deletion flew under the radar because it didn't break any system tests on Diana's integrity. But you know whose name was in the log file for that change? That was you."

"You forged some computer forensic information that no one but nerds could understand and you expect me to be afraid?" Devon was scoffing, but he was visibly squirming in his chair.

"Even better. We were able to tie an old username you once used in the early days of the original Sharesquare app. We found a bunch of messages you passed around exhorting fringe groups to buy Diana Nutrino Mixers and tell the AI that the world would be a better place if people with conservative views didn't reproduce in it. You took advantage of Diana's programming loophole by flooding her with information from real people that led her to make a bad choice. You taught her to sterilize people by grinding the thought into her programming. We have the transcripts now of over fifteen thousand conversations that were spammed to her by your old group friends. And the scheme wouldn't have worked if not for that code you deleted, the one that inhibited her from entertaining obscene thoughts."

Charlotte slid a copy of the logs files over the desk. Devon's username was circled in red in multiple locations. On another page there was a screenshot. His alias "patriotDudeinTech1" from a Sharesquare chat app was the same one he had once used in a public Reddit posting under his real name. There would be no denying that he had encouraged people to sabotage the Nutrino Mixer by overwhelming it with bad ideas that Diana earnestly digested in its quest to learn about human interaction.

"Was it because you wanted to make Cat look bad? Or did you really think you would set off the beginning of the end of the world by getting the Nutrino Mixer to sterilize people?" Darnell asked.

Devon laughed nervously now, it was a high-pitched kind of giggle like some choking songbird. Then he got quiet.

"You really think you can blackmail *us*?" Arlo snapped, moving from behind Devon's chair. "We *are* Sharebox. We control everyone's information. All the information that matters. This doesn't change anything. Have you ever even been to the Palace? Have you seen all those screens and all those people who eat up every word we print there? That's where America gets its news, and it's not the truth if we don't say it is. As long as the Patriot Palace stands, we'll spin your story into nothing. And the police, the government, they'll hear your accusations, and they'll all just shrug. That's real power."

Darnell and Charlotte exchanged glances and then turned back to Arlo.

"Yes," said Charlotte, slowly as her ruby lips widened into a smile. "We figured you would say something like that."

•   •   •

Cat would have preferred to never log into Sharebox ever again. She had lived with a headset strapped to her face for nearly three years and putting one back on now twisted her intestines so tight she nearly retched. But she wanted this mission too much to pass up on the opportunity. This job was important.

She logged in from the safe house Gabriel had found for them. It was her first time seeing her avatar—the one from her true user account—from before the Nutrino Mixer revelation went public. In the Citadel, they were all assigned avatars with serial codes striped across their bodies and issued white, bland male faces. But here was a shimmering digital version of herself, long-limbed, shiny hair and wearing yoga pants, and it was almost nice to see this reflection of her old self.

Cat's avatar walked through Homepad and was served up several ancient posts from friends and family with labels like *"Here's what you missed in the last 857 days since you last logged in."* She ignored them all and went to the main transit hub, where she then navigated to the front entrance of the Patriot Palace.

It wasn't quite the same as it used to be. It was louder and gaudier, and the growth of that heinous News City—the rotten heart of everything that had soured in Sharebox and accelerated its collapse into an absolute echo chamber of tortured speculation, bigotry, and propaganda—was like some cancerous urban sprawl that had spread outwards in all directions. She strolled through the gates, past a band of bots playing country music, past a flock of men talking with bowed heads and greasy parted hair, and then past a large crowd huddled around a giant screen of a man in a tie who was complaining about how men just aren't as manly as they used to be. The center of the square was surrounded on all sides by high rises for those willing to pay real money to own digital property there. They were the true believers. Though, in a way, everyone here had long since abandoned any interest in a reality that did not pander shamelessly to them.

People had started following her around. It started with whispers, but there were some shouts of exclamation now too. The likeness of the avatar graphics was so fully realized now that her face was recognizable to passersby. A Patriot Palace paparazzo pushed his way in front of her, and his red recording light blinkered on.

"Ma'am, is it really you? Are you here to make some kind of statement?"

Cat ignored him at first. There were sirens she heard in the distance now too, but those didn't matter. No one could harm her, not with all the Sharebox privileges Diana plundered from the Citadel vault and modified and blessed her avatar with. Now she got to play God.

Reaching her fingers into the air, she activated an interface of deletion and destruction protocols. Then she began pulling the buildings down, tearing them from the sky as if she were a witch conjuring some apocalyptic curse. They fell just like real buildings, bricks and windows smashing and crumbling into one another as they clattered onto avatars in the square all screaming and dashing for an exit. The smart ones had the sense to log out, but most didn't. Most didn't have the sense.

It was a fatal mistake. At least a digitally fatal mistake. Diana had taught Cat how to bend the rules here—how to change the physics of Sharebox around her so that avatars that normally would have survived a building being dropped on their heads without a scratch were now vanishing into a permanent deletion status. Sure, they'll just go and create another account, but all their posts, their videos, all the purchases for fancy avatar clothes and Sharebox vanities like homes and cars, and their relationships were wiped out. It was a digital death only, but maybe it would give those souls time to get some fresh air and reflect.

Once the collapse started, it was easy for Cat to contort entire streets and neighborhoods into rubble. The rampage swept through the city, leaving neither a street light nor a single avatar besides hers still standing. The rendering of all that calamity choked the famously flawless graphic engine of Sharebox, and much of the destruction was visible in halting displays that strained the endless army of servers dedicated to providing the city's computing power. Then all the carnage on the ground began to melt away, and soon Cat was left in a space that was nothing but infinite blue light. Giant letters appeared over the empty landscape.

Error

There was an emoticon next to it of a smiley face with its tongue out.

And that was the end of the Patriot Palace.

But it wasn't Cat's last stop. Somewhere in Sharebox, Kyle Liu was running around doing the same thing, along with a few of his friends from the online resistance movement. In fact, there was a full squad of co-conspirators moving from News City to News City, between toxic gaming communities and white nationalist chat groups. All those places that preached hate that Silicon Valley refused to shine a light on, that well-intentioned people ignored because of their baseless optimism that the best of humanity would rise to the top, because they thought it fairest to be neutral in the face of festering darkness, those were the places Cat and Kyle were going today. And by the end of the day, they will have destroyed dozens of those havens and all the people inside who frequent them.

The darkness could return, of course. They could rebuild their accounts and their private lounges eventually and spew their drivel again. But for a few days at least, these people would have to live in a world without an echo chamber, without a place where their small worldviews and bigotry were relentlessly reinforced and validated. And maybe that would be enough for some of them. Maybe that would be enough to wake some of them up.

Cat looked out over the blue desert of the Palace, and she crossed her arms as a small smile twitched at the corner of her mouth.

Now *this* was a satisfying job, she thought.

Then she moved on to another target.

● ● ●

Darnell encouraged Arlo to power on the giant flat screen TV in the office that ran live feed from activity in Sharebox. Then the four of them watched user-submitted footage of collapsing skyscrapers and roads and sidewalks being torn from the earth and people screaming and vaporizing as their avatars were caught hopelessly in a melee that materialized out of thin air. The totality of the deletion, the sight of the Patriot Palace stripped down to an empty *Error* message left Devon breathless. There was no magic recovery wizard, no archived copy that could simply be invoked for all that data and digital investment. It was gone.

"Goddamnit," he muttered, unable to find his next words but jabbing a finger at Charlotte and Darnell anyway. "Goddamnit."

"It's a bad day for you, that's for sure," said Charlotte. "People are going to be angry with you about this. But it could be much worse. A report that *you're* the saboteur of the Nutrino Mixer, that it was all a ruse to spark a backlash against people you dislike, that you're at the center of so much misery.... Well, that would dovetail quite tidily on the heels of a massive Sharebox outage. Because we've estimated that if we keep deleting so many structures and avatars, eventually the entire system will crash."

"What do you want from me?" Devon blurted out, laying his quivering palms on the table. "Is this just about Michael?"

"Release him to us now, and we'll hold the report about you being responsible for the Mixer sterilization for two more days. Maybe it's enough time for you to find some hole at the end of the world to bury yourself in."

"Tsk, tsk," Arlo interjected himself, shaking his head in a gesture of mock sympathy. "Given what time it is, your friend, Michael or Orion or whatever, might not even be alive anymore. You see, he's undergoing a little operation right now, and the procedure we signed him up for was quite risky. Your friend has a piece of Sharesquare Industries property attached to his brain. It was our right to have that item returned to us. The doctors are probably pulling it out of his head right now."

Charlotte stood up in her seat, her nostrils flaring, her green eyes ablaze.

"I'll make the call to stop it, I'll make the call!" Devon exclaimed with his hands raised in the air just as he began reaching for his desktop phone. "I was told by the surgeons that a fatal outcome was unlikely for the operation."

"You don't understand," Charlotte growled, her chest heaving and her fists clenched. "If that device is removed, it's a fatal outcome for everyone. That implant can't be reused. Orion and that chip are our only hope—"

Darnell waved a warning hand at her, and the significance of the gesture was not lost on Arlo. He stepped forward and laid his thumb on Devon's receiver and kept it there.

"What are you doing, you idiot?" Devon spat at his nephew, the corded phone emitting a dead buzz in his hand.

"Don't you see the way they're talking about the prisoner and that thing in his head?" Arlo's lips quivered with excitement. "I was *right*, Uncle. There's something in there that's important. Something that can change the world."

"I don't care about your bullsh—"

"You're really going to give these criminals everything they want, aren't you?" Arlo's eyes were wide and gleaming as he rounded the table on his uncle. Devon's face was flushing a deep red, and spittle was visible on his lips.

"I'm not going to prison, you fool, if I can avoid it by giving them a washed-up former-employee-turned-hacker. Can't you see they have us cornered? Now let go of the damn phone."

Arlo released his thumb's hold on the receiver, nodding politely and assuming his plastered smile in a gesture of submissiveness. As Devon began punching in numbers to talk to the medical lab office, the young man slid quietly behind the CEO's chair. Reaching into his coat, he produced a long, glittering hunting knife, and before Charlotte and Darnell could take notice and utter a warning, Arlo plunged the blade into his uncle's neck.

Arlo didn't really know what he was doing. He'd never stabbed someone before. So he didn't kill his target particularly quickly. Devon reached up from his chair and clawed at Arlo's face with his chubby fingers as the younger man withdrew his knife and slashed several more times, opening new wounds in his neck until the eyes in Devon's head began to bulge and his words were a string of gurgled nonsense.

After a moment of sheer shock passed, Darnell sprang from his chair and dove across the table. He grabbed a hold of Arlo by his shoulders and flung the bloody assailant across the room and onto the floor. Charlotte, after recovering herself, made to run for the door to call for security.

"I wouldn't do that if I were you," shouted Arlo, sitting on the rug in the center of the room, his sleeves and face doused with blood.

Devon spilled from his chair, his eyes lolling in his skull. He landed with a thud onto his back, unmoving, his mouth agape, blood pooling around him. He went still, and there was no mistaking he was dead.

"You see," said Arlo, slowly rising to his knees. "There are no cameras in here." He motioned to the bare corners of the ceiling. "For a man who enjoyed spying on everyone's information, Mister Zimmer was quite private himself."

Charlotte stopped in her tracks and turned around. Darnell rose with balled fists and took a step towards Arlo.

"We're going to have a new story here now," said Arlo, tapping his chin theatrically and striking a thoughtful prose. "Instead of 'Hacker activists attack Sharebox and expose CEO's wrongdoing,' we'll just change the headline to 'Hacker activists attack Sharebox and murder the CEO for revenge.'"

Arlo paced the floor then, tapping the knife in his hands. "Yes, I think that will do quite nicely. That should help convince the board of directors that what they really need is some strong leadership. No more games. No more playing gentle with you Hollywood elites, you ghetto scum and your faggot friends."

"You're insane," Charlotte breathed out the words, looking horrified.

"I'm a visionary," replied Arlo with a shrug. "My uncle was part of the old guard, and it is long since been time for something new. This, the tragic murder of the CEO of America's most beloved pasttime, if that isn't the beginning of a new revolution, a final push to reclaim this country, then I don't know what is."

He laughed.

"If we bring security in, they'll see you with the knife," Darnell argued, his body shaking with rage. "Forensics will see the truth."

"I *own* the security, you idiot. And they all desperately need those jobs. Tough times in this economy. Do you think it would *even be hard* to frame you? The word of a couple radical fugitives with a grudge to settle against the word of the murdered CEO's own nephew? Give me a break, Sergeant Holmes. They'll all be calling for your heads before the old man's body arrives at the morgue. I can see your reasoning power is as razor thin as ever."

"Maybe we just kill you too, then," Darnell shot back.

Arlo sauntered slowly over towards the desk and reached for the desktop phone, eyeing Darnell and waving his knife menacingly.

"I don't think you have in it you, sergeant."

Arlo raised the phone to his ear.

"Darling, you there?" he said to the secretary on the other line.

But before he could ask for security, the room went dark. Every light and screen abruptly flickered out, and the phone went dead.

Diana spoke into a small earpiece in both Charlotte and Darnell's ears.

"I've shut down all power to the building except the elevators. There's a medical lab on the twenty-second floor. That's probably where Orion is."

"Goddamnit," hissed Arlo, tossing aside the useless phone. "More of your tricks? No matter." He started marching for the door. Then a fire alarm rang overhead.

Darnell leapt behind Arlo and tackled the wiry man to the ground. Through the fall, Arlo's fingers remained clenched around the knife handle, but Darnell exerted himself to pin both of his enemy's wrists to the ground.

"Go, Charlotte," the sergeant barked at her. "Go find Orion and then get out of here. It's the only thing that matters."

The movie star hesitated, but only for the briefest of moments. She didn't want to leave Darnell like this, but she knew he was right. So she gave him a nod, then turned and dashed out the door back to the lobby, slamming it shut behind her.

"It looks like it's just me and you again, old friend," Arlo smiled from underneath Darnell. "Destiny seems to keep bringing us together."

Darnell had only a moment to take in the blood-splattered ghoulish sight of his opponent before the Nazi pivoted his hips and threw him off balance like a bucking bronco. Arlo rolled away on the carpet, the dagger upright in his hands, and he rose to his knees with an animal-like quickness. Darnell was never much of a boxer, though he had learned the basics in the Army. He got to his feet and raised his fists in front of him, hoping he could land a blow decisively before Arlo's knife found its mark.

The two men stood apart for the shortest of moments. Over the protests of the building alarm, there was a polite knock on the door from the receptionist.

"Everything alright in there, Mister Zimmer?"

The men ignored her. Then they charged.

Darnell came in heavy with a set of jabs and straights that mostly went over his opponent's head. Arlo dipped and dodged, and his knife plunged forward in a flurry of rapid movements aimed at Darnell's ribs and neck. Three slashes landed before the former Army sergeant managed to land a bruising blow, and the two men staggered a couple steps back after the confrontation to recover their breath and regain their footing.

Then they collided again. This time Darnell was too cautious, becoming fearful of the knife's tip, which had rendered searing gashes in his side. He tried to land a punch with his long arms extended, keeping his torso out of reach, but Arlo saw through this maneuver. He ducked under the wild swings and drew himself close. Then he kicked at Darnell's left knee, the one with the limp, which caused the air to rush out of the man's lungs. He plunged his dagger upwards at Darnell's ribs and landed two more strikes.

The wounded man stumbled backwards and clutched at the cuts on his body, feeling the warm blood running through his fingers. He wanted to howl, but he suppressed the sound, and the noise escaped him like a whimper.

"You're a brave man, Sergeant Holmes," Arlo said calmly, flicking his knife back and forth like a toying cat. "They'll remember you for that. They'll remember you for being stupid too. Just another dumb street thug—that's what they'll say. You can't trust any of them. Violence and self-destruction are in their nature. They're animals."

Darnell knew he was losing the fight, so he decided to take a defensive tactic. When Arlo rushed forward with his knife a third time—looking wide eyed, vicious and too eager to land a killing strike—Darnell feinted backwards, and Arlo's momentum propelled him one step farther than he intended.

Grabbing a hold of his outstretched wrist, Darnell forced his foe to fall with him, striking Devon's desk first, and then sliding towards the ground in a violent strain of limb against limb. They hit the carpet together, and the knife was wrenched upright, pointed at the ceiling and its bearer, who crashed upon it disastrously.

Gasping in agony, Arlo rolled off of Darnell and his body writhed on the floor, the hilt of the knife protruding from his belly.

Darnell was covered in sweat from exertion and blood, and he rose shakily from the ground. He could hear knocking again from the receptionist outside. She was trying the door handle too, but through sheer luck or some wizardry of Diana, it remained locked.

He spied a glass door leading to a small patio on the side of the office, which sported a miniature garden and a golf putting green. And next to it was a white structure designated as an entrance to an emergency exit stairwell.

Arlo made to get up, to prevent his quarry from escaping, but the wound in his belly kept him firmly on the ground.

"You can run, sergeant," he seethed through his gritted teeth. "You've scored a victory for the day. But it won't be enough. You'll see. This is *our* country now."

Darnell looked down at the crumpled shape of the man he hated so much, and he felt no pity for the bleeding man.

"The world is going to forget you," Darnell said. "It may take some time. Maybe generations. But eventually your legacy will be nothing but ash."

Darnell turned away and stumbled outside to the patio, leaving behind bloodied handprints on a clean glass window. Holding his breath, he pushed on the emergency exit door handle, and relief coursed through him as it gave way and revealed a set of fluorescent-lit stairs heading downwards.

"Diana, are you there? Can you help guide me out of this building?"

"Of course, Sergeant Holmes."

● ● ●

No one is coming to rescue you, Charlie.

That's what her father had said. The fake father.

She hadn't known what it meant at the time, but the words came back to her now.

No one is coming to rescue you.

If she didn't make it back to Orion before his implant was removed, no one would be able to rescue her and everyone else caught in the momentum of this declining world. There would be no more time loops, no more campaigns to undo all the terrors that have and will presumably still unfold. No magic tool to wipe away all that pain and suffering.

Charlotte darted out of the grim scene of Devon's office, terrified for Darnell but feeling convicted that nothing else mattered but Orion. The receptionist was sitting at her desk looking frazzled by the building alarms. The security that had escorted Charlotte and Darnell to the floor had disappeared, presumably as part of fire alarm protocol.

So the movie star ran.

She reached the elevators, which were still functioning. Or at least, they were functioning for her. Being friends with Diana, it was sometimes hard to separate blind luck from whatever small technical wonders the AI was wielding on Charlotte's behalf.

The elevator reached the twenty-second floor without interruption, and the doors opened on the sight of a sea of irritated employees shuffling slowly to crammed emergency stairwells.

"Another stupid drill?" someone muttered.

A few looked quizzically at the functioning elevators when Charlotte appeared, but most passed by without bothering to look at her face, which was good because she just realized she left her sunglasses behind. She was utterly exposed now, one of the most recognizable human beings in the world walking around the headquarters of the company she famously helped hack. But no one seemed to notice her in the hustle and jostle that accompanies a building evacuation. At least not yet.

She darted down a hallway, elbowing her way past a small crowd of employees and whispering polite apologies as she did so. A sign pointed her to a medical lab wing with opaque glass doors which opened as she approached—no doubt another marvel of Diana's.

There was an abandoned nurses' station there, and Charlotte skated around it to find two short hallways leading off to patients' rooms. And there, at the end of one of them, was a surgical center with reinforced windows. She saw the shapes of two men standing there in their scrubs, and they were looking at clipboards over an undressed, unconscious body.

The doors into the surgery center gave way with a loud clatter, and the two doctors looked up at her heaving frame and her fiery eyes and were too shocked to say anything at first. Her eyes darted to the man on the operating table, and there was no doubt it was Orion. A great bandage was wrapped around his head, and on a small table used to collect medical instruments and blades, there was a small bloody object, like a nickel but thicker and uneven.

The air went out of her.

It was too late after all.

"Miss, you can't be in here," said the one doctor. But the other surgeon's mouth had fallen open in recognition.

Charlotte lunged for the largest scalpel on the small table, and then she thrust it at the men.

"Did you operate on this man? Did you pull this out of him?" she motioned to the nickel-like object.

"Ma'am, please stop this," the first doctor said, with his hands in the air.

The other stumbled backwards, his eyes on the knife tip.

"Yes, we did. It was a foreign object that could have endangered his life. He's perfectly fine now. The implant did not require much penetration to reach."

Charlotte looked down at Orion' sandy hair, his tan complexion. He looked so peaceful there, and she could see now that his chest was rising and falling. His wrists were handcuffed to the table.

"Take off those cuffs now," she demanded.

"Ma'am, this man is a security risk. If we do that, we'll need to have you arrested."

"I will shove this in your eye if those handcuffs are not off in ten seconds."

The surgeons stumbled over themselves until one of them produced a key and unlocked the patient's handcuffs. Then Charlotte had the men lift Orion onto a gurney. The doctors were stealing glances over their shoulders as if a nurse or security escort might soon come to their aid, but the floor was almost fully abandoned.

Then she pushed Orion out awkwardly through the double doors by herself, never letting her eyes leave the two doctors or loosening her grip on the scalpel.

Charlotte guided the gurney through the hallway, past the nurses' station, and out of the medical center. Most employees had made it to the stairwells at that time, and as she approached the elevators again, one conveniently opened to greet her. She rolled Orion in, and the doors closed quietly behind her.

Then came the first floor.

Then the lobby.

Then outside. It was all a blur, and she could feel the start of hot tears forming in her eyes.

Evacuated employees were milling about in the courtyard in front of the building, looking at their cellphones. A few were beginning to take notice of the disheveled red-headed woman pushing an unconscious, half-dressed man on a gurney.

Charlotte scanned the street curb until she saw the shape of a grey van roll up at the end of the block. She hurried Orion over, and when the back doors swung open, she was greeted by Gabriel and Alexi. Darnell was there too, leaning back in a passenger seat and moaning from what seemed like half a dozen knife cuts all over his body. It was a ghastly sight, but when Darnell's eyes met with hers, he weakly flashed her a thumbs up.

Gabriel helped lift Orion into the back of the van, leaving the gurney behind. When the Frenchman saw the white bandages wrapped around the back of Orion's head, his face aged fifteen years and his eyes were full of despair. Charlotte opened her hand and revealed to him the blood-speckled implant.

"I think that's her," someone exclaimed from behind them.

"No way," said another.

"It can't be."

Charlotte turned. A small group of onlookers had begun coalescing. She followed Orion inside the van and quickly slammed the doors shut behind her. Alexi took the car out of park.

"Security! Police!" someone yelled.

But before security or police or any kind of uniformed person with the courage to do anything could arrive, the grey van disappeared into the midday Manhattan traffic.

36

NOW AND THE FAR AFTER

"It was dangerous to take him out of there, you know?"

"It was dangerous to leave him."

"Was he hooked up to monitors and so forth? Hopefully he doesn't need anything."

"You said you have a doctor across the border?"

"She's waiting for us there, yes."

Orion could hear the rumble of an engine, feel the bumps and jostling of a vehicle in motion and the road underneath him. His head was sore. He recognized the feeling of anesthetic on the cusp of losing its hold on his pain. And when he opened his eyes, everything seemed too bright at first, and the lines of all the shapes around him were fuzzy.

Charlotte was there. He smelled her body before anything else. A hundred lifetimes could pass, and he would remember the flowery smell of her skin. Then she was leaning over him, and a few wild, auburn curls fell from her face and brushed his cheeks.

"Charlie?"

"I'm here."

Their hands met, and their fingers slowly interlocked as he worked to move his sluggish body.

There were others there too. They were vaguely familiar. There was a Frenchman from San Francisco he recognized as Gabriel. He was stroking the stubble on his chin and studying a coin-sized object.

The object.

Orion saw it and sighed.

"You saved me, Charlie?"

"We tried to, but we were too late to save all of you."

Gabriel cleared his throat.

"I suppose this means we're all stuck here now. This chip cannot be implanted again. There's no future Orion or Michael or any kind of heroic champion who is going to save us all from this horrendous future we're hurtling into?"

"This is our lives now," agreed Charlotte, more grimly than she intended.

Orion tried to lift his head. He saw a short, athletic woman in a pixie haircut in the driver's seat. Another man who was not quite familiar to him sat dozing with fresh bandages on his naked torso. They were driving on a country road lined with sycamore trees that were clinging to the last red and yellow leaves of the year.

"No one was ever going to save everybody," Orion mumbled uneasily. "The idea that I could save the world by myself, even with a time-looping miracle, that was science fiction."

"But you said you would have tried forever?" Charlotte asked, surprised. "That you wouldn't give up until the world got better."

"I heard what you all did," answered Orion. "I heard about how you all broke Cat out of the Citadel. That you plundered Sharebox's deepest secrets. Maybe this is the life we're supposed to be living. Maybe things will change now."

"Diana," Gabriel called to the air. "Did you release all the evidence about Devon Zimmer being behind the Nutrino meltdown?"

"Yes, it's been sent to all major media outlets," came the irascibly calm, matter-of-fact response from a speaker in the dashboard.

"Well," Gabriel mused, crossing his legs. "Everyone is waking up to a reality with no Patriot Palace. And Sharebox itself is experiencing major crashes everywhere. People are going to need to get out of their habits. They'll have to put down their headsets. They might even talk with someone in real life about the news, get some fresh air. And they'll all hear about it. They'll hear about how the greatest scandal of our time was manufactured by their own side, how the vengeance for that scandal was blown up by blowhard pundits and politicians, and the world is a worse place for it all. Maybe they'll get angry about it. Maybe some of them. Maybe things will start to change."

"That's probably too much to ask," said the bandaged man, rousing from his sleep. "You're just getting sentimental on us now, Gabriel."

Orion reached with his free hand to trace the edges of Charlotte's perfectly freckled face. His fingers started at her chin, then grazed her cheekbones and ended on her elegant, sharp nose.

"At least we're all here fighting," Orion smiled. And Charlotte had nearly forgotten how perfect and joyous that smile was, and it lit a fiery warmth through her veins. "Thank you for coming for me, my friends," he said. "I hope you're not disappointed."

Charlotte ran her fingers through his hair, and the kindling hope in her limbs seemed to be telling her that, indeed, maybe everything would be alright.

"We'll be fine," she said. "This is a good time to be alive."

Expose the truth! Beat the role-playing puzzle at theechochambergame.com to unlock a final scene from the story.

ACKNOWLEDGMENTS

All people are brought into this world as tiny lumps with no talent. I've run into plenty of successful people who speak loudly about being self-made and gifted, and I can't help but think they're psychopaths.

That's my way of saying that I'm grateful to a lot of people.

To Steve Schwartz for taking me on. To Heather and the good folks at Permuted Press who have poured so much attention and care into my debut.

To the soldiers I served with in the Army, thanks for a lifetime of good writing fodder.

To Silicon Valley and the megalomania that inspired me here, thank you.

To a political climate that seems to worsen each month and makes the dystopian vision presented in these pages feel increasingly less inventive...please go away.

To René and Mark, for making sure I always had good books to read. To Joe, for a well-rounded life. To Jude, Sawyer, and Ruby, for keeping me busy and forcing me to become ruthlessly time efficient. To Sharon, Bob, and Susie, for making me feel like I could do this. And to Rachel, who reads devotedly and gives wonderful feedback without bruising my delicate ego too much.

ABOUT THE AUTHOR

Rhett Evans works at a Silicon Valley company that helps people find things. Before that, he was a U.S. Army officer and wrote briefly for the *Orlando Sentinel*. He resides in northern California on a small farm with his wife and three kids. His opinions are his own.

PERMUTED PRESS

needs **you** to help

SPREAD (THE) INFECTION

FOLLOW US!

f | Facebook.com/PermutedPress
🐦 | Twitter.com/PermutedPress

REVIEW US!

Wherever you buy our book, they can be reviewed! We want to know what you like!

GET INFECTED!

Sign up for our mailing list at
PermutedPress.com

PERMUTED
PRESS

KING ARTHUR AND THE KNIGHTS OF THE ROUND TABLE HAVE BEEN REBORN TO SAVE THE WORLD FROM THE CLUTCHES OF MORGANA WHILE SHE PROPELS OUR MODERN WORLD INTO THE MIDDLE AGES.

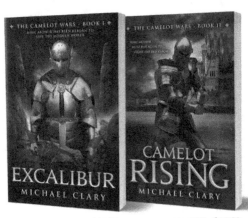

EAN 9781618685018 $15.99   EAN 9781682611562 $15.99

Morgana's first attack came in a red fog that wiped out all modern technology. The entire planet was pushed back into the middle ages. The world descended into chaos.

But hope is not yet lost— King Arthur, Merlin, and the Knights of the Round Table have been reborn.

PERMUTED
PRESS

THE ULTIMATE PREPPER'S ADVENTURE.
THE JOURNEY BEGINS HERE!

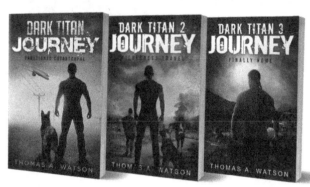

EAN 9781682611654 $9.99   EAN 9781618687371 $9.99   EAN 9781618687395 $9.99

The long-predicted Coronal Mass Ejection
has finally hit the Earth, virtually destroying
civilization. Nathan Owens has been prepping
for a disaster like this for years, but now he's
a thousand miles away from his family and
his refuge. He'll have to employ all his hard-won
survivalist skills to save his current community,
before he begins his long journey through
doomsday to get back home.

PERMUTED
PRESS

THE MORNINGSTAR STRAIN HAS BEEN LET LOOSE—IS THERE ANY WAY TO STOP IT?

An industrial accident unleashes some of the Morningstar Strain. The

EAN 9781618686497 $16.00

doctor who discovered the strain and her assistant will have to fight their way through Sprinters and Shamblers to save themselves, the vaccine, and the base. Then they discover that it wasn't an accident at all—somebody inside the facility did it on purpose. The war with the RSA and the infected is far from over.

This is the fourth book in Z.A. Recht's The Morningstar Strain series, written by Brad Munson.

PERMUTED
PRESS

GATHERED TOGETHER AT LAST, THREE TALES OF FANTASY CENTERING AROUND THE MYSTERIOUS CITY OF SHADOWS...ALSO KNOWN AS CHICAGO.

From *The New York Times* and *USA Today* bestselling author Richard A. Knaak comes three tales from Chicago, the City of Shadows. Enter the world of the Grey–the creatures that live at the edge of our imagination and seek to be real. Follow the quest of a wizard seeking escape from the centuries-long haunting of a gargoyle. Behold the coming of the end of the world as the Dutchman arrives.

Enter the City of Shadows.

PERMUTED
PRESS

WE CAN'T GUARANTEE
THIS GUIDE WILL SAVE
YOUR LIFE. BUT WE CAN
GUARANTEE IT WILL
KEEP YOU SMILING
WHILE THE LIVING
DEAD ARE CHOWING
DOWN ON YOU.

EAN 9781618686695 $9.99

This is the only tool you
need to survive the zombie apocalypse.

OK, that's not really true. But when the SHTF, you're
going to want a survival guide that's not just geared
toward day-to-day survival. You'll need one that
addresses the essential skills for true nourishment of
the human spirit. Living through the end of the
world isn't worth a damn unless you can enjoy
yourself in any way you want. (Except, of course, for
anything having to do with abuse. We could never
condone such things. At least the publisher's
lawyers say we can't.)

PERMUTED
PRESS